A LIFE FOR A LIFE

Tim Ellis

Published in 2010 by YouWriteOn Publishing

First Edition

British Library C.I.P.

A CIP catalogue record for this title is available from the British
Library.

ABOUT THE AUTHOR

Tim Ellis was born in London and grew up in Manchester. He joined the Royal Army Medical Corps at eighteen and completed twenty-two years service, leaving in 1993 having achieved the rank of Warrant Officer Class One (Regimental Sergeant Major). Since then he has worked in secondary education as a senior manager, in higher education as an associate lecturer/tutor and consultant, and as Head of Behavioural Sciences in a secondary school. He has a PhD and an MBA in Education Management and an MA in Education. He lives in Essex with his wife and five Shitzus.

Also by Tim Ellis:

Warrior
(Genghis Khan)

Path of Destiny
Scourge of the Steppe

The Knowledge of Time
(Young Adult Science Fiction)

Second Civilisation

Detective Chief Inspector James Harte

Solomon's Key

Collected Short Stories

Untended Treasures

ACKNOWLEDGEMENTS

I would like to thank the YouWriteOn.com team for a marvellous site for unpublished writers, the site members for their constructive and valuable reviews, which were a constant source of help and encouragement.

To Pam, with love as always

And in memory of my mother June Enid Susan Ellis

Show no pity:
Life for life, eye for eye, tooth for tooth, hand for hand,
foot for foot.

Deuteronomy 19:21

ONE

Tuesday 14TH January

The machine swallowed Greg Taylor's day-return ticket to London. He stepped through the automatic barrier as it opened; unaware that he would be dead before he reached his house. Glancing up, he saw that the large railway clock above the station exit displayed six-thirty. The shop was still open, and it crossed his mind to buy a bar of chocolate to eat whilst he walked the short distance home, but he knew his wife Debbie would kill him if he didn't attack the promised stew and dumplings with a ravenous hunger.

Zigzagging round a rather slow-moving plump woman with a walking stick, he trudged out of Chigwell train station and turned left towards Station Road. The one orange streetlight barely lit his way. He was tired, his back ached, and his eyes were stinging. All day he had sat in a windowless air-conditioned seminar room at the International Hotel on the water's edge at Canary Wharf listening to someone prattle on about improving GCSE performance in History. He was looking forward to getting home, eating his meal, and relaxing in his armchair in front of the television with his family. Year 8 would have to be happy with a quiz on Tudor Monarchs tomorrow, he'd get up early to do an Internet search and print a quiz off.

After passing Dennis the Bakers, the 24-hour Mart, and Harrison's estate agents, he turned into Lakeside Road. There used to be a lake and the road used to run beside it, but now there was no lake, only a road with houses. He headed up the hill towards Ralston Drive; hands stuffed deep into coat pockets and his nose snuffled into his scarf. Snow had been promised, but none had materialised yet. The North already wore its blanket of white – maybe the South would get it tonight. With luck, the Headteacher might close the school. He could do with a couple of days off to catch up with the marking.

As he turned sideways to let someone wearing a black coat with a hood pass him on the narrow pavement, he felt a pain in his chest that shot up his neck, exploded in his brain, and took his breath away. He glanced down and saw a gloved hand wrapped around the handle of something protruding from between his third and fourth thoracic ribs.

'Time to die, Mr Taylor,' the stranger whispered.

It was the last thing Greg Taylor heard as he slid down the garden wall of 29 Ralston Drive onto the pavement, just two doors away from his home.

Before he walked away, the hooded stranger stooped and slipped something small into the dead man's mouth and said, 'For Johnny Tomkins.'

***

Staring out of the window of her bedroom at 33 Ralston Drive, seventeen year-old Kishi Taylor was listening to *Shut Up* by the Black Eyed Peas on her iPod when she saw her father walking up the hill.

She went to the bedroom door and shouted down the stairs, 'Dad's here.' Then she returned to the window and waited for him to appear at the gate and walk up the path so that she could wave at him. When he didn't arrive, she began to doubt that she had even seen him at all.

'I thought you said your father was here?' her mother called up to her.

A LIFE FOR A LIFE

She padded onto the landing in her pink slippers and nightdress, and leaned over the banister clutching the pink rollers in her hair. 'I saw him, I'm sure I did.'

Just then an insistent knocking came from the front door. Kishi went down the stairs as her mother opened it. She could smell the stew and dumplings bubbling in the kitchen, and hoped her father had arrived – she was starving. Maybe he's lost his keys, she thought.

'Debbie call an ambulance, the police.' It was Mr Mayhew from across the road, horror seared into his face.

'Hello, Harry,' her mother said. 'Oh dear, what's the matter?'

'It's Greg, he's been stabbed.'

Kishi didn't understand. It was as if Mr Mayhew was speaking in a foreign language.

Her mother stood holding the door open, letting the cold air in. She looked around at Kishi with her mouth agape like a mountain tunnel as if she didn't believe Mr Mayhew was actually speaking to her.

Mr Mayhew walked into the hall uninvited, picked up the phone and dialled 999. 'Hello, yes, ambulance and police please. There's been a stabbing…'

Kishi heard Mr Mayhew provide the 999 operator with the required details as if she were listening to a conversation through a padded wall with cotton wool stuffed in her ears. Her father… stabbed… What did that mean?

'Come on,' Mr Mayhew said grasping her mum's elbow. 'He's outside number 29. I was closing my gate when I saw what looked like a teenager walk past your husband. Then Greg collapsed on the pavement, and the boy walked away as if nothing had happened.

I saw him as well, Kishi thought, but it wasn't a boy, it was a man.

Looking at Kishi, her mother said, 'You'd better stay here.'

Ignoring her, Kishi pushed past them and rushed along the path to the gate. She stopped and looked down the hill expecting to see her father walking towards her, but instead, in the glow from the orange streetlight, she saw a man slumped against the wall of number 29.

Her mother reached the gate and placed a hand gently on Kishi's shoulder. 'You should have put your dressing gown on, love, you'll catch your death dressed like that.' Then she saw Greg Taylor, the man who used to be her husband, and screamed as she ran along the road. 'Oh God! Greg, what's happened to you?' She knelt down and hugged him, but he didn't respond. Then she shook him, crying and calling out his name.

Kishi stood behind her mother. She felt numb. Was that really her father? Was he really dead? She'd miss her A Level Psychology tomorrow morning. Oh God!

'What's going on?'

It was Ryan, her twelve-year-old brother. He'd been in his room playing on his Xbox, they'd forgotten about him.

'What's wrong with dad?' he asked. 'And why's mum crying?'

'Dad's been stabbed,' Kishi answered him. It was as if someone else had said those words.

Ryan looked at her as if she were pulling his leg. 'Don't talk stupid.'

Her mother stood up. There was blood all over the front of her beige blouse. Her father didn't move. 'Come inside you two,' her mother said trying to shepherd them back towards the house.

'Is dad not coming?' Kishi asked.

'No, love,' her mum said.

'Dad?' she called to him. 'Dad, get up. Mum's made your favourite – stew and dumplings.'

'Come on, love,' her mum said wrapping an arm around her shoulders. 'Your dad can't come with us now.'

She shook herself free of her mother's embrace, and knelt down on the freezing pavement next to her father. Touching her dad's cold hand, the truth of his death spread up her arm like a virus and made her eyes flood with tears. I love you dad. You're the best dad in the whole world. What am I going to do without you? She squeezed his hand. He couldn't be dead. Things like this only happen to other people, not to us. Then, she felt strong hands, like her fathers, lifting her up.

'Come along, Kishi,' Mr Mayhew said. 'Your father wouldn't have wanted you to freeze to death out here in your nightdress.'

She went along meekly.

Just then the ambulance arrived followed by a police car, and both had flashing lights. Heads began to appear around net curtains, but no one came out, it was too cold.

'You take the children inside, Debbie,' Mr Mayhew said. 'I'll deal with things out here.'

'Thank you, Harry,' she managed to say.

Kishi followed her mum and Ryan inside. The smell from the kitchen reminding her she was starving. I shouldn't still be hungry after my dad has been killed should I? What's wrong with me?

***

After finding no carotid pulse, or pupil reaction to the light from his pen torch, Mortimore Strange closed his emergency box and stood up. He had dealt with enough of these knifings in the three years he'd been a paramedic to realise that it was now a murder crime scene, and he should leave the body where it lay. Although he could have pronounced the man dead himself, the law stipulated that a qualified doctor must perform the task.

A policewoman came up and stood behind him. 'I'm PC Mary Richards from Cheshunt Police Station,' she said. 'Is he dead?'

He could see by her fresh face, and the way she kept looking around, that Mary Richards was new. He was surprised at how small she was. He was six foot, but her eyes barely reached his shoulders. 'Yep, although officially I'm not supposed to say that. Died of a knife wound to the heart.' He wondered if she was single. Maybe it was the blue canvas trousers she wore as part of her police uniform, but he thought her hips looked a bit wide. Beggars couldn't be too choosy though, and he was definitely a beggar. He hadn't been with another woman since his girlfriend, Babs, had got tired of his shift work and thrown him out six months ago.

'Who is supposed to say he's dead then?' Mary Richards asked.

'A doctor.'

'Is one coming?'

'No, we take him to the Accident & Emergency at King George Hospital in Redbridge. A doctor will pronounce him DOA there, and fill out a death certificate.'

'Dead on Arrival?'

'You learned something whilst you were in training then, Mary Richards?'

Mary Richards smiled.

She had good teeth, clear bright eyes and wore her long dark hair in a ponytail. If he was going to ask her out, now was the time to do it. His heart rate increased. 'Would you like to go out for a meal sometime?'

'Sometime? Is that a new day they've invented and added to the week between Sunday and Monday?'

It was Mortimore's turn to smile and he did. He had his foot in the door, but before he could close the deal a grey-haired old man interrupted him.

'Excuse me?'

'Yes?' PC Richards said turning towards the man.

'Harry Mayhew, I saw what happened. I live across the road at number 32. Mr Taylor was a neighbour. Are you going to cover him up?'

'It's a crime scene, Sir. We have to wait for the Scenes of Crime Officers to arrive and secure the area.'

'Yes, of course,' Mayhew said. He was wearing a vest, shirt and a sleeveless cardigan, and the cold was making him shiver. 'I only popped out to close the gate.'

'What did you see, Mr...?' Mary Richards asked pulling out her notebook and pen.

'Mayhew... Harold Mayh ew. Greg... Mr Taylor was walking up the hill when a teenager wearing a hooded coat stabbed him as they passed each other.'

'Would you be able to recognise the teenager again?'

'No. As I said, he had a hood covering his face. I was across the road. I'm all in favour of the council saving money, but these orange streetlights are useless for seeing anything. I'm not even sure it was a teenager, it could have been a man. I just... I got the impression it was a teenager, but...'

'And you saw this person stab Mr Taylor?'

'Well no, but after the boy had walked past, Mr Taylor fell to the pavement. Who else could it have been? Greg didn't stab himself, did he?'

'Then what did you do?'

'Well, I went and knocked for Debbie... Mrs Taylor, and whilst I was there I used their phone to call for you two.'

'You didn't come and see if Mr Taylor was alive or dead?'

'Well no… I mean… I'm not trained in first aid or anything like that… I was an accountant… retired now. I thought the best thing to do was to get his wife, and call the emergency services.'

'I'm sure you did the right thing, Mr Mayhew.'

'Thank you, officer, very kind. This is all terribly dreadful. It used to be a nice neighbourhood you know, but now… well… it's the immigrants. I blame the government. They've got no education, no skills, and no jobs, but they still let them in. And…'

'Thank you for your help, Mr Mayhew,' Constable Richards said. 'You look as though you're freezing. I would go home and get warm. If there's anything else we need to ask you, we know where to find you.'

'Yes, I am a bit cold. I'll go home if you're sure? Will someone look after Debbie and the children?'

'Don't worry, Mr Mayhew, someone will look after them.'

TWO

Parish realised he had "mug" written on his forehead.

'Holidays, sickness, poor recruitment strategies, lack of quality candidates, and global warming has meant that I've got no Detective Inspectors left,' the tall stick-like Chief Superintendent Walter Day had said to him an hour ago. 'You're it, Detective Sergeant Parish. Get out there and solve your first murder. You'll be applying for promotion before too long, and if you don't make a dog's dinner of this case I'll give you a good write up. Think of it as on-the-job-training.'

Originally a working-class lad from Barnet, Walter Day had risen through the ranks to reach his current position, and was proud to tell his tale. He had no family, and his wife had died of breast cancer three years ago. Now, with eighteen months left until retirement, he had come to the end of the road in more ways than one. Parish, like most of the station, knew the Chief had recently been diagnosed with prostate cancer, and some sick bastard in Vice had opened a book on the date of his likely demise. With chemotherapy and regular radiotherapy sessions at King George Hospital making him look like a walking corpse, Parish wondered whether the Chief would even reach the end of the month.

'On my own, Sir?'

'You'll report directly to me. I want an emailed update at the end of every day, and pop in and see me at eight-fifteen each morning. I'll deal with the press. You solve the case. For all intents and purposes you'll be a DI, but without the rank or the pay – budget constraints unfortunately.'

He had no idea how 'global warming' affected the number of DI's at Hoddesdon police station, but he wasn't about to argue with the Chief. A chance to be in charge of a murder investigation, and show what he could do would give him an edge in the promotion lottery. This was an opportunity to get his nose in front. He was a lean mean thirty-six, had been a DS for seven years, it was about time he got his shot at the big time.

'Which detectives have you allocated me, Sir?'

'Well, here's the thing, Parish, I don't have any. DI Paterson has got one on the Bingley house murders, DI Mullins has taken another two to investigate the death of the MP's wife, and then there's one on training, two on long-term sick that we can't seem to get rid of or replace, and another four on maternity leave. I'm sorry to have to land this on you, Sergeant, but it's only another knifing, so it shouldn't be too difficult to solve.'

The Chief had left the squad room before Parish could think of a suitable response. He heard one of the secretaries sniggering behind him, but when he turned round they both looked as if rock cakes wouldn't melt in their mouths.

***

It was five-past seven when he climbed out of the three-year-old Ford Mondeo he'd haggled from the car pool, and headed towards the small female Constable talking to a paramedic outside 29 Ralston Drive. There was also a paper-suited SOCO collecting evidence within the yellow demarcation tape of the crime scene. Well, he hoped it was evidence. Some DNA pointing directly to the killer would be good, he thought.

'Constable...?' God she was young. He wondered if they were recruiting straight out of school.

'Richards, Sir.'

'Well, Constable Richards, I'm DS Jed Parish from Hoddesdon police station.' Her tiny hand nearly got lost in his bear paw when he shook it. 'Are you sure you're old enough to wear that uniform, Richards?'

'I was twenty-one last week, Sir.'

He shook his head. 'Okay, what have you got for me?'

PC Richards opened up her notebook. 'Mr Gregory Taylor, aged forty-nine, lived at 33 Ralston Drive.' She turned and pointed – like the tour guide of a famous murder site – to a house with all its lights on. 'Just there, Sir.'

He liked being called, 'Sir.' There were clearly advantages to being the boss.

'Okay, carry on.'

'He was walking home from Chigwell train station,' she pointed down the hill.

'You don't need to point to everything, Constable, I know where the train station is.'

'Sorry, Sir.'

Yes, he could get used to being a 'Sir.' He'd just have to make sure he solved the case, and quickly.

'It was approximately six-thirty-seven when he reached here,' she pointed at the dead man. 'Sorry, Sir…' The hint of a smile touched her lips and she blushed. 'A hooded teenager, or man, stabbed him in the chest.'

His eyes narrowed. 'A hooded teenager or man? What does that mean?'

'There's a witness, Sir.' She turned and pointed across the road. 'A Mr Harold Mayhew who lives at number 32, but he's not sure whether the killer was a teenager or a man.'

It might be a robbery, or a gang initiation, he thought. God, what was the world coming to when a life could be traded for a couple of pounds, or entry into a teenage street gang?

He slipped on a pair of latex gloves that he kept in one of the pockets of his Rannoch weatherproof coat, and knelt down to check the dead man's inside pocket, left wrist and ring finger. The wallet, gold-plated Seiko wristwatch, and gold wedding ring were still there, which probably ruled out robbery. He'd have to get the man's wife to check if there was anything else missing.

He stood up and took off the gloves. 'Good. You're doing well so far, Constable Richards. Carry on.'

'There's no murder weapon, Sir. The killer must have taken it with him.'

'The killer was male then?'

'Well... the witness said it was a male.'

'Let's not close any doors until we're sure. Anything else?'

'He... Mr Taylor, was a history teacher at Chigwell secondary school... He used to be my teacher, Sir.'

A teacher! The killer could be one of his students - three possibilities now.

'Did he? What about the family?'

'They're in the house, Sir.'

'Have you interviewed them?'

'No, Sir. I thought...'

'It's all right, Constable, but... You're not going off-duty, or out on a date with that paramedic are you?'

She blushed and looked at her wristwatch. 'No, Sir... I finish at eight-thirty, I've got another hour-and-fifteen minutes before my shift ends.'

'Good. You can accompany me when I go and see the family.'

'Okay, Sir.'

An idea jumped into his mind. 'Which station are you from?'

'Cheshunt, Sir.'

'Waltham Cross?'

'Yes, Sir.'

'Do you think they'd miss you?'

'What do you mean, Sir?'

'I need someone I can trust to work with me.'

Her eyes widened as if Parish had told her she'd won the lottery. 'I've only been a Constable for three weeks, Sir. They won't even know I'm not there.'

'Do you want to come and work for me?'

Her face lit up like a flare in the night sky. 'Oh, yes please, Sir.'

'You'll have to wear civilian clothes.'

'Like a real detective, Sir?'

'Yes, Constable, like a real detective. Ring your Duty Sergeant and ask him if it'll be all right.'

Mary Richards could hardly contain her excitement as she took out her mobile phone. 'Yes, Sir.'

He turned to the SOCO, a thin-faced man with unusually bushy eyebrows, a twisted nose, and yellow teeth who was kneeling by the side of the body. 'Name?'

'Gregory Taylor, Sir.'

'Your name, you idiot.'

'Sorry. Paul Toadstone, Sir.'

'Well, Mr Toadstone... unusual name?'

'It's derived from mythology, Sir. People believed...'

'All right, Toadstone, I'm not writing a book about it. Can the paramedic take the body away before *rigor mortis* sets in?'

'*Rigor mortis* is caused by a chemical change in the muscles, Sir. Cold merely slows it down.'

'Don't be a smart arse, Toadstone, you know what I mean.'

'Yes, I've finished with the body, Sir. A post mortem needs to be done now.'

'Sir?' It was PC Richards.

'Yes?'

She thrust her mobile phone towards him. 'The Duty Sergeant wants to talk to you.'

He took the phone. 'Hello, Jed Parish here.'

'Tony Pollack. Are you sure you want Constable Richards on a murder case, she can't even make a decent cup of tea?'

'We've got no one available at Hoddesdon, and she's performed well so far.' He smiled at Richards' eager face looking up at him. 'If it's all right with you, I'll show her the ropes.'

'How long for?'

'Let's say a couple of weeks,' Parish said, but he hoped he was going to have the case solved in less than a week.

'You'll take care of her?'

'As if she were my daughter.'

'Okay, I'll clear it with my Inspector. We'll call it on-the-job-training.'

'Thanks, Tony, I owe you one.'

'Yes, you do.'

The line went dead, and he passed the phone back. That's two of us doing on-the-job-training, he thought.

'Is it all right, Sir?'

'Yes, Richards, for the next two weeks you belong to me.'

She grinned like the Cheshire cat on cocaine, and clapped her hands together.

'Did you give that paramedic your number?'

Richards blushed again, and shuffled her feet like a young girl on her first date. 'I... I don't know what you mean, Sir.'

'I'm a detective, Richards, I notice things. Do you want me to ask the paramedic myself?'

She stared at him with shock etched on her face. 'No, Sir. Yes, I've given him my number.'

'Good. Go and tell him he can move the body. King George Hospital I presume?'

'Yes, that's what he said, Sir.'

'Good. It helps to know where they're going to do the post mortem. Well, off you go then.'

Parish turned back to Toadstone. 'Have you found anything I can use?'

'I won't know for sure until I carry out my analysis, but I'm not hopeful. There might be something on the clothes, but I won't get those until after the PM.'

'Okay thanks, Toadstone.' He passed the SOCO one of his cards. 'Give me a ring if you do find anything of value.'

Toadstone glanced at the card. 'Yes... Sergeant.'

It was nice while it lasted, Parish thought.

Richards came back.

'All sorted?'

'Yes, Sir.'

'Right, let's go and see the family.'

Parish walked the short distance up Ralston Drive and opened the gate of number 33. With PC Richards following, he trudged along the concrete path and knocked on the door. A skinny boy of about twelve-years-old with a pale face opened it.

'Is your mum in?'

'Yeah.'

Just then, the door opened wider. A woman with a black-streaked face and copious amounts of congealed blood on her cotton top stood before him. He wondered why she hadn't changed her top.

'Mrs Taylor?'

The woman nodded.

15

He showed his warrant card, and introduced himself and PC Richards. 'I'm sorry for your loss. I know this is a difficult time, but I need to ask you some questions. Would it be all right if we came in?'

She nodded again, and trudged along the hall to the kitchen. He left PC Richards to shut the door after them.

A young girl of about seventeen with bright pink rollers in her hair sat at the kitchen table staring into space. The boy stood leaning against a cabinet watching him.

'Please sit down,' Mrs Taylor said. 'Would you like tea?'

Parish could smell stew or something, and realised he was starving. He hadn't eaten since the cheese and onion roll from the canteen at ten this morning. 'If its not too much trouble,' he said. He knew that keeping busy was a common method of coping with bereavement.

She didn't reply, but occupied herself filling the kettle, laying out cups and saucers, and putting tea bags in a plain white teapot.

He thought he'd ask his questions whilst she was distracted. He didn't really want to spend any longer in the house than was necessary. 'Do you know if your husband had any enemies?' he asked.

'Enemies?' she repeated glaring at him as if he were the enemy. 'He was a teacher for God's sake.'

Parish expected that was a "no". 'What about hobbies, or clubs outside school?'

'He read a lot, liked historical fiction and westerns. Watched Arsenal play on the television.'

'Have you seen anyone strange in the neighbourhood?'

'No.'

'I saw him, you know.' It was the girl who spoke.

Parish looked at the girl sat at the end of the wooden table. She was ghostly pale like the boy, and her eyes were red and vacant. He didn't know much about shock, but wondered whether the paramedic was still outside. 'Who did you see?'

'The man who killed my dad. I saw him when he passed our gate.'

'Where were you when you saw him?'

'I was looking out of my bedroom window.'

'Did you see his face?'

'No, but Mr Mayhew said it was a teenager. It wasn't, it was a man.'

'What makes you say that?'

'I just know.'

'Definitely a man, not a woman?'

'It was a man.'

Mrs Taylor put a cup of tea in front of him. 'Help yourself to sugar,' she said.

He usually had four sugars in his tea, but took only two lumps from the sugar pot.'

'Where will they take my dad?' the girl asked.

'King George Hospital,' he said.

'Are they going to cut him open?'

'They have to carry out a post mortem, it's the law. I'm sorry.'

The girl began to cry.

Parish felt awkward all of a sudden, took a sip of tea, and looked down at the table. 'I'm afraid you'll have to formally identify your husband's body in the next couple of days, Mrs Taylor. Someone will call to arrange it.'

She nodded.

'Do you happen to know whether he was carrying anything of value?'

Mrs Taylor rounded on him again. 'He was a teacher, not a diamond smuggler, just an ordinary teacher with a

17

family. The only thing of value he was carrying, besides his life, was probably some money in his wallet. Have you checked his wallet?'

'Yes, it wasn't taken.' He took a card from his jacket pocket and placed it on the table. 'If there's anything, anything at all that you think of which might help, please don't hesitate to call me. I'll do everything in my power to find the person responsible.'

'You won't catch him,' the girl said.

He opened his mouth to reassure her, but knew it was pointless. The only response was to find the murdering bastard. He stood up, and then remembered something.

'Have you got a Victim Support leaflet in your car, Constable?'

'Yes, Sir.'

'Go and get one and bring it back, will you?'

Richards nodded and made her way towards the front door.

'The leaflet will explain who Victim Support are,' he said. 'There are people who can help you come to terms with your loss.'

He hated intruding on people's grief, but it was a necessary part of the job. He'd attended training sessions, but until you actually did it in real life, you had no idea what it was really like.

He walked towards the front door. The boy followed him out.

Richards came back with the leaflet. He took it and passed it to the boy. 'Give that to your mother.'

The door closed behind them.

'It's horrible isn't it, Sir?'

'What is?'

'All of it, Sir. I was about that girl's age when the police came to our house to tell my mum and me that my dad had been killed in a petrol station robbery. And now I've been on the other side of it.'

'I'm sorry about your father, Richards,' he said.

'It was a long time ago, Sir. It's what made me want to join the police.'

'Did they catch the killer?'

'Yes, Sir, there were two of them.'

'I'm glad.'

They made their way across the road to number 32 Ralston Drive. Parish was about to knock on the door when it swung open. A squat man with grey hair and a paunch stood before him.

'Mr Mayhew?'

'Yes.'

Parish showed his warrant card. 'I'm Detective Sergeant Parish, and I believe you know PC Richards.'

'Yes, please come in.' Mr Mayhew moved to one side and closed the door behind them. 'Come through,' he said and ushered them into the front room. 'Can my wife get you anything to drink?'

'No thank you, Mr Mayhew, we're fine,' Parish said as he and Richards sat down next to each other on the green floral sofa, and Harold Mayhew sat in one of the two matching armchairs opposite. Mrs Mayhew was nowhere to be seen.

'Can you tell me what you saw?' Parish asked the old man.

'Didn't the Constable tell you what I told her?'

'Yes she did, but I would like to hear it first hand and clarify some points.'

Mr Mayhew sighed. 'It was shortly after six-thirty, I know because the six o'clock news had just finished. I went out to close my gate because it was banging in the wind. I happened to look up and saw Greg... Mr Taylor walking past number 29. A hooded teenager was coming

19

from the opposite direction. Greg turned to let him pass, but the stranger seemed to stop in front of Greg. When the teenager did walk past him, Greg was slumped on the ground against the wall.'

'You say a teenager, could it have been a man?'

'Yes... I just got the impression is was a teenager.'

'What about a female?'

Mr Mayhew looked at PC Richards as if seeking support. 'Well, I suppose its possible, but I don't think it was. You can tell by the way a person moves, even from a distance, whether they're male or female.'

'How tall was this person?'

'As tall as Greg Taylor, maybe slightly taller.'

Parish realised that he had no idea how tall the victim was. He'd have to get that information from the pathologist tomorrow morning.

'What about build? Was he thin, medium, or fat?'

'It was difficult to say in the dark, but he looked average.'

'So the person wore dark clothes with a hood, was of average build, and stood as tall as Mr Taylor?'

'Yes.'

'Then what happened? Did the person run away?'

'No, that's what was strange, he simply walked away as if he didn't have a care in the world.'

'And did you shout out, or go and see what had happened to Mr Taylor?'

'Well no, I didn't shout out because I was in shock. And as I explained to the Constable, I don't know anything about first aid, so I went to get Greg's wife, Debbie, and call the emergency services.'

Parish didn't understand why Mayhew hadn't raised the alarm by shouting out, and then gone over to see if his neighbour was still alive, but he didn't read anything sinister into it. He knew it took all types to make the world go round. Standing up he offered his hand and said, 'Thank you, Mr Mayhew. I'd be grateful if you could come to Hoddesdon police station tomorrow and make a formal statement.'

'Certainly,' he said and showed them out.

THREE

'Right, Richards,' Parish said as they left 33 Ralston Drive, 'before your shift ends let's go and sit in my car out of the cold and see what we've got.'

They walked across the road and climbed into the Mondeo. Parish switched on the ignition, the heater and the interior roof light. The digital clock on the dashboard showed seven fifty-five.

'Write my ramblings down in your notebook, Richards,' Parish said once they were settled. 'In no particular order, we've got three possible motives. The first is robbery, although if it was robbery we have no idea what was taken because the victim's wallet, wristwatch, or wedding ring weren't removed. Second, gang initiation, which will be difficult to prove, or to identify a killer because the victims are usually chosen at random. Third, the killer had a grudge against Mr Taylor, possibly one of his pupils.'

'I can't believe a pupil would kill Mr Taylor, Sir.'

'Why not?'

'Well, he was a good teacher. When I was at school, everyone liked him. He made history interesting.'

'That was then and this is now, Richards. Times have changed. Every week somebody becomes a victim of a knife crime in London. In America they shoot you, here they knife you.'

'Will we have to go to the school, Sir?'

'Why, do you have a problem going back to your secondary school?'

'No, Sir. It'll just be weird that's all.'

'You don't mind if we carry on do you, Richards?'

'Sorry, Sir.'

'As far as we know, Mr Taylor had no enemies who would resort to murder. The killer was either a male teenager or a man. So yes, we'll have to go to Chigwell secondary school and see if there are any likely suspects there. I'll also contact my informers and see if there's any word on recent gang initiations. Then, we'll have to see if Mrs Taylor can spot anything missing from her husband's effects. Anything else you can think of, Richards?'

'Me, Sir?'

'Yes you, Richards. You're now half of the Parish-Richards duo, so you need to contribute your share of the ideas.'

A worried expression spread over her face. 'If you say so, Sir.'

'I'm joking, Richards. You'll get used to my sense of humour, or lack of it. What I'm really saying is that if you do have an idea, speak up. I don't care how ridiculous it sounds I'm not going to shout at you, or make fun of you – well, not much anyway.'

'Thanks, Sir, I think.'

'Have you got your own car?'

'I've got an old Beetle, Sir. It's a rust-bucket, but it goes.'

'Okay. How about you drive to Hoddesdon in the mornings and leave your car in the car park. We can then take a pool car, and at night we can go home from there?'

'That's okay with me, Sir.'

'And you can stop calling me, "Sir". As much as I like being a Sir, I'm not there yet. Sergeant will do from now on.'

'Oh, okay, Sir. What time do you want me in the morning?'

'Meet me at eight-thirty, and from there we'll go to King George Hospital and find out when they're going to do the post mortem. With any luck, that might give us

23

some evidence we can use to narrow down the motive. Have you seen a post mortem before, Richards?'

'No, Sir.'

'You're not squeamish are you?'

'I don't think so, Sir. I saw my dad dead.'

'A post mortem is slightly different, Richards. I'd wear some clean underwear tomorrow morning.'

She looked at him and blushed again.

'That was another joke, Richards.'

'Okay, Sir... What about the rest of your team?'

'We're a team of two, Richards. I'm the acting DI, but without the rank or the pay, and you're the Detective Constable without the training or the experience.'

Richards smiled nervously. 'If you say so, Sir.'

'Don't worry, Richards, I've been a DS for seven years, there's not much I don't know about murder investigations. We're just going to be spread a bit thin that's all. There'll be no time for romantic assignations with paramedics, that's for sure.'

Richards blushed again.

'We also haven't got the manpower for a house-to-house, so we'll do a drop instead. I'll type something up later asking for information, make copies, and then sometime tomorrow we'll pop back and drop them through the letterboxes on both sides of the street. It shouldn't take us more than half an hour.'

'That's a brilliant idea, Sir.'

'Thanks, Richards. Right, anything else before we say goodnight?'

'I don't think so, Sir.'

'Okay, off you go then, and thanks for all your help tonight, Constable.'

She smiled and blushed. 'You're very welcome, Sir.'

As she opened the door and climbed out of the car it began snowing like the beginning of a nuclear winter.

Back in the small cold flat, the athletic-looking man took off his duffel coat and gloves and threw them on the back of the threadbare armchair. He pushed the hood back from his dark wavy hair and smiled. There was no joy behind the smile. Joy was an emotion that had been stolen from him many years ago. The smile was in recognition of his accomplishment. The murder of Mr Taylor had gone the way he had planned it would – no more, and no less.

He picked up the marker pen from where he'd left it on the Formica-topped coffee table that he had bought for three pounds from a charity shop, and walked towards the wall above the bed. A photograph of Mr Taylor grinned at him. He scored a black cross through the face and stepped back to view the effect.

'Not grinning now are you, you bastard?' he said out loud. He felt nothing. It was as if he had successfully completed a mundane task that had been outstanding for some time.

It had taken him two years to find a job and get settled after his release from prison for grievous bodily harm, and another three years to find out where they all were, but eventually he had found them. Now, it was simply a matter of a life for a life, fulfilling the promise he had made to himself and the others, tidying up the loose ends of the past so that accounts could be closed.

He stared at the next picture. He was tempted to put a cross through the woman's face, but he controlled himself. There was no rush. Instead, he went to the kitchen to get a beer, and slipped a ready-made meal into the microwave.

***

It was eight-forty when Parish walked into the station. He waved at the night shift playing poker downstairs whilst it was quiet. The detective's squad room on the second floor was cold and eerie, and he felt as though he'd walked into a deserted building. He sat down at his desk and switched on the computer. Like everything else in the station, it needed replacing. It took him ten minutes to get to the login screen and bring up his email. As usual, his inbox was full of mostly rubbish. Of the thirty-seven emails, he deleted all but two of them. He opened a new email and wrote his report for the Chief. It included everything he'd found out about Greg Taylor's murder, what he thought the possible motives were, and his loan of PC Mary Richards from Cheshunt police station. The last thing he did was to design a leaflet requesting that anybody with information about the murder should contact Hoddesdon Police Station. He gave the station telephone number rather than his mobile number because he didn't want to be answering phone calls from crazy people all day tomorrow. After printing the leaflet, he copied it a hundred times.

Outside in the car park, he had to brush the fresh snow from his three-year-old Ford Focus before he could get in and go home. Three inches of snow had fallen and stuck in an hour and a half. It was still snowing, and he guessed the Siberian weather would cause him no end of problems with his investigation.

He arrived home at nine-fifty. The ground floor flat, just off Conduit Lane behind the Conservative Club, had one bedroom and that was the best he could say about it. He called it home, but it wasn't really a home. It was just somewhere he parked himself when he wasn't working – like an automaton recharging its power cell. He hadn't bothered to put pictures up, or fill the empty surfaces with ornaments or photographs. What was the point? He lived alone. He was alone. His parents had died in a car crash when he'd been two years old, and confined him to the care system. They were poor, and they left him nothing except a senile old woman in a home who had died many years ago. There was an Aunt in Australia and an Uncle in Japan, but they didn't want to know him. He had no memories of being a child before he went into long-term fostering at eight years old. He had no brothers or sisters, no friends, and no relationships. When did he ever get the chance to meet anyone who wasn't a copper, a victim, or a suspect?

He took a one-person meal out of the one-person freezer, and put it into the one-person microwave. He didn't even bother to find out what the meal was, because they all tasted of plastic anyway.

He only had a small television in the kitchenette that he watched the news on, so he had treated himself to a wireless laptop last week. Against his better judgement he had logged on to an Internet dating agency a few days ago in the hope of finding someone to share his lonely existence with. At the moment he was browsing, learning the ropes, filling in his biography, which was obviously important because he didn't want to appear too desperate.

He powered up his laptop and logged on to the FindLove.com website. He smiled. God, he could just imagine his colleagues at the station finding out about his new hobby. They'd think he was a sad loser, and maybe he was. Sometimes, he wondered what he was doing, what it was all for.

The microwave pinged. He got up and put the plastic container on a tray, shook the salt and pepper pots on the steaming meal, and took it back to the armchair. Whilst he was browsing, he put forkfuls of the unappetising meal in his mouth, chewed and swallowed. He decided to finish his biography tonight, and put up the photograph he'd taken of himself with his mobile phone. It had needed a few tries to get a picture with a chin. He seemed to have a natural instinct to tuck his chin in every time he pressed the button. In the end he decided not to look at the camera, and that seemed to work. The photograph made him look intellectual, staring off into the distance as if he were contemplating the theory of everything. His black hair was slightly too long, but he thought it added to the illusion of mystery. His biography contained some little white lies, mainly about his interests and hobbies. He didn't want to sound like a lonely workaholic even if he was, so he had said he socialised, did hang gliding and walking in the Lake District. He expected everyone stretched the truth a bit on their biographies. Once he'd finished describing the person he'd like to be, he published it.

Let's see what we get, he thought. It was a bit like fishing, and he was the bait.

He closed down the laptop and went to bed. He tried to read a chapter of a novel about frozen Russian bodies in Gorky Park, but he couldn't concentrate. His mind was on the hundreds of beautiful women that were reading his biography and licking their lips in anticipation. He switched the light off and journeyed into the dark place to confront his nightmares again.

***

Wednesday, 15th January

It was five-fifteen when he woke up sweating. After peeing, he padded into the living room in his bare feet and boxer shorts, powered up the laptop and logged on to FindLove.com. Whilst it was loading, he made a mug of strong coffee to kick-start his internal organs.

There were three messages in his inbox. One was from a thirty-nine year-old who "liked it rough", and wanted him to use his handcuffs and truncheon on her. No thank you, he thought and deleted the message. The next one was from a twenty-eight-year-old with three children. A ready-made family, he pressed *delete*. The final message sounded more promising. It was from a thirty-year-old who, if the picture was to be believed, looked like a model. Her name was LoopyLou, but he suspected that it wasn't her real name, just as his wasn't Brad Russell – a combination of Brad Pitt and Russell Crowe. She ran her own clothes shop in Chigwell, and also liked to socialise and take walking trips in the Lake District. She wanted to meet him. He wrote a short note back:

LoopyLou: Thursday night, eight o'clock in Chigwell. You choose where. Brad.

As soon as he'd sent the reply he began getting palpitations. He had to stand up, bend over with his hands on his hips and take deep breaths to calm down. A reply came back almost immediately:

Eight o'clock at The Ram Inn on Curzon Street, I'll be in the yellow dress. LoopyLou.

Another early riser, he thought. He sent back:

Looking forward to it. See you there. Brad.

Smiling, he logged out and closed down the laptop. It was six-thirty and time he got ready for work. A date already, maybe his life was about to change.

He had two pieces of liberally buttered toast and another coffee for his breakfast. When he switched on the television news, he learned that whilst he'd been sleeping, another three inches of snow had fallen. Pictures of cars in stationary queues were shown to illustrate the chaos on the roads. A spokesman for the council gave a convoluted excuse about why the gritting hadn't made things any better.

Wishing that he owned a sled and a team of huskies, he left the flat at seven-thirty.

***

Even though he had left the flat in plenty of time to drive the mile and a half to the station, he still managed to arrive five minutes late.

Debbie, the Chief's secretary, hadn't arrived yet, so the Chief had made a pot of coffee, and offered Parish a cup. It looked and tasted like treacle, but he smiled, nodded his thanks, and put the cup down on the table. He didn't want to tell a terminally ill man his coffee sucked.

'Good report, Sergeant Parish,' the Chief said, 'but what's this about a PC Richards from Cheshunt?'

Parish could see that the Chief had printed his report out and had it on the desk in front of him. He wondered why a man with probably terminal cancer would still come to work in the mornings when he could easily get early retirement and do the things he'd never had chance to do.

'Because of the staff shortages here, Sir, I thought I'd try my luck co-opting someone from Cheshunt, and it worked. I've got her for two weeks.'

'Two weeks! I hope its not going to take you that long to solve a simple knifing, Sergeant?'

'I didn't say that, Sir. In a worst case scenario, I have the option of PC Richards' help for that length of time.'

'If I get a request to pay PC Richards' salary for the two weeks, you'll lose her, you know that?'

'I expected as much, Sir.'

Referring to the report, the Chief said, 'You've suggested three possible motives, Parish. What's your gut feeling? Is it a random knifing, or was Mr Taylor the target?'

'Too early to say, Sir, but from the limited information I have of Greg Taylor, it seems likely it was a random knifing. He was a teacher, hardly the stuff targets are made of.'

'Okay, good, I'm pleased with your progress so far, Parish, keep it up.'

Parish stood up, leaving the coffee untouched. 'Thanks, Sir. We'll know a lot more today after the post mortem.'

The Chief nodded, and Parish left.

He looked at his watch and realised that the five minutes he'd lost he still hadn't found, it was eight thirty-five. He looked out of the window overlooking the car park and saw PC Richards wrapped up in a red quilted coat, yellow snow boots, hat, scarf and gloves. She was occupying her time by building a snowman at the back of her VW Beetle.

***

'I hope this is not going to become a habit, Richards?' he said to her when he reached the car park.

'What, Sir?'

'You building a decidedly shabby snowman whenever you have to wait five minutes for me?'

Parish couldn't determine whether Richards was blushing or not, because she had healthy ruddy cheeks due to the exercise and the biting wind.

31

Richards threw a snowball that hit him on the arm and said, 'It's a better snowman than you could build, Sir.'

'I'm getting too old for snowball fights, Richards, and I have no desire to build snowmen.'

She threw another snowball, which hit him on the forehead, and then ran off behind a car.

He wiped the snow from his forehead. 'I'm beginning to regret asking you to help me, Richards,' he said angrily. 'We're involved in a serious murder investigation, and…'

Richards stood up and began to walk towards him. 'Don't say that, Sir, I was only…'

A snowball hit her on the top of the head.

'Sirrr?' she squealed.

They were both laughing as Parish ran off along the road towards the car pool garage with Richards chasing him.

'A truce, Richards?' Parish said when they reached the garage.

Richards had a snowball in her gloved hand that she threw in the air and caught again. 'Its not another one of your tricks is it, Sir?'

'No trick, Richards.'

'Okay, Sir,' she said warily moving away from him, but still holding onto the snowball.

'What's your driving like?'

'I think its good, Sir.'

'In this weather?'

'I can manage it.'

'I don't want to die.'

'Neither do I, Sir.'

'Okay, Richards, I'll let you drive and we'll see if we're still alive when we get to the hospital.'

'If we're not, Sir, we'll be in the right place.'

'Yes, very good, Richards.'

Once they were moving south along the A1112 towards Goodmayes Parish said, 'Tell me about yourself, Richards.'

'Really, Sir?'

'Yes, really.'

'There's not a lot to tell.'

'I want to know who's got my back.'

'Well, you know I went to Chigwell Secondary School, Sir. I left there with four A levels and went to the University of Greenwich to do a degree in Criminology and Criminal Psychology. Then I went to Hendon, then Cheshunt, and here I am.'

'That tells me where you went and what you achieved, but it doesn't tell me who you are, Richards. Surely you must have done the 'Who am I?' exercise at university?'

Richard's face dropped. 'Yes, Sir. I was the one the teacher picked on.'

'Good. So tell me, Richards, who are you?'

'I'm an only child, Sir. You know I lost my dad in a petrol station robbery, and that's what made me want to become a copper.'

'Do you still live with your mother?'

'Yes, Sir. We're best friends. I don't see any reason to leave home.'

'What drives you?'

Richards didn't speak for some time, and Parish had to check that her eyes were still open.

'I'm still thinking, Sir.'

'Okay.'

Eventually she said, 'I'm ambitious, Sir, but its fairness that drives me. I believe that everybody should be treated fairly.'

'You're in the wrong job, Richards.'

'And you're a cynic, Sir.'

'I know.'

'Who are you, Sir?'

'I'm your boss for the next two weeks, Richards that's who I am, so keep your mind on what you're doing.'

Parish found he was still in one piece when they arrived at King George Hospital. He had to admit that Richards was a good driver. Admittedly, the snow had turned to slush on the main roads and the traffic crawled along at five miles an hour, but she managed to get them to the hospital alive and that was the main thing.

Although he had been to the hospital on numerous occasions, Parish hadn't noticed before that the Mortuary was not identified on the main display board as a department. He imagined that the Board of Directors didn't really want to advertise that there was a whole department, which specialised in death.

He knew the way to the Mortuary anyway. Richards followed him through the main reception area where he bought a paper, then he took a right past the Fracture Clinic and the Outpatients Departments, another right past Beech and Ash Wards to the end of the corridor. The Mortuary was in Block 1 opposite the Catering Stores.

FOUR

The completely bald sixty-one-year-old Doctor Maurice Michelin stood five foot ten with brown eyes and a grey goatee beard. Apart from the wrinkles of time, his skin was blemish-free and it was clear that he played sport to keep in shape. He had nearly finished the post mortem of Greg Taylor and looked up when DS Jed Parish and PC Mary Richards arrived at the Mortuary.

The cadaver lay on the stainless steel table with its torso open from throat to groin like the gateway to hell. Doc Michelin was rummaging around inside as if he were searching for a childhood keepsake that had been mislaid many years before.

Parish glanced at Richards as she put her hand up to her mouth and turned a ghostly white.

'Are you going to be okay, Richards?'

'I'll be okay, Sir.' She moved back to the door. 'I'll wait for you over here.'

Parish stepped up to the table and peered into the empty cavern of Greg Taylor. It had been a long time since dead bodies had affected him. With all the organs removed and sitting in jars on the side for analysis, he could see the spinal cord glinting in the light.

'No DI with you this morning, Sergeant Parish?'

'I'm the DI today, Doc.'

'Are congratulations in order?'

'Not really, I've just been given the dirty end of the stick, no rank and no pay, just the work.' He introduced PC Richards.

'You'll be all right with Sergeant Parish, Constable, he's one of the good ones.' Michelin stood up straight and massaged his lower back with his left hand. 'Well, hopefully I've got some good news for you, Sergeant.'

Tim ELLIS

'You found a DNA match and you know who the killer is?'

Michelin gave a snort. 'Not that good, I'm afraid.'

'Go on then, make my day.'

'Two things. First, the victim was stabbed in the heart. Death would have occurred almost immediately. The wound, however, is not your usual knife wound.'

'In what way?'

'Its round instead of oblong.' He went over to a small whiteboard fixed to the wall behind him and drew the shape of a normal knife wound. 'This is your common or garden knife wound, which is usually bevelled towards the cutting edge, but most definitely oblong.' He drew a circle next to it. 'This is Mr Taylor's wound.'

'A knitting needle?' Parish suggested.

'Larger than a knitting needle, and tapered.'

'What then?'

'A marlinspike.'

'Never heard of one.'

Michelin went back to his computer and brought up the picture of a metal spike with a piece of string attached to it. 'That's what I think was your murder weapon.'

Richards edged closer, but kept a perfumed handkerchief over her nose and mouth. 'Looks like a tent peg,' she said when she saw the picture.

'Unlike the tent peg, Constable, which is hollow and a uniform diameter along its length, the marlinspike is solid and tapered.'

Parish scratched his head. 'What's it for, fishing?'

'In a way, yes. It's a tool used in rope work apparently.'

'So we might be looking for a sailor, or a fisherman?'

'I'm not saying that, Parish. What I'm saying is that Taylor was killed with a marlinspike. It might be that the killer found it in a charity shop and is simply using it as his murder weapon, but he has no idea what it is.'

Parish could see that knowing the murder weapon was a marlinspike wasn't going to be of much help unless they caught the killer, then it would probably condemn the bastard to life imprisonment. 'Okay, thanks Doc, what's the second thing?'

Michelin stood up. With his rubber wellingtons flopping on the floor, he walked over to where Mr Taylor's organs were sat in clear glass jars of formaldehyde. He slid a small evidence bag towards him off the top next to the spleen, and passed it to Parish. 'This little trinket was in the corpse's mouth.'

Parish looked at the small round metal coin with the number 27 stamped on it. He turned it over, but the obverse was blank. He looked enquiringly at Doc Michelin.

'Yes, you may well wonder what it is, Parish. You don't see them anymore, but they used to be produced in all shapes and sizes. This one looks as though its made from copper, but they were also made from brass, pewter, aluminium and tin.'

Parish passed the bag to Richards and said, 'It looks like a coin.'

'In a way it is,' Michelin agreed. 'It's a token, and might very well have been used as currency when it was produced.'

'Might?'

'Usually, the currency tokens had the value and the issuing authority stamped on them.'

'Doesn't the twenty-seven indicate a value?'

'Possibly, but possibly not. There's no issuing authority, and the twenty-seven has no denomination such as pence or cents.'

'So you're saying its not a currency token?'

'I'm not saying anything of the sort. Stop putting words into my mouth, Parish, next you'll be wanting me to sign a confession which says I did the dastardly deed.'

Parish smiled. 'So what are you saying, Doc?'

'It might be a currency token, but its more than likely not.'

'What other types of token are there?'

'There are railway tokens, but its not one of those. There are telephone tokens, but its not one of those either. There are barter and trade tokens, but again they usually had a value and issuing authority on them. More recently there are slot-machine tokens, but they have the casino stamped on them. There are variations on the themes, but I would say that this is not any of those.'

'Now that you've told me what its not,' Parish said feeling exasperated. 'What is it?'

'I have no idea, Sergeant. My suggestion would be to find someone who knows something about tokens.'

'The way you've been going on about them, I thought you were the resident expert.'

'No, I did a bit of research out of curiosity when I found the token in the victim's mouth, but I've exhausted my knowledge now.'

'Okay, did you take a picture of the token before you put it in the bag, so that I can show it around?'

'We're not complete amateurs in the suburbs you know, Sergeant.' Doc Michelin went to the printer and produced a 12" x 8" photograph incorporating blow-ups of both sides of the token and passed it to Parish. He also gave him a memory stick. 'That photograph, as well as others, is on there as a Jpeg.'

'You're a genius, Doc,' Parish said.

'It has been said on many occasions. Now, if there's nothing else, I need to get on. I'll send over the full report tomorrow morning, but you already know the important details.'

'One last thing. How tall was the victim?'

Doc Michelin referred to a clipboard with the outline of a human on a chart. 'One point seven eight meters.'

'And in old money?'

'Ah, you're one of those fossils are you? Five feet ten inches.'

'Someone's got to keep the flag flying, Doc.' Parish turned towards the door. 'Have a good one, and thanks.'

***

In the car outside, Parish stared at the photograph and wondered what the significance of putting the token in the victim's mouth was. He then looked at the paper to see what had been said about the stabbing.

Police have launched a murder inquiry after a man died of a stab wound in Chigwell, Essex.

Officers received reports of a man with stab wounds at 6.40pm on Tuesday night in Ralston Drive, Chigwell. Although paramedics rushed the man to hospital he was pronounced dead at 8pm. Forensic officers cordoned-off the area to conduct a search. No arrests have been made. The victim has not been identified and police have not released details of his age, though he is believed to be an adult. Chief Superintendent Walter Day of Hoddesdon Police Station said his murder team has begun an investigation and would release further details later. The number of recorded violent crimes increased by 3% in Chigwell from 2008 to 2009. The figure is twice the national average according to the British Crime Survey.

Parish's lips curled into a wry smile. ...his murder team... If the press only knew, he thought.

'Its freezing in here, Sir,' Richards said.

It *was* freezing. He recalled the female weather forecaster at the end of the morning news saying that temperatures were unlikely to go above $-5°C$, and that more snow was expected. It wasn't snowing yet, but the gunmetal sky looked as though there was a bucketful to come.

The engine was running and the heater was set to three. 'It'll soon get warm,' he said passing the photograph to Richards. 'What do you think this means then, Constable?'

She took her gloves off and blew on her hands. 'If the killer put the token in Mr Taylor's mouth...'

'I think we can take that as read, Richards. The victim was hardly sucking on it like a lozenge before he was murdered.'

'But Mr Taylor could have put it in his own mouth as a message to us.'

He hadn't thought of that. 'That's a damned good observation, Richards, well done, but I think we'll stick with the killer putting it in there. The simplest explanation is usually the right one.'

'Okay, Sir.' Richards stared at the photograph as if the solution was hidden somewhere on the paper like a magic eye illusion. 'Well, if the killer put it in there then he was telling us something.'

'Excellent.'

'Also, I don't think it was a random killing, Mr Taylor was probably the target.'

'Not necessarily, a gang member might be using the token as a tag.'

'What, you mean like a signature, Sir?'

'Yes.'

Richards didn't say anything.

'I know it sounds far-fetched, but it's early in the investigation and we shouldn't rule out an avenue of inquiry so soon.'

'Its not that, Sir, I was thinking about someone using a token as a signature. It might not be a gang member, it could be someone else.'

'Slow down, Richards, we don't want to start travelling down that road.'

'Sorry, Sir, it just came into my mind and with the marlinspike thing... well. I was watching a programme about the signatures of serial killers on the Crime Channel last night, and I started to think...'

'This is Chigwell in Essex, Richards, let's keep it real shall we? And stop using the Crime Channel as a substitute for proper police training.'

Richards blushed. 'Sorry, Sir. I suppose I am getting a bit carried away, but...'

'No buts, Richards. This will be an isolated murder with a logical explanation. We just have to keep collecting the jigsaw pieces until we find some that fit together and the picture starts to make sense. The last I heard, Anthony Hopkins was writing a cookbook somewhere in South America, he's not visiting Chigwell.'

Smiling, Richards said, 'What next, Sir?'

'Chigwell High Street.'

As they pulled out of the car park the day became night, and the snow fell from the sky like confetti at a wedding. Richards needed the lights on main beam and the windscreen wipers on ultra fast so that she could see where she was going.

When they reached Chigwell High Street Parish didn't bother getting out of the car but signalled to a couple of youths huddled in a doorway to come over. Yes, they'd heard about the murder. No, neither of them knew anything about it being gang-related. He told them to keep their ears open and contact him if they did hear something.

'They weren't much help, Sir.'

'No.' Parish looked at his watch. It was quarter to twelve. 'What about lunch, Richards?'

'That's very nice of you, Sir, but I have to watch my weight.'

'It wasn't an invitation, I have to eat to keep going. Drive down the road and park at the Chigwell Arms. You can watch me stuff my face with burger and chips, and feel good about yourself.'

***

The date of 1805 had been affixed to the outside of the pub. Inside, the crooked ceilings were designed for people of below average height, and Parish kept banging his head on the beams as he made his way to the bar.

They sat at a small round table with a beer mat under one leg. Parish had a pint of extra cold Guinness, Richards a diet coke.

'This snow isn't helping us is it, Sir,' Richards said absentmindedly.

'If necessary we'll walk, Richards,' Parish said. 'Okay, in the light of the two jigsaw pieces Doc Michelin has kindly given us, let's consider the motives for the murder again.'

Richards pulled her notebook and pen out. 'Robbery was the first one, Sir.'

'Do you think it was robbery, Richards?'

'No, Sir. I think that the token in Mr Taylor's mouth means something. If we find out what that is, we'll be able to solve the case.'

'I see. So, you don't think a robber, or a gang initiate left the token as a signature?'

'No, Sir. A robber wouldn't leave something so he could be identified, and as far as we know nothing of Mr Taylor's was stolen. I think we can forget about robbery as a motive, Sir.'

An unshaven man in a striped apron and hat brought Parish's burger and chips with the instruction to: 'Enjoy.' After liberally sprinkling the condiments over his plate he began to eat. With his mouth half-full he said, 'Okay, I agree with you. Cross robbery off our list of motives, Richards. Now, what about a gang initiation?'

'The marlinspike and the token make that unlikely, Sir. Gang members carry knives. The marlinspike looked a bit effeminate to me, like a large sewing needle. I don't think someone in a gang would be seen dead with one of those.'

'What about the token?' Parish said before stuffing a quarter of the burger in his mouth.

'Gang members use graffiti tags, Sir, not tokens. Not only that, the token was old. Where would a gang member get an old brass token from? I don't think they would be bothered with them, Sir.'

'So, should we cross off gang initiation then?'

'Yes, Sir.'

'Do it. That just leaves Mr Taylor as the target. And you said he was so nice that no one in their right mind could possibly harm him.'

'I know, Sir, but maybe whoever did murder Mr Taylor wasn't in their right mind.'

'I think we can safely assume that was the case, Richards. Murder is hardly a rational behaviour.'

'What happens now, Sir?'

'Well, all we've got left is Mr Taylor. You've eliminated everything else apart from the marlinspike, which I don't think is going to be much use until we catch the killer. I agree with you that the token is an important piece of the jigsaw, so we need to find out everything we can about it. We also need to dig around in Mr Taylor's life to find out why someone would want to kill him. Is that okay with you, Richards?'

Mary Richards smiled. 'We make a good team, Sir.'

'We certainly do, Richards. Did that paramedic ring you last night?'

Richards looked towards the bar as if something had caught her eye. 'No, Sir.'

Parish ate the last of his burger and drank the dregs of his Guinness. 'Richards, you're dealing with a professional here. I know when people are lying to me. When have you agreed to see him?'

Richards blushed. 'Saturday night, Sir.'

He raised an eyebrow. 'You might be working.'

'Then I won't see him. He knows I'm on an important case.'

'You'd better tell him that Hoddesdon Police Station was built over the remains of a medieval castle. When contractors were doing repairs to the boilers last year they found a set of stairs beneath the cellar. Those stairs lead to one of the castle's dungeons, which is in excellent condition. Implements of torture covered in dried blood were found inside that dungeon, Richards, and from time to time we take suspects down there, away from the tape recorders, the video cameras, and the two-way mirrors to extract confessions.'

Richards sat opposite him with her mouth open. 'Really, Sir?'

'What do you think, Richards?'

She laughed. 'You tell a good story, Sir, you had me going.'

'What I'm saying is, tell him he better look after you, or he'll find himself in that metaphorical dungeon.'

Mary Richards put her hand on his. 'Thanks, Sir.'

'Right,' Parish said getting up and putting on his coat and scarf. 'Enough of this touchy-feely crap. Let's go and do the drop at Ralston Drive. After that, we'll visit Chigwell Secondary School and see if we can identify any likely suspects, then before we call it a day we'll go and find someone who knows something about tokens.'

The leaflet drop took them less than half an hour because Richards turned it into a competition. As soon as Parish realised that he was in a race he was already two houses behind her, and although he put on a spurt he couldn't make up the ground he'd lost.

Richards crossed the road to meet him as he came out of the last house. 'You lost, Sir.'

They began to walk back up the road towards where Richards had parked the car.

Once Parish had brought his breathing under control he said, 'I didn't even realise we were racing, Richards.'

She turned to stare at him. 'I think I can spot when people are telling me lies as well, Sir.'

'Good for you, Richards,' he said and smiled.

FIVE

They arrived outside the locked gates of Chigwell Secondary School at two forty-five. A group of children were building a snowman on the pavement.

'Crap,' Parish said. 'A bit of snow and these bloody teachers close the school and give themselves more holidays.'

'It could be closed for a few days, Sir.'

'Thanks for being so helpful, Richards. Any idea where the Headteacher lives?'

'No, Sir, it's a different one from when I came here, but I didn't know where the last one lived either.'

'Very helpful.' He got out of the car and peered at the school sign. 'It says the Headteacher is Mrs Juliet Rambler, BSc (Hons), Cert Ed, NPQH. Is that the new one, Richards?'

'I suppose so, Sir,' Richards said through the open window. 'I don't know her.'

'Okay let's go and poke about in the local council offices, and see if we can't find someone who knows where she lives. If Mrs Rambler has rambled off to London shopping I'm going to arrest her for obstructing a police investigation.'

Parish got back into the car, and Richards put her window up.

'Where are the council offices, Sir?'

'Redbridge, Richards. Go down the B173 towards the A12.'

Once Richards was heading in the right direction along the B173 she said, 'You don't really think the killer is a pupil at the school do you, Sir?'

'Probably not, Richards, but we still have to eliminate it as an avenue of enquiry. Also, if we don't find any suspects among Mr Taylor's pupils or ex-pupils then where do we look? You heard Mrs Taylor, he was a teacher and had no enemies.'

At the reception desk in the foyer of Redbridge Council, Parish flashed his warrant card to the plump ginger-haired receptionist and asked for the Director of Education.

After a quick telephone call, the Receptionist told him that Mr Arnold Tindale wouldn't be available until five o'clock. As it was just coming up to four o'clock, they had an hour to kill.

'Where are we going to find a token expert, Richards?'

'We could look in the Yellow Pages.'

'Good thinking,' Parish said and interrupted an old woman complaining about her bin not being emptied. The Receptionist gave him a look of disgust, but passed him the Yellow Pages anyway. He riffled the pages to 'T', but as expected he found nothing resembling 'Tokens'. Then he turned to 'C' for 'Coin & Medal Collectors' and struck lucky. There were only a few in the local area, and one was located close to the Market Square.

'Remember this address, Richards.'

'Okay, Sir,'

'25 Lanyan Road. Got it?'

'Yes, Sir.'

Parish closed the Yellow Pages, and left it on the counter where it lay. 'Right, let's go,' he said.

'Now, Sir? Will we have enough time?'

They glanced up at the large clock above the reception desk. It was four-fifteen.

'Fifteen minutes to get there, fifteen minutes for a question and answer session, and fifteen minutes to get back. Come on, Richards, we haven't got much time.'

He strode out with her chasing after him.

It took them twenty-five minutes to reach the address and park the car in a snowdrift against a garden wall. As soon as they climbed out of the car it began to snow again.

Stanley Shawcross: Medal & Coin Collector, was located in the cellar of a town house, and they had to clatter down a metal spiral staircase to get to the entrance. There was no bell on the door and no sound in the shop when they entered. The room they were in wasn't a large room, which was made even smaller by the stacks of old books and magazines, and a floor-to-ceiling cabinet containing trays presumably full of coins and medals. There appeared to be no heating in the shop, and it reeked of mould.

'Hello?' Parish called.

'Yes?' A sallow unkempt man with straggly grey hair and a week's growth of beard appeared from behind a stack of magazines.

Parish said, 'Are you open?'

The man took off a pair of slim reading glasses and stared at Parish before he answered. 'Was the shop door locked?'

'No,' Parish said and then realised that it was a ridiculous question. How else could he have been in the shop talking to the proprietor if the door had been locked? Then he felt stupid when he became aware that was the purpose of the question.

'Then we must be open,' the man said. 'What can I do for you?'

'Tokens.'

'I have a few, but they're not really something I specialise in.'

Parish produced his warrant card. 'I'd like your help with something?'

'Why not, it's not as if I have a rush on.'

'I presume you are Mr Stanley Shawcross?'

'Yes, I'm a one-man band.'

Parish pulled the photograph of the two sides of the token from his coat pocket and gave it to Mr Shawcross.

'Yes, its definitely a token,' Shawcross said.

'What we're interested in is who issued it and where it might have been used.'

'I doubt whether you'll be able to find those things out. Usually, the issuing authority, or where it can be redeemed, is stamped on the token. This could have been used anywhere for any purpose. Often, businesses would make and use them internally for various reasons, not simply as a replacement for money. Twenty-seven might mean many things such as, twenty-seven pence, number twenty-seven in the queue, or a person identified as number twenty-seven instead of a name. I could think of some more if you want me to?'

'That won't be necessary, Mr Shawcross, I get the message.'

'Let's not give up too soon though. As I said, I'm not the expert on tokens, but I know a man who is.'

He disappeared behind the stack of magazines, then reappeared holding a scrap of paper. 'Arvid Carlgren, that's who you want. If anyone can tell you anything useful about your token, it'll be him. He lives in Sweden, but here's his email address.' Shawcross passed the bit of paper to Parish. 'Just tell him I recommended him and he'll answer your questions if he can. You'll obviously have to send him the picture of the token as an attachment.'

'You've been very helpful, Mr Shawcross, thank you very much.'

'You're welcome, have a good day.'

Outside it was dark and the falling snow reflected in the orange glow from the streetlights.

'It's five to five, Sir,' Richards said. 'We're never going to get back to the Council offices for five.'

'Mr Tindale will wait for us.'

Richards pulled a face. 'If you say so, Sir.'

'Now who's being cynical?'

It was twenty-five past five by the time they got back to Redbridge Council offices. There were no lights on and the glass front doors were locked.

Parish kicked one of the doors. 'I'm going to arrest everyone connected with Redbridge Council,' he said. 'And then I'm going to take them down to the dungeon at Hoddesdon Police Station one by one and torture them.'

Richards smiled. 'We'll just have to come back tomorrow won't we, Sir.'

Parish's anger dissipated. He sighed, hunched himself into his coat, and started walking back to the car. 'Bloody local politicians. I hate them, Richards they're all as bad as each other. They climb aboard the gravy train and pay themselves ridiculous salaries from our money to lord it over us, and then when we want them to do something for us there's always some reason why they can't do it. We should line them up and pour excrement over them.'

They reached the car and climbed in.

'What do you think, Richards?'

'I'm sure you're right, Sir.'

'I knew you'd agree with me.'

'Back to Hoddesdon, Sir?'

'We've got nothing else better to do.'

When they reached the station, Richards took the pool car back to the garage and then went home in her VW rustbucket. Parish trudged up to the squad room. Once he'd logged on to his computer he wrote and sent the Chief a report and emailed Arvid Carlgren in Sweden. Attached to both was a Jpeg of the token.

Thursday, 16th January

'A bloody token in the victim's mouth, Sergeant,' the Chief said when Parish knocked and entered for his meeting. 'What's that about?'

'I wish I knew, Sir.' He was surprised at how ill the Chief looked this morning. His eyes were like sunken galleons in two dark whirlpools.

'And you've ruled out robbery, and a gang initiation?'

'Yes, Chief.'

'Have you heard back from the Swede yet?'

'Not yet, Sir, but they're an hour ahead of us, so I should hear something soon.' Parish's mind went back to earlier in his flat when he had powered up the laptop and logged on to FindLove.com. There had been five messages from eager females wanting his attention. He had laughed out loud as he realised he was in demand by women for the first time in his life. Three of the messages were from women who could devour him whole and he had deleted them, but the other two looked promising. There was no rush to respond though, he was seeing LoopyLou tonight. He'd see how the date went and then decide whether to respond. If they were that keen, they'd wait 'I'm sorry, Sir, what was that?'

'This murder investigation isn't disrupting your sleep patterns is it, Parish?'

'No, Sir, I started thinking of the token again,' he lied.

'A bit of a puzzle that's for sure, but you'll work it out. I have every confidence in you, Sergeant.'

'Thank you, Sir.'

'Is PC Richards holding up okay?'

'Best partner I've had in a long time, Sir.'

51

'I rang Cheshunt yesterday and thanked them for letting her work with you. Are you interested in making it permanent?'

'Are you sure, Sir? She'll be jumping over hundreds who want to be detectives.'

'If we get her transferred here, she's new and wouldn't cost us the same amount as a proper detective. We could then give her to you on special assignment.'

Parish realised that the Chief's prime motive was saving money. 'I'll speak to her, Chief, see whether it's what she still wants to do. She was keen at the start, but the novelty might have worn off by now. After working with me for a couple of days, she might want to go back to pounding the beat.'

'Let me know tomorrow, Sergeant, I'll set the cogs in motion. So, what's your plan for today?'

'I need to find out about the victim. His wife said he had no enemies and PC Richards said he was a really nice bloke who everybody liked, but someone clearly wanted him dead. The token was a message, we just don't know what that message is yet. Hopefully, the Swede will respond soon and decipher its meaning for us.'

'Well done, Parish. The investigation is proceeding apace. You'll soon have the killer in custody.'

Parish realised he was being dismissed. 'I hope so, Sir,' he said as he stood up and left.

It was eight-forty. He looked out of the window. Richards had already collected the pool car, and was working on the rough edges of her snowman. She had obviously come prepared because her work of art now had a stony stare and smile, a carrot for a nose, an old black and white striped scarf round its neck, and large orange buttons down its front.

Outside in the snow-covered car park, Parish said, 'How old did you say you were, Richards?'

'When I'm building a snowman, Sir, I'm with my dad and I'm five years-old.' She smiled and stood back to admire the snowman. 'Not so shabby now, hey Sir?'

Parish bumped his hip against her arm. 'Not so shabby, Richards. I'm sure your dad would be very proud of you.'

'Thanks, Sir.' She was quiet for a moment then said, 'I checked and Chigwell Secondary School is still closed. Are we going to Redbridge Council to arrest everybody now, Sir?'

'We certainly are, Richards, especially the Director of Education, Arnold Tindale. We'll handcuff him and bring him back to that dungeon I was telling you about deep underneath the station and torture him. Once we've done that, I'm sure I'll feel much better.'

***

The same ginger-haired receptionist stood behind the enquiry desk at Redbridge Council offices when they arrived. According to a green badge her name was Astrid, and she looked at Parish as if he'd been sleeping in the park with skunks. She rang Mr Tindale's secretary only to discover that he had flown to Bermuda on a fact-finding mission.

Parish nearly said something that would have finished his career, but Richards nudged his arm before he did. Instead, he asked if he could see Mr Tindale's secretary.

They went up to the fourth floor in the lift.

Richards whispered, 'You nearly said something then, didn't you, Sir?'

'Thanks to you, Richards, I still have a career.'

'I'm getting to know you, Sir.'

'What you see is what you get, Richards.'

The lift pinged and the doors opened. Mrs Julia Preston, Mr Tindale's secretary, a thin woman in her fifties with a severe-looking bun on top off her head, met them in the corridor and, after finding out what they wanted, gave Parish Mrs Rambler's address in Surrey.

'Surrey!' Parish said exasperated. 'Have you got a telephone number for her, there's no way we'd make it to Surrey in this weather?'

Mrs Preston took the paper back, wrote down a telephone number, and then returned it to him.

On the way down in the lift Richards said, 'Asking questions over the telephone isn't going to be very good is it, Sir?'

'What choice do we have?'

'I was thinking that the Deputy Headteacher, Miss Lupin, lives locally. She's been at the school forever, and would probably know more than the new Headteacher about Mr Taylor.'

'And you're telling me this now instead of yesterday because?'

'Sorry Sir, it only just occurred to me.'

As they stepped outside it started snowing again.

'Do you know where Miss Lupin hibernates during the winter?'

'Yes, Sir.'

'Let's go then shall we.'

***

It was a large house set back from the road close to Chigwell Golf Course. A car covered in ten inches of snow stood in the drive. The path beyond the gate hadn't been scraped, and it was an obstacle course to reach the front door.

Nobody answered, but a dog barked.

'Doesn't look as though Miss Lupin is in,' Parish said.

'Her car is still here.'

They walked in opposite directions and met at the rear of the house. There were no footprints except there own, and the curtains were all closed. They returned to the front door and knocked one more time. The dog barked, and Richards squatted to look through the letterbox.

'I can see the dog, Sir. It's a Yorkie, and the mail is all over the hall carpet. I think something has happened to Miss Lupin.' She put her mouth to the opening and shouted. 'Miss Lupin, are you there?'

The dog barked louder, but Miss Lupin didn't answer.

Parish tried the front door and it opened. Richards fell forwards onto her knees.

'Sirrr?'

The dog ran forward adopting the pose and facial expression of a guard dog, but without the bulk it wasn't really going to be taken seriously.

Richards stood up and shouted Miss Lupin's name again, but received the same response. 'Should we go in, Sir?'

'You lead, Richards.'

'Me, Sir?'

'You're not scared are you?'

Richards tried not to step on the assortment of letters, free and paid-for newspapers, pizza leaflets, and so forth, but there was at least four days worth. The dog barked, growled, and backed-up.

'Can you smell it, Richards?'

'Yes, Sir.'

'You feed the dog and call for an ambulance, and I'll see if I can find Miss Lupin.'

Richards headed for the kitchen. Parish didn't have far to look. A decomposing Miss Lupin was dead in an armchair in the lounge, her eyes were still open. The television was on mute, and she had an open book in her lap. It didn't look as though she had been murdered. He closed the old woman's eyes and used a throw from the sofa to cover her up so that Richards didn't have to see her old teacher.

This case was turning to shit in a handbasket, he thought. Another morning wasted. He took out his mobile and the paper Mr Tindale's secretary had given him and rang Mrs Rambler's number.

'Hello?' It was a child's voice.

'Can I speak to your mother please,' he said.

'Hello?' The phone was now in the hands of a woman.

'Is that Mrs Juliet Rambler, the Headteacher at Chigwell Secondary School?'

'Yes, who is this?'

'I'm Detective Sergeant Parish from Hoddesdon Police Station.'

'What can I do for you, Sergeant? Has there been a break-in?'

'No, there hasn't been a break-in. I have information for you, Mrs Rambler, and I suggest you sit down.' He leapt straight in. 'First, I'm sorry to have to tell you that Mr Gregory Taylor was stabbed and killed on Tuesday night outside his home.'

There was a long silence from the phone. 'Are you still there, Mrs Rambler?'

'Yes, I'm still here, Sergeant. What else?'

'At the moment I'm stood in Miss Lupin's lounge. I'm sorry to have to tell you that it appears she has died of natural causes. I'm waiting for the ambulance to arrive at the moment.'

'Oh my God,' Mrs Rambler said. 'Perri Lupin dead? …And Greg Taylor?'

'I came here to talk to Miss Lupin about Mr Taylor, but I obviously can't do that now, so I'll have to talk to you.'

'Is that the third thing?'

'Yes. We think that Mr Taylor was the intended target rather than a random killing.'

'I didn't know him very well, but I find that hard to believe. He was well liked by faculty and pupils alike.'

'I was going to ask you if Mr Taylor had any enemies – current or ex-pupils?'

'As far as I am aware there is no one, but I haven't been at the school long.'

'Is there someone who lives locally that we could talk to about Mr Taylor?'

'Mr Bell, Mr Taylor's Head of Department, lives in Chigwell. Just a moment while I get his address…' The phone went dead for over a minute. 'Sorry Sergeant, someone had moved my briefcase. Have you got a pen and paper?'

'Yes.'

'45 London Road.'

'Yes, I know where it is,' Parish said.

'I'll have to drive up there, speak to the Governors, the Director of Education, and…'

'Mr Tindale is on a fact-finding mission to Bermuda apparently.'

'Yes… Is there anything else, Sergeant, I have a million things to do as a result of your phone call?'

'No, but you….'

'Thank you, Sergeant. Goodbye.'

The call disconnected. Bitch, he thought. He was going to offer his condolences.

Richards walked in. 'I've fed the dog, Sir, and the ambulance will be here soon. I've also rang the RSPCA to come and collect the dog, unless you want it?'

'What would I do with a dog, Richards? Are you okay?'

'Yes, I'm fine, Sir. Did Miss Lupin die of natural causes?'

'Looks that way.'

'Who were you talking to?'

'Mrs Rambler. I told her about the two deaths and asked her about Mr Taylor. She's pointed me in the direction of Mr Bell, Head of History.'

'Yes, he's been at the school for a long time as well.'

The ambulance arrived. They told the two paramedics everything they knew and left.

'Number 45 London Road, Richards. Let's hope Mr Bell is still alive.'

SIX

It was ten-past twelve as they drove past a café with steamed-up windows on the way to 45 London Road.

'Pull in here, Richards,' Parish said. 'I'm starving.'

Richards parked outside the *Hungry Hippo* café on High Road in Chigwell. The café boasted: "The Best Breakfast in Essex". Parish licked his lips in anticipation.

Inside, the café was reasonably busy with a mixture of truckers and families. Parish ordered the Olympic Breakfast and a tea, whilst Richards eventually chose brown toasted bread with organic jam and a water.

'You've got no chance of being in the 2012 Olympics, Sir. Your cholesterol level must be sky-high. Do you always eat like this?'

'Are you doing a survey for the NHS, Richards?'

'I'm just thinking of your health, Sir. Would you like to come to my mum's house for Sunday lunch?'

'Do I look like I need a decent meal?'

'Yes, Sir?'

'What time?'

'One o'clock.'

'Thanks, I'd like that, Richards. It obviously depends on what's happening with the case.'

'Of course, Sir.'

'Are you sure your mother won't mind?'

'No, Sir, she'll be pleased as Punch.'

'You're not trying your hand at matchmaking are you, Richards?'

'Me, Sir? I wouldn't know how.'

'I bet.'

Just then the food arrived and Parish focussed all his energies on devouring the cooked breakfast.

Richards barely touched her brown bread and jam.

'Today isn't going so well is it, Sir?'

'I've had better days, Richards. Up to now, we've wasted a whole morning, and this afternoon doesn't look too promising either. It's not a pupil, and seeing Mr Bell is purely a process of elimination.'

'We haven't got any other suspects, Sir. What will we do after we've seen Mr Bell?'

'At the moment, Richards, I have no idea.'

'What about going to see Mrs Taylor and asking her about Mr Taylor's past. If Mr Taylor was the intended target, then the killer must have had a reason to kill him. And if the killer isn't a pupil, then who else would have had a reason to murder Mr Taylor? He's been teaching History at Chigwell Secondary School for at least ten years, but what did he do before that? Maybe Mr Taylor's past came back to stab him in the heart.'

'You were doing well until you started getting overdramatic, Richards.' He pulled his phone out and found the number for the Mortuary in his contact list. Only a copper would have the Mortuary on speed dial, he thought.

'Michelin?'

'Hi Doc, its Parish.'

'What can I do for you, Sergeant?'

'Has Mrs Taylor been in to formally identify her husband yet?'

'Three o'clock this afternoon.'

Parish checked his watch. It was five to one. He had two hours. 'I'll be there, I need to talk to her. Thanks, Doc.'

'Glad to be of assistance, Sergeant.'

Parish disconnected the call.

'Maybe this afternoon isn't such a good time to speak to Mrs Taylor, Sir,' Richards said. 'She'll be upset from identifying her husband.'

'I'm as empathetic as the next guy, Richards, but we need to keep the momentum going. We haven't got the luxury of time.'

He gulped down his tea. 'Have you finished starving yourself?'

'Yes, Sir.'

He went up to the till and paid.

Outside, he spotted an Internet Café two doors away. 'You go and warm the car up, Richards, I'm going to see if there's an email from Arvid Carlgren. Maybe today won't be a waste after all.'

The place was filthy, with filthy monitors and keyboards positioned around the room. A group of Goths dressed all in black stared at him as if he were the *Marquis de Sade* carrying a whip and chains. He ignored them and sat down at a free computer.

Arvid Carlgren had sent him a short email. He printed it off. There was also an email from the Chief changing the time of tomorrow's meeting from 8.15 to 10.15. He was out on the town with LoopyLou tonight, and God-knows what else afterwards if he was lucky. A lie-in might be just what he needed.

He collected the printout, paid £2.50 for the pleasure, and went out to the car.

'Was there an email, Sir?' Richards asked.

Parish opened the folded printout and read it out:

Without the issuing authority stamped on the token it is nearly impossible to give you any relevant information. However, if you provide me with the metal content of the token, I should be able to help you. I have other tokens with only numbers on, but I have none with the number 27 on, which might be relevant.

Arvid Carlgren

Token Specialist
Stora Herrestad'

'That sounds promising, Sir.'

'Yes, we'll have to go and see Mr Toadstone in forensics and get him to analyse the metal content of the token, if he hasn't already done it.'

'Mr Bell's house?'

'When you're ready, Richards.'

She pulled out and headed towards London Road.

'I also received an email from the Chief postponing my eight-fifteen meeting with him until ten-fifteen, which means we can both have a lie-in tomorrow morning. Come to the station at eight thirty-five instead of eight-thirty, Richards.'

'Don't be mean, Sir.'

Parish grinned. 'All right, I don't want you thinking I'm some kind of mean-spirited dictator, make it nine-thirty.'

Richards smiled. 'Thanks, Sir.'

'And whilst we're on the subject of being mean, the Chief wants to know if you'd like to be transferred to Hoddesdon?'

The car swerved. 'To be a detective, Sir?'

'Try not to kill us both, Constable.'

'Sorry, Sir, but…'

'To be a detective it takes five years on the beat, and then you have to do a three-phase competency-based course over twelve months at the end of which you sit the National Investigators Examination.'

'Then…'

'Once you're at Hoddesdon, the Chief will allocate you to me on special assignment.'

'Is that allowed, Sir?'

'It's seriously bending the rules, Richards. If you do something wrong, heads will bounce in the basket. Especially mine.'

'When?'

'If you say yes, I'll let the Chief know in my daily report. He'll then start oiling the machinery. It should be a done deal by the time your two weeks are up.'

'Okay, Sir. I like this work better than what I was doing before.'

'That was the wrong response, Richards.'

'Okay, I like working with you, Sir.'

'Now we're getting somewhere, but it won't be a walk in the park you know. Everybody will hate you for pole-vaulting over the hundreds that are waiting for their chance to become detectives. You'll become a pariah.'

'Don't you want me to say yes, Sir?'

'I want you to come into this with your eyes open, Richards. I like working with you. You've shown initiative and I need someone I get on with that I can bounce ideas off. So yes, I do want you to say yes.'

'Thanks, Sir.'

'Also, you're lucky because I'm a Tutor Detective, which means I can train you to be a detective so that when the five years are up, and you're ready to go on the course you'll be way ahead of everyone else.'

'Does that mean we're partners, Sir?'

'I guess it does, Richards. Now stop talking so much and drive the damned car.'

The grin was sculpted onto Mary Richard's face. 'Yes, Sir.'

***

Constable Mary Richards pressed the bell of 45 London Road in Chigwell, and Mr Roland Bell opened the door.

'Yes…?' The bald-headed man was sloppily dressed in a pair of grey tracksuit bottoms and an Arsenal shirt. He stared at Richards more closely. 'I know you don't I?'

'Mary Richards, Sir.'

'That's right, you got an A* in your History A Level… three years ago?'

'Yes, Sir.'

'So, why are you ringing my doorbell when school is out?'

Parish showed his warrant card and introduced himself. 'Constable Richards is working with me, Sir.'

Bell turned back to Richards and looked wistful. 'A policewoman already. It only seems like yesterday that I was telling you to stop chewing gum and sticking it under the table.'

Richards blushed.

'So, you've come about Greg Taylor?'

'Yes, Sir,' Parish said.

'The Head – Mrs Rambler – rang me about thirty minutes ago, I've had time for it to sink in. He'll leave a massive hole in my department, he was an excellent teacher.' Remembering where he was he said, 'Oh sorry, we don't want to be standing out here on the doorstep freezing to death do we, come in.' He stood to one side whilst they entered, then he shut the door. 'Please, follow me,' and he led them into a dishevelled living room. 'Excuse the mess, I was trouncing my son on the Xbox.'

'Huh, as if,' came from another room.

Mr Bell smiled. 'I'm one of the four hundred thousand divorced men paying a fortune to the CSA, but I can stretch to a cup of tea?'

'Thank you, Mr Bell, but we've just had lunch. I'd like to ask you a couple of questions about Mr Taylor if I may?'

'Of course, I'll tell you what I can.'

Richards had her notebook and pen ready.

'How long has Mr Taylor been at the school?'

'His whole teaching career. Well, that's not strictly true. He used to be at Ravenscroft School before it amalgamated with Chigwell in 1994 under the Conservatives Grant-Maintained initiative.'

'Was he always a teacher?'

'As far as I know. He never mentioned having done anything else.'

'Which university did he attend?'

'Bristol.'

'From what I understand, he had no enemies?'

'The pupils loved him.' He looked at Richards and she smiled. 'And apart from the odd squabble, none of which were life-threatening, he was well-liked by the staff.'

'A past pupil?'

'No one springs to mind. Yes, there have been some toe-rags, but I'm sure none of them are killers. You don't teach people for five years or more without knowing what they're capable of.'

Parish stood up and extended his hand. 'Thank you very much for your time, Mr Bell.'

'I'm sorry I couldn't identify the killer for you. I hope you catch the bastard.' He glanced at Richards. 'Sorry, Mary.'

'That's okay, Sir, I've heard you say it before.'

'Are you trying to get me arrested?'

Parish led the way to the front door.

'I was thinking, Sir,' Richards said to him as they were climbing into the car. 'We need to see Mr Taylor's personnel file, that will give us his career history.'

Parish smiled. 'It was a good day when I chose you, Richards, I was thinking exactly the same thing.'

'Thanks, Sir.'

He looked at his watch. It was one-fifty. 'First though, we've got to get to the Mortuary for three o'clock to see Mrs Taylor.'

'I'm not sure that's a good idea, Sir.'

'Oh?'

'Well, all she will tell us is probably what Mr Bell told us, and it'll be based on her memory. I think we'd be better getting Mr Taylor's file, it will give us objective facts.'

'Objective facts! Are those something they told you about at university, Richards?'

Richards blushed. 'You know what I mean, Sir.'

'All right, Constable, we'll go in search of these objective facts you're so fond of.'

After ringing Mrs Rambler to obtain her secretary's number, he called the said secretary – Mrs Rowena Lovitt – who lived locally, and arranged for her to meet them at the school to hand over the file at four o'clock.

'Four o'clock, Sir? We could go now.'

Parish still had an idea that he might be able to talk to Mrs Taylor after the identification process. 'Someone has to witness the formal identification, Richards, it's the law.'

'Oh, I didn't know that, Sir.'

'Three weeks on the job, I'm sure there's a lot you don't know.'

'Does it have to be us that attends, Sir?'

'No, usually when victims are being formally identified someone at the Mortuary will ring the station. The Duty Sergeant will send a Constable at the specified times.'

'Oh.'

'Now drive, and stop talking.'

'Yes…' She closed her mouth when Parish's head swivelled to stare at her.

***

When they arrived at King George Hospital there was still thirty minutes to fill before the formal identification, so Parish suggested that they go up to the hospital restaurant and get a cup of tea.

At the counter, he helped himself to a triple chocolate muffin as well as a mug of tea. He saw Richards looking at him as she took a bottle of water from the cooler shelf.

'Don't say a word, Richards. If I don't have my daily intake of chocolate I get really crabby. And anyway, they've found that chocolate prevents cancer.'

'You won't have to worry about cancer, Sir, you'll have died of a heart attack long before that.'

'You couldn't help yourself could you, Richards?'

Parish paid and they found a table.

'This is becoming a difficult case isn't it, Sir?'

The muffin was like glue sticking to his upper palate, and he had to swill his mouth with tea so that he could talk. 'Let's say that I was hoping to have it solved by now.'

'I'd hate my first murder case to go on the unsolved pile, Sir, especially as its someone I know.'

He gave up with the muffin and pushed the plate to one side. 'In a way, Richards, this is my first case as well, in charge anyway, so it's not going on the unsolved pile.'

'I'm glad, Sir.'

Mrs Taylor was sat on a wooden bench with her two children outside the Viewing Room waiting to formally identify her husband. It was five to three. Parish and Richards nodded respectfully as they approached, words would be superfluous.

Parish told Richards to stay with the family whilst he went into the Mortuary to speak to Doc Michelin.

'Did you get the post mortem report, Sergeant?'

'I haven't been back to the station since early this morning, Doc, anything new in it?'

'Nothing, I gave you everything I had yesterday. Any progress on the token?'

He told him about Arvid Carlgren in Sweden and his request for the metal content of the token.

'Yes, I suppose that would be a bit like a fingerprint. Oh well, lets get this identification over with. One of the more unpleasant aspects of my job unfortunately.'

Parish followed the Doc out into the corridor. 'When you're ready Mrs Taylor, if you'll follow me.'

Mrs Taylor stood up and followed the doctor into the Viewing Room.

Richards held her arm.

Gregory Taylor lay on a stainless steel table. His head was showing, but a starched white sheet covered his body.

It was over very quickly. When asked by Doc Michelin if the corpse was her husband, Mrs Taylor nodded. Her face was a map of wrinkled grief. She turned and rushed back into the corridor, and her children hugged her. The doctor informed Mrs Taylor that she could arrange the funeral as soon as she wanted to. Richards made encouraging noises.

Parish realised that Richards had been right. There was no way he could have asked Mrs Taylor any questions. Richards was good, he had to admit it. She seemed to know instinctively what to do. And better still, she wasn't afraid to speak her mind. It made a nice change to have a partner he got on with. His last partner – DC Toby Gorton – had been a right miserable bastard. All he'd wanted to do was study the horse racing form guides. And he smelled. God, you had to make sure you stood upwind, because if you were downwind the rancid stench of an unwashed body would have put you in the hospital. The deterioration began after his wife had left him and taken the kids with her. He was addicted to gambling. Everything and everyone became subordinate to that addiction. When he hadn't been to work for two weeks, Parish went round to his house. He had to break the door down because Gorton was sat naked in a heavily stained bath with hundreds of horse racing form guides looking for the perfect winner. They committed him to Claybury Mental Hospital on the outskirts of Chigwell, and as far as Parish knew he was still there.

That had all happened four months ago, and Parish decided then that he'd do without a partner for a while. Of course, that was until the Chief had given him this case, and he'd co-opted PC Mary Richards.

***

It was three thirty-five when they climbed back into the Mondeo in the hospital car park.

'The school, Sir?'

'Yes.'

'That wasn't very pleasant was it, Sir?'

'It never is, Richards, but you did a good job in there, well done.'

'Thanks, Sir. I nearly became a nurse like my mum, but in the end I decided on the police.'

'Nursing's loss is our gain. Is your mum still a nurse?'

'Yes, she works in the Intensive Care Unit in the hospital.'

'You could have gone up and seen her if you'd said.'

'She's not there, Sir, she's on night duty. Finishes Friday night.'

'Just in time to make my Sunday lunch.'

'Yes, Sir.'

They were five minutes early, but the gates of the school were unlocked and the front door was open.

A natural blonde-haired woman with more than her fair share of mammary glands met them just inside the door. Another man, who was either her husband or the caretaker, stood to one side like a bodyguard, but wasn't introduced.

'Can I see some identification before I hand over the file,' the woman said.

Parish produced his warrant card.

'Thank you.' She gave the file to Parish and glanced at Richards. 'You used to be a pupil here didn't you?'

'Yes, Miss Lovitt, I'm Mary Richards.'

'So you are, and a policewoman now? Well, I hope you're going to catch whoever killed Mr Taylor?'

'We will, Miss Lovitt.'

She turned back to Parish and adopted a stern expression. 'When can I have my file back, Sergeant?'

'When is the school going to be open again?' he countered.

'When it stops snowing.'

'That's when you'll get your file back then.'

'Oh!'

SEVEN

'Back to the station, Richards.'

She pulled away from the front of Chigwell Secondary School and headed towards Hoddesdon Police Station. It was nearly completely dark and the streetlights had come on.

'What does the file say, Sir?'

'This is not a speaking file, Richards, and I don't like reading whilst I'm a passenger in a car it makes me feel sick.'

'What are we going to do when we get back to the station?'

'We'll create an incident board and try to make sense of what we've got so far. And when we do find a suspect, I'm going to let you interrogate him, Richards. I have a feeling no one could hide anything from you for long.'

'If you want me to stop asking questions, Sir, you only have to say so.'

'A detective that doesn't ask questions is like an elephant without a trunk.'

She glanced sideways at him and said, 'Okay, Sir. If you say so.'

They reached the station at four thirty-five. Richards dropped Parish off, and he told her to take the car back to the garage and then come up to the second floor of the station. It was time he introduced her to everyone.

After telling PC Susan Meredith on the desk to let Richards up to the squad room, he made a detour via forensics before they closed up for the night. When he got there Toadstone had his coat on and was heading for the door. Parish told him he wanted the metal content of the token analysed, and Toadstone said he'd do it first thing in the morning and email him the results by nine-thirty.

The squad room was beginning to empty for the night as Parish walked in.

'Sergeant Parish, as I live and breathe,' DI Ray Kowalski said. 'Just got back from your holidays?'

The two were old friends, and regularly swapped banter in passing.

'I haven't had a holiday since 1990, Ray, you've taken them all.'

Ray Kowalski was often mistaken for the side of a house. He was thirty-eight, had cropped blonde hair, and had begun to sag around the jowls and the waist, but he still looked like a formidable opponent. Criminals didn't argue with DI Kowalski. 'Rumour has it that you've got a new partner at last, Jed?'

'You've obviously got nothing else better to do if you're listening to rumours, Ray.'

'A good looking Constable so the rumour goes.'

'She'll be here in a minute you can take a look for yourself, but if you hit on her I'll tell her about how you like wrinkled old grannies, the older the better.'

They both laughed.

'You just want her for yourself, Jed.'

Just then Richards walked into the squad room.

'You didn't tell me she was a supermodel, Parish. Are you going to introduce me?'

Richards blushed.

'This is DI Ray Kowalski, Richards. Take no notice of him, he talks rubbish most of the time.'

'You don't think I look like a supermodel then, Sir?'

'Stop fishing for compliments, Richards.'

'Sorry, Sir.'

Richards introduced herself and shook hands with Kowalski.

'Have you been promoted and nobody's told me, Sergeant?'

'Come on, Richards, you're not sashaying down the catwalk now, we have work to do. Go and arrest someone Kowalski, and leave PC Richards alone.'

'You know that if you need some help, Parish, you only have to ask,' Kowalski leered at Richards. 'You as well, Constable. In fact, especially you.'

She smiled at Kowalski. 'Thank you, Sir.'

'Richards,' Parish called.

'Coming, Sir.'

Parish found a training room with a white board and marker pens. Richards followed him in and closed the door.

'Don't...' he began.

She touched his arm. 'Don't worry, Sir, I know what DI Kowalski was after, I've met his type before.'

Parish busied himself moving the whiteboard into position and collecting up the marker pens. 'Yes, well just so long as you do know. And remember, Richards, you're under my protection now, so don't hide things from me. If any of those idiots out there step over the line, I want to know about it, okay?'

Richards sat down at the table. 'Okay, Sir.'

'Right, let's get this wrapped up, I'm going out tonight.'

'Anywhere nice, Sir?'

'Need to know, Richards.'

'And I don't need to know?'

'Correct. Right, first of all let's do a timeline of Mr Taylor's life.' He passed Richards the personnel file whilst he stood at the whiteboard, marker pen poised.

Richards opened the file and began skimming. 'He was born in West Ham to Elizabeth and Albert Taylor on 4th February 1961, went to St Nicholas Church of

England Primary School, and then to Standahl Grammar School. He did a degree in History, which included a Post-Graduate Certificate in Education, at Bristol University between 1979 and 1982. He then joined the Housing Department of Redbridge Council as a Rent Advisor until 1986. His first teaching post was in the history department of Ravenscroft School in September of 1986, which as Mr Bell said closed and was amalgamated with Chigwell school in 1994.

Parish said, 'Has he got a disciplinary record in there?'

Richards riffled through the pages and eventually said, 'No, Sir.'

'What about complaints?'

'Nothing, Sir.' She pulled the India tag through the holes of the file and started making piles.'

'Mrs Lovitt isn't going to like you, Richards.'

'I know, Sir, I'll get expelled for this.'

'What are you doing?'

'Making sure we don't miss anything. I'm putting the pages into piles based on content such as training, references, annual reports, and so on.'

Parish sat down and waited until she'd finished. 'Okay, go through each pile and see if there's anything in there.' He picked up the smallest pile.'

'I knew you'd pick that one, Sir.'

'Someone had to, Richards.'

They found nothing but glowing reports. Greg Taylor was the perfect teacher.

'At least we found out that he worked for four years at Redbridge Council, Sir. We didn't know that before.'

Parish picked up the pile containing references and found the one from Redbridge Council. It was a standard reference dated 12 July 1986 and said nothing useful. The signature block stated: Herbert Micklethwaite, Director of

Housing. He passed the reference to Richards. 'We'll go to Redbridge Council again tomorrow, see if anyone remembers Greg Taylor, and find out what his work entailed.'

'It doesn't sound promising, Sir.'

'What else have we got, Richards? Everything we've read and heard indicates that Gregory Taylor was an exemplary teacher with no enemies. If that's the case, then he either upset someone outside teaching, but according to his wife he had no outside interests, or he upset someone in his past and that's what we need to investigate next.'

'Maybe we're wrong, Sir?'

'Wrong! That's not a word I want you to use near me, Richards.'

'Sorry, Sir, but maybe it was a random killing, and the token is a signature of some kind.'

'Let's not give up until we've exhausted all other avenues of inquiry. If you're going to be a good detective, Richards, you need perseverance. In most cases you turn down blind alleys, reach dead ends, and stumble around in the dark before you find something that helps everything else make sense. All we've got at the moment is fragments of the whole. We need to be patient. Right, go home, and remember nine-thirty tomorrow morning. Get the pool car then come up here. I've got to send an email to our man in Sweden, and then see the Chief before we go anywhere. Whilst I'm doing that you can arrange an appointment with someone in Housing at Redbridge Council, and find out whether Mrs Taylor is up to answering our questions yet.'

Richards got up and put her coat, scarf, hat and gloves on. 'See you tomorrow, Sir, and have a nice evening tonight wherever it is you're going.'

'I will, Richards, and don't think about following me.'

'Good night, Sir.'

'Good night, Richards.'

Parish went to his desk in the squad room. Whilst he was waiting for the login screen to appear, he skimmed through Gregory Taylor's post mortem report. Doc Michelin was right, there was nothing more of interest. He put the file in his pending tray, logged onto the computer and wrote his report for the Chief. It was a short report. Maybe Richards was right, he thought, maybe they had taken a wrong turn. He'd give it tomorrow and then review where they were.

It was six-thirty when he switched the lights out in the squad room and made his way out to the car park.

***

Diane Flint had been preparing her quarterly report for the Council's Social Care, Children & Health Committee all day long only to be informed at six-thirty that the scheduled meeting was cancelled due to the inclement weather. It wasn't the first time she had been the last to know. As Redbridge Council's Director of Social Services, she expected a certain level of respect from the Council's elected members, but since Mrs Emily Catchpole had been appointed as the new Chairperson of the Committee, that level of respect had declined to an unacceptable level and she had no idea why.

As she packed her briefcase and then put on her coat, she wondered whether it was time to take early retirement. At fifty-three years old she had been a Social Worker all of her working life, and she wasn't getting any younger. She had no life to speak of – her husband had left her long ago. There were no friends, and no family. She was alone. All she had was her work, and if they took that away from her, well what was left? Lately, she had been wondering what it was all for. Maybe now was the time to go. Maybe she had reached that crossroads in her life and it was time to make a decision.

It was six-fifty as she entered the lift and descended four floors to the basement car park. There was no one about that she could see, and only a few cars remained. Although there were CCTV cameras in the car park, she still felt nervous at this time of night.

What would she do when she arrived home, but work? Yes, she had a cat, but one cat did not a life make. She had squandered her life helping other people. Although, some would say meddling in other people's lives. Her intentions had been honest. She had worked within the rules. It was clear that some parents didn't deserve to have children, and that some children didn't deserve to have parents. She had done her best, and that was all anybody could ask of her. In that moment she smiled, and knew in her heart that she wanted to retire, to enjoy the autumn of her life. In fact, have a life.

The locks on her Lexus GS 450h SE sighed open as she walked towards it. She didn't hear the man dressed all in black with a hood covering his face move from behind a concrete pillar and follow her.

'Excuse me?' the man said.

Diane Flint's heart might have leapt into her mouth as she turned around if it hadn't been for the marlinspike, which had pierced her thoracic cavity between the fourth and fifth thoracic ribs, entered the left atrium and severed the aorta. Her mouth opened to call out, to scream, but she was already dead as she slid down the rear door of her silver Lexus GS 450h SE. She didn't even hear the man whisper, 'Time to die Mrs Flint.'

She also didn't feel the man place a token on her tongue, close her mouth and say, 'For Joseph Dobbs.' Nor did she see him walk out of the empty car park.

***

He caught the bus back to Chigwell, back to the cold dreary flat, back to the confines of his life.

He put a black cross through the newspaper picture of Diane Flint's austere face that he'd stuck to the wall above his bed. It had all started with her. She had been the one who had altered the course of many lives. But for her, he could have been an astronaut exploring distant galaxies, or an aircraft pilot shooting down enemy planes, or a teacher like Mr Taylor. He could have been someone different, someone who didn't have a rucksack full of guilt, pain and regrets strapped to his back. Someone who liked people, and who had a future. Someone who could see the footprints of a life to follow stretched out before them. But, he was a ghost, had been for as long as he could remember. A ghost of someone he might have been.

It had taken him twenty-four years to keep his promise – a life for a life – that was what he had sworn to himself and the others. It was simple arithmetic, cancelling out both sides of the sum.

He lay down on the bed and waited for the nightmares to come, as they always did. Brian Ridpath's picture mocked him from the wall. Anger welled up inside him, but he controlled it. What was the point of anger now? The time for anger had long since passed under the bridge. Now, it was time for revenge. Tomorrow, Brian Ridpath would die. A life for a life, he chanted inside his mind until the darkness came.

EIGHT

By the time Parish got back to his flat he only had fifty minutes to shower, get ready and travel to the *Ram Inn* in Chigwell to meet LoopyLou. Ripping off his clothes, he called a taxi for twenty to eight, and then dived into the shower. He was ready to go by seven thirty, so he had a quick tidy up of his flat just in case it went the distance. He didn't want anyone thinking he was a slob.

It was two minutes to eight when he walked into the *Ram Inn*. A real log fire crackled in the hearth, and thankfully the music was low and easy to listen to. He saw the yellow dress immediately. She was sat at the bar with a horde of admirers. Her laughter was soft, and her long light brown hair sparkled like tinsel in the firelight.

'Extra cold Guinness,' he said when the barman asked him what he wanted. He felt embarrassed, and didn't know how to let LoopyLou know he was here. The pub was quite crowded for a Thursday night. Then, as if by magic, her admirers faded away. He cleared his throat and she turned around.

'Brad Russell?'

'LoopyLou?'

She smiled.

He was glad he had decided to meet her. There had been moments earlier in the day when he had thought he was being foolish, that he was too old for dating.

His mobile activated. He didn't want to answer it, but he knew he had to. 'Sorry,' he said to her, and pressed accept.

'Yes?' There was a resigned quality to his voice.

'Is this a bad time, Sergeant?' It was Doc Michelin.

'Will you go away and bother someone else if I say yes?'

79

'I could, but then you'd be in the shit.'

'Why are you ringing, Doc?'

'I'm in the basement car park of Redbridge Council. Mrs Diane Flint, the Director of Social Services, is lying next to her car with a hole in her heart and a token in her mouth that has the number 32 on it.'

'Shit. Okay Doc, I'm on my way.'

He turned to LoopyLou, shrugged and walked outside to ring Richards.

'Hello, Sir, are you having a nice time?'

'I'm at the *Ram Inn* on Curzon Street, Richards. Come and pick me up we've got another body.'

'I'm in my pyjamas, Sir.'

'If I were you I'd get changed, Richards. And don't be long its bloody freezing out here.'

Stamping his feet outside the pub, he rang the Duty Sergeant and told him to get a SOCO over to the Council offices.

He could hear her VW Beetle coming towards him before he actually saw it. She was right, it was a rustbucket. He climbed in and fastened the seatbelt. She had music he'd never heard before playing softly in the background.

'You didn't tell me I'd be working twenty-four hours a day and have no life, Sir.'

'Redbridge Council,' he said.

She turned the car around and headed out of Chigwell on the B173.

'Detectives are special people, Richards. If you want a life you should go and be a secretary or a shop assistant.'

He said it in such a way that didn't invite a reply, and he didn't get one. He wasn't happy. The first time he'd arranged to meet a woman in months, years even, and he gets called out. It was true what he'd said to Richards, if he wanted a life he should go and be a bin man or a petrol station attendant, something that didn't overflow into time off. He chose to be a detective and it was no use moaning about it now, things weren't going to change anytime soon.

They arrived in the underground car park of Redbridge Council at eight fifty, thirty-five minutes after Doc Michelin's phone call. There was an ambulance with a flashing light and two paramedics stood beside it talking, the unmarked forensics van, a police car with a constable trying to look important, and the Doc's Renault Espace.

'Did you come via Manchester, Sergeant?' Doc Michelin said.

'I didn't have my car with me when you called, and Richards took forever to pick me up.'

Affronted, Richards said, 'Sirrr!'

He moved to where the body lay slumped against a silver car. She was a short, plump woman, probably early fifties, smartly dressed with straw-like blonde hair that had obviously been dyed. He squatted, and looked more closely at the stab wound and the woman's face, but there was really nothing to see.

'My guess is that she was surprised from behind. When she turned around, the killer stabbed her. Like the last victim, she died almost instantly. He knows what he's doing with that marlinspike, Parish. Okay to move the body?'

'Has forensics finished with it?' He looked around and saw Toadstone on his hands and knees near the lift doors. He also spotted a CCTV camera in a metal and wire mesh housing on the wall.

'Some time ago. He's scouring the area now, but I doubt he'll find anything.'

'Is that your paramedic, Richards,' Parish said.

'He's not *my* paramedic, Sir.'

'Well, whoever he belongs to, tell him to take the body to the Mortuary.'

'Yes, Sir.'

He turned to the uniformed Constable. 'Who found the body?'

'The security guard doing his rounds, Sergeant. He's up on the ground floor behind the reception area.'

There was nothing left to do at the crime scene, but before he went up to speak to the security guard, he asked Toadstone to analyse the metal content of both tokens just in case it wasn't obvious to him.

'It might be a bit later than nine-thirty, Sergeant.'

'Why?'

'Well, I won't get in until late. They don't pay us overtime, you know. We have to take time off in lieu where we can.'

'So you're going to take your time off in lieu tomorrow morning?'

'That's right. It'll probably be after lunch now.'

'I should arrest you for obstructing an ongoing investigation, Toadstone.'

'You could, but then you probably wouldn't get the analysis done at all. They're a bit thin on the ground in forensics.'

Parish realised the conversation wasn't going anywhere. 'Just get it to me when you can, Toadstone. Remember, lives could be at stake.'

'Yeah, the other detectives play the guilt card as well. It'll be my fault if someone else dies. It doesn't work, you know.'

Parish walked towards the lift. 'Richards, when you're ready.' He held the lift doors open for her.

Inside the lift Richards said, 'We've got a link between the two victims haven't we, Sir?'

82

'Have you been watching the Crime Channel again?'

She smiled and her brown eyes sparkled. 'Yes Sir, but its true isn't it?'

'Yes, Richards, it's true. Well done. Redbridge Council seems to link Greg Taylor and Diane Flint. How, is something we now need to investigate, if we're still on the case in the morning.'

'What do you mean, Sir?'

'Well, what you seem to have missed is that we're now hunting a serial killer. The same *modus operandi* has been used on both victims – they were stabbed through the heart with a marlinspike, and a numbered token was inserted into their mouths.'

'But why would they take you off the case, Sir?'

'Serial killers usually get their own task force. I might be lucky and get put on it because I've been working on the case, but you've got no chance.'

'That's a bit mean, Sir.'

'It's what happens, Richards. Not only that, they won't have a lowly DS heading up the hunt for a serial killer, not senior enough. They'll probably put a Detective Chief Inspector in charge.'

The lift doors opened and they stepped out into the Council reception. A security guard came towards them with his arm outstretched.

'Paul Cummins, I used to be on the job.'

Parish shook Cummins' hand, and introduced himself and Richards. He wondered what Cummins had done wrong to end up as a security guard.

'I was stabbed in the line of duty if you're wondering why I'm a security guard Sergeant,' he said. 'I couldn't carry on after that.'

'Sorry to hear that, Cummins. Have you checked the security disc?' Parish asked.

'Yes, the murder is on there.'

Richard's eyes opened wide. 'We've got the killer on tape, Sir?'

'Don't get too excited Richards, remember he wears a hood.'

They followed Paul Cummins through a door at the side of the reception desk, along a corridor and into the security room. There was a bank of six televisions showing split-screen views of various parts of the Council building, and they were all connected via a box to a single computer.

Cummins sat down facing the computer. 'Are you ready?' he asked.

'Go,' Parish said.

They watched the murder unfold. As expected, the killer was dressed completely in black with a hood hiding his face.

Cummins took the disc out of the drive, put it in a case and gave it to Parish. 'I expect you'll be passing it to forensics to see if they can enhance the picture.'

'I expect so,' Parish said putting the disc in his pocket. 'Well, thanks for your help, Cummins.'

'You're welcome, Sergeant, I hope you catch him.'

They caught the lift down to the car park. It was nine thirty-five. Everyone had left. Diane Flint's silver Lexus had been locked and left where it was.

'Let's go home, Richards.' He was drained. Hadn't been sleeping well lately. Maybe he wasn't ready to lead a murder investigation. And now that they were looking for a serial killer, the stakes were that much higher. He expected he'd be relieved to hand the case over. At least he was confident that he'd done everything by the book. Nobody could criticise him for a sloppy investigation. He'd try to keep Richards on the team, but it depended who took over. Before he went to bed he'd have to send the Chief another email to update him on what had happened tonight. Give him a list of leads they planned to pursue, and offer to step aside. The Chief had enough problems without him kicking up a stink. He'd get another chance before too long. They all knew he could do it now, and he'd get promoted to DI at the next promotion board.

'We're here, Sir.'

'Thanks, Richards.' He wasn't in the mood for conversation. 'I'll see you in the morning.'

'Good night, Sir.'

He closed the door and she rattled off in her rustbucket.

***

Friday, 17th January

It was five a.m. when he woke up sweating. As usual, he couldn't remember the nightmare, but he was sure he had been allocated token number fifty-five. What that meant he had no idea, but the case was obviously getting to him. It was probably a good idea that he was handing it over, his sleep patterns would return to normal.

He got up, made a coffee and logged on to FindLove.com. He'd clearly blown it with LoopyLou, but there were others. Now that he wasn't pursuing a serial killer maybe he'd make some time for himself.

LoopyLou had sent him a message, which contained a lot of swear words and some travel advice. Who could blame her? He deleted the message. There were a further seven women eager to find out who he was. He opened the first of the two messages he'd left in his inbox yesterday. It was from a twenty-eight-year-old with three children. He decided he'd be no good as a father and deleted the invitation for a family meal. The next message was from a sixty year-old grandmother of seven who wanted to know if he was interested in becoming a toy boy. He pressed the delete button.

The other messages were much the same and he deleted each one in turn.

'And then there were none,' he said out loud. It was the story of his love life. He smiled. A love life was stretching the truth to snapping point. There was no love, and the life he had was a lonely journey towards old age and death. There had been a couple of women, but they never seemed to hang around for more than a couple of months. As soon as they realised that the job came first they were waving goodbye, and who could blame them. If they had stuck it out their lives would be going nowhere like his was.

He shaved and showered then watched the news on the small television in the kitchenette. He would have eaten a couple of pieces of toast, but the bread in the packet had turned a furry green. He made a mental note to do some shopping on his way home. The local news had picked up on the "horrific stabbing of the Redbridge Director of Social Services," but had failed to link Greg Taylor's death to Diane Flint's. Well, of course, they didn't know about the marlinspike and the tokens, or Greg Taylor's earlier life as a Rent Advisor at the Council, and the Chief wasn't going to do their work for them. He knew they'd find out soon enough, and then the hunt would be on for someone to blame, someone's career to ruin. Yes, he was relieved that it was no longer his case. The sooner he offloaded it onto a senior officer the better.

Then he remembered that he had some time this morning. It was seven-thirty, he could stop off at a café on the way to the station and have a fry-up with all the trimmings. He could take his time, and savour the moment. Life was looking up. He could even do a spot of shopping and store it in the boot of his car until he knocked off later. It would save him time tonight, and instead of hunting for a serial killer in Chigwell he could hunt for a woman on FindLove.com.

***

As he walked into the station at nine-fifteen he felt stuffed. Usually, meals were snatched, grazed, or plastic. It made a nice change to take his time eating a decent meal.

The usual banter accompanied him to his desk. He had just over half an hour before his meeting with the Chief.

Richards rustled in at nine-thirty in her snow boots and quilted coat.

Kowalski shouted a greeting to her, and she waved and smiled at him.

'Good morning, Richards,' Parish said.

'Good morning, Sir.'

'I'll be handing the case over to a senior officer soon, so lets go into the incident room and cobble together a summary of where we are and what the next steps might be.'

She followed him to the incident room and stripped off her coat, hat, gloves and scarf.

'Do you want a coffee, Sir?'

'You mean you'd like a coffee?'

'I'll make it, Sir, I saw the kitchen when I came in.'

'Go on then, but be quick, and remember I have four sugars in mine.'

'I'll never forget that, Sir.'

She had pulled the door closed before he had formulated a reply. This tiredness was making him slow, he thought. Normally, a withering response would have screeched off his tongue like a mad dwarf wielding an axe, but he felt a bit muggy this morning. Maybe he was coming down with something. It was the flu season after all.

Richards came back with the coffee.

'We've got two murders.' Parish said drawing two lines on the whiteboard. One was headed Gregrory Taylor, and the other Diane Flint. 'Both victims were stabbed in the heart with a marlinspike, and both had a token with a different number inserted into their mouths. Its clearly the same killer, but apart from the *modus operandi* the only other connection between the two victims is Redbridge Council.'

'The link is a bit weak, Sir. Although we know Mr Taylor worked at Redbridge Council, how would the killer have found out?'

Parish was quiet for some time and sipped his coffee. Eventually he said, 'Because he already knew.'

'But... that would mean the killings are related to something that happened between 1982 and 1986.'

'If that's true, Richards, why was Diane Flint killed? Did she work for the Council during that period as well? Whilst I'm meeting with the Chief, ring someone at the Council and find out. It would be good to hand over the case with a large portion of the jigsaw completed.'

'Okay, Sir.' She wrote down the task in her notebook.

He took the security disc from Redbridge Council out of his pocket and handed it to her. 'Take that up to forensics and ask them to magic up a face for us. Oh, and get the keys to Diane Flint's house off Toadstone.'

'I don't know where forensics is, Sir.'

'You're a detective now, Richards – detect.'

'Yes, Sir.'

'Also, we still need to see Mrs Taylor so try and arrange an appointment, and Ring Doc Michelin to find out when he's doing Diane Flint's post mortem.' Richards wrote furiously on her 'to do' list. 'Have I missed anything?'

'Do we need to go and look at Diane Flint's house?'

'Yes we do, Richards. Okay, follow me. You can sit at my desk and use the phone there.'

'Did we get any information from the leaflet drop we made on Ralston Drive, Sir?'

'Not a squeak, Richards.'

She grabbed the pile of clothes off the chair and followed Parish out to the squad room.

'And don't talk to DI Kowalski. He's married with seven kids, and you know he only wants you for one thing.'

'Stop worrying about me, Sir, I can take care of myself.'

'Yes well, I'm only along the corridor if you do need me.'

'I'll be all right, Sir, have a good meeting.'

***

Parish walked along the corridor, knocked and stuck his head round the Chief's door.

'Come in, Parish,' the Chief said.

Even before he'd sat down the Chief started on him. 'What's this about you wanting to hand over the case?'

'Well...'

'During my radiotherapy at the hospital, I was on the phone to the Chief Constable. Following my recommendation, he convened an emergency promotion board. You're a Detective Inspector now, Parish, but if you're now telling me you can't handle the pressure, that

89

you want to hand the investigation over to a more senior officer, that you want to remain a Sergeant for the rest of your doomed career…'

'A DI, Sir?'

'That's what I said, Parish. With immediate effect, and this time you'll get the pay.'

He stood up, grasped the Chief's hand and shook it as if he were pumping water at a well.

'Remember I'm not the man I used to be, Inspector.'

Parish dropped the Chief's hand. 'Sorry, Sir, I got carried away. Thank you.'

'You deserve it, Parish, I've been really impressed with how you've handled this case so far. No one could have done more, and getting PC Richards from Cheshunt to help you showed real initiative.'

It wasn't often Parish blushed, but he felt his face burning up as if he'd stepped too close to the sun. 'Considering what you're dealing with yourself, Sir, I'm very grateful you had time to think of me.'

'Pah! The cancer will either disappear or it won't. Some days I think it's the cure that's killing me, not the cancer. Anyway, it's not worth worrying about things we can't change. So, what's your next move?'

'Redbridge Council, Sir. We have a tenuous link between the two victims. What we need to find out now is whether Diane Flint worked there at the same time as Gregory Taylor. Also, once we get the metal content of the tokens from forensics, I'll send them to Carlgren in Sweden and see what he comes back with. There's also the security disc from last night's murder which Richards has taken up to forensics, maybe they can extract a face for us.'

'Good. I've called a press conference for two o'clock. Time to introduce our new DI to the press. I'll take the lead on this one, but then you'll be on your own.'

'Okay, Sir.'

'Are you going to sit here all morning, or go out there and do some work, Detective Inspector Parish?'

He stood up. The sound of Detective Inspector Parish sounded like music to his ears. At the door he turned and said, 'Thanks again, Sir.'

'Oh, by the way, Parish, Kowalski tortured me until I told him, so don't be surprised if he's decorated your desk with banners or something equally obnoxious.'

'Bloody hell, Sir.'

NINE

Parish tried to sneak out, but Kowalski was waiting for him in the corridor.

'Don't think you can disappoint your fans, Parish,' Kowalski said herding him back towards the squad room like a stray sheep.

'Come on, Kowalski, you know how I hate things like this. How much do you want?'

'Trying to bribe a police officer is a crime, Parish.'

He knew he wasn't going to get anywhere with Kowalski, so he resigned himself to the embarrassment of a party. His colleagues were all gathered in the squad room clapping. The Chief was right, his desk was adorned with banners and bunting. The detectives congratulated him and slapped him on the back as he walked amongst them like the Second Coming.

The Chief had probably put his hand in his pocket for the cakes, orange juice, coke and lemonade. Ten-thirty in the morning was far too early for alcohol, but the crowd were all going to *Dirty Nelly's* at five-thirty and he'd been invited to buy the first round.

'Congratulations, Sir,' Richards said when he'd spoken to most people, some of whom he hadn't seen for months.

'Thanks, Richards.'

'Does that mean you're still on the case?'

'It means we're both still on the case. Did you do what I asked you to do?'

'Of course, Sir. Forensics said someone will have a look at the disc but they make no promises. Redbridge Council confirmed that Diane Flint worked for them between those dates as a Social Worker. Mrs Taylor is staying with family in Derbyshire and will be back on

Monday for her husband's funeral, and Doc Michelin is not doing Diane Flint's post mortem until ten-thirty tomorrow morning.'

'Well done, Richards. Have we got a contact number for Mrs Taylor?'

'Yes, Sir.'

'Are we going to be able to speak to her on Monday?'

'She'll be burying her husband, Sir.'

'Is that a *no* then?'

'I would leave it until Wednesday as a mark of respect.'

'Wednesday! Okay, Richards, I'll go along with you this time. Give Mrs Taylor a ring, ask her to come into the station at nine o'clock on Wednesday morning to provide us with a formal statement. You can ask her about Beech Tree Orphanage then.'

'All right, Sir.'

'This morning we need to go to the Council offices to find out what happened during those dates that links the two victims together, and have a look around Diane Flint's abode.' He checked his watch. It was ten forty-five. 'Or should I say, what's left of this morning. I've got to be back here for two o'clock for a press briefing.'

'Are you going to be on the telly, Sir?'

'So it would seem.'

'I'll be able to point you out to my mum before Sunday, but you could do with a haircut, Sir.'

'Have you finished having a good time partying, Richards?'

'It's your party, Sir, I was simply joining in.'

'I hate parties, Richards.'

'I knew you would. As soon as they started organising it after you'd gone in to see the Chief, I knew you'd hate it.'

'I might have to consider getting a new partner, Richards, one that doesn't keep trying to analyse me every five minutes.'

Richards smiled and flicked the hair out of her eyes. 'I'm ready to go when you are, Sir.' She went to his desk and started putting on her coat, scarf, gloves and hat.

'Going so soon, Parish?' Kowalski said.

'Work to do, Kowalski, something you wouldn't know a lot about. I don't want to get busted back down to Sergeant for partying all day.'

'You could leave Richards here. I'll look after her.'

'Get a life, Kowalski, she's far too young and pretty for you.'

'See you at five, Parish. Bring your piggy bank with you. It'll be a long night.'

Richards followed him out. On the stairs she said, 'DI Kowalski's a moron isn't he, Sir?'

'I've been trying to tell you that all morning, Richards'

'Do you really think I'm pretty, Sir?'

'Stop fishing, Richards.'

'Sorry, Sir.'

It had been snowing again, and the dark ominous sky promised more of the same. The gritters were out, but they were fighting a losing battle. The snowdrifts made the local area look like the Arctic, but without the polar bears. Some people had abandoned normal modes of transport and were in sledges, on skis or snowboards, and one entrepreneur had opened up a stall at the side of the road to rent out teams of huskies.

'Everybody goes mad when there's a bit of snow, Sir.'

'Not everyone, Richards, keep your eyes on the road.'

***

Diane Flint had lived in a four-bedroom town house on Middleton Road in Redbridge overlooking the frozen wastes of Valentines Park and the golf driving range. Parish opened the UPVC door of number seventeen using the key Richards had obtained from Toadstone in forensics.

There was a heap of post on the hall floor and Parish picked it up and put it on the telephone table. He wondered who would open her post. Diane Flint seemed to be just like him, putting a question mark in the Next of Kin box on official forms. They'd learned she had no next of kin. He wondered where her money would go. At least he had some distant relatives both in terms of geography and DNA, and they would probably inherit his debts.

Richards switched the lights on.

'I've noticed that you're a female, Richards,' he said, 'so you can stay down here and look in the bedrooms.'

'You're very observant, Sir. What am I looking for?'

'Anything that might give us a clue as to why she was killed. I'll go upstairs and rummage around in the other rooms.'

'Okay, Sir.'

Upstairs there were no photographs in frames on the sideboard or the table. The pictures hanging on the walls looked as though they came with the house, much the same as smiling photographs in the clear plastic section of a new wallet or purse. This was a human garage similar to his own flat. A place for sleeping, eating, and re-charging batteries in-between work shifts. He looked in drawers and cupboards, but found only insurance policies, car documents, and other paperwork belonging to a lonely person. There were no letters from loved ones, no fridge magnets with *Smile if you Love a Social Worker* or *Did*

Someone Say Chocolate? There was no address book filled with friends and relatives, and no nik-naks from family days out cluttering up the surfaces.

On the coffee and dining tables were research reports, longhand notes, open books on ethics, anti-discrimination, and child protection, with sections highlighted in green, orange, and yellow. He switched on a laptop computer, which he knew would contain Council reports, budgets, and personnel appraisals and he was not disappointed. In the Internet search history he found only social work terms. It was as if a person with no past or future lived here.

On the bookshelves were books on Social Work, Psychology, Sociology, Politics and Local Government, there were no novels or biographies – nothing personal – not even matching bookends.

Richards appeared. 'There's nothing in the bedrooms, Sir. If it weren't for the clothes, I wouldn't be able to tell you who lived here.'

'It's the same up here, Richards. Let's go. I'm depressed. We'll find nothing of interest here.'

***

It would take at least a week before he received his new warrant card, and before that happened he'd have to go and get a passport photograph taken. He hated those damned machines they were designed by idiots for idiots. He couldn't get the hang of the seat, the flashing light, where to look, or anything else about them. And the photographs that came out always looked as though he was one flash away from the asylum.

It was a different receptionist at the desk in the Council offices. Paula, the new receptionist, was a lot friendlier than Astrid had been.

'Detective Inspector Parish,' he said holding his warrant card up, but with his finger strategically placed over the *Sergeant*. It sounded so good when he said it that he wanted to say it again, but he also knew that if he did he'd look like an idiot so he restrained himself. Maybe later, when he was in his flat, he could practice in front of the mirror. It was important to get these things right.

'Yes, Sir, how can I help?'

Paula had red hair, freckles and a wonderful smile.

'I'm here about the murder of Mrs Flint, and I'd like to see the person in charge of the personnel records.'

She picked up the phone, dialled an internal number and spoke softly into the mouthpiece. 'Mr Chivers is on his way down, Sir, he's the Director of Personnel.'

'Thank you, Paula,' Parish said.

'You're welcome, Sir.' And she was moving on to the next visitor as if she was genetically programmed to be a receptionist.

Mr Reginald Chivers, a tall angular-faced man in his fifties, and dressed in a three-piece suit took them up to a rather plush office on the fifth floor with a deep-pile carpet, mahogany desk and brown leather chairs. He offered them real Colombian coffee. Richards declined, but Parish needed a caffeine fix and accepted asking for milk and only two sugars.

'We're all very shocked about the murder of Diane Flint, Inspector, and the Director of Security has instigated a full review of our security measures.'

'I understand, Sir, and we're doing everything we can to bring her killer to justice. To assist us, we need to look at two of your personnel files. A Mr Gregory Taylor, who was employed in the Housing Department during the period 1982 to 1986, and of course, Mrs Flint.'

'Mr Taylor? Yes, I saw the report on the news. Did he work here at the Council? I thought he was a teacher?'

'According to his personnel records from Chigwell Secondary School, he was employed here during that period before he went into teaching. There was a reference signed by a Mr Micklethwaite.'

'Ah yes, Herbert Micklethwaite was Director of Housing then. He's dead now though.' Mr Chivers leaned back in his chair and crossed his legs. 'So, you think the same person who murdered Mr Taylor killed Diane Flint?'

'We're not sure of anything yet, Mr Chivers, that's why we need to look at the personnel files.'

Mr Chivers went to his desk and pressed the button on the intercom. 'Carrie, could you bring in the personnel files for Diane Flint, and a Mr Gregory Taylor who worked in the Housing Department between 1982 and 1986 please.' He came back and sat down. 'It might take some time, we only keep active files in the office. What specifically are you interested in, Inspector?'

'Whether the two worked together on anything. A project or something they were both involved in. Maybe a client who didn't like the service he received from either Mrs Flint or Mr Taylor. I suppose we could start with Mrs Flint's cases and go from there.'

'You're making the assumption that we have a record of all the cases Mrs Flint worked on between 1982 and 1986, Inspector, I'm afraid we don't. It was nearly thirty years ago for goodness sake. What we do have are all the files that Social Service employees worked on during that period, which probably amounts to between five and ten thousand. Mr Taylor's files in Housing were destroyed many years ago. I have no doubt that the two may have communicated on cases where Diane Flint's clients were allocated Council housing, but the only way we would be able to identify those instances would be to read every case file during that period, clearly an impossibility.'

This wasn't going as he'd hoped. In fact, he didn't really know what he had expected. He'd been optimistic that the answer to the murders lay in the old files, but going through five to ten thousand was clearly beyond his resources - what now? He had no idea. Maybe there were people who had worked with either or both victims, but asking them to recall events from twenty-eight years ago would be hit and miss. Someone might remember the numbered tokens from that period. They were certainly unusual. Maybe he could persuade Mr Chivers to send all Council employees an email with the picture of the token. He could ask them if they recalled seeing the numbered tokens between 1982 and 1986 and give his contact details. There would only be a few employees who had worked at the Council that long though.

Just then, a striking blonde-haired woman came in with the two files. She was in her early thirties wearing stilettos, a pencil skirt and a translucent white blouse that showed clearly a silk patterned white bra.

'Thank you, Carrie,' Mr Chivers said to his secretary.

She smiled and lit up the room.

Parish couldn't help but stare as she leaned down and put the files on the coffee table in front of him. He would have watched her walk out, but Richards nudged him.

'The files, Sir.'

'Thank you, Richards, I can see them.'

'Would you like to take them with you?' Mr Chivers asked. 'I expect you want time to examine them properly?'

He thought he'd like to examine Carrie properly. Taking Richards by surprise, Parish stood up and extended his hand. 'Thank you very much, Mr Chivers. I have one request if I may?'

'By all means, Inspector.'

Mr Chivers confirmed that they had the ability to email all employees at the press of a button, and agreed to send an email out requesting information. Parish needed to compose it first and asked for an email address he could send it to. Mr Chivers gave him Carrie Holden's email address.

***

It was twelve thirty-five when they walked out into the snowstorm beyond Redbridge Council offices.

Richards squealed, turned away from the direction of the wind and pulled her hood up.

'Let's go and have lunch, Richards,' Parish said, 'I'm famished.' Looking around he saw an Italian restaurant opposite the Council. 'Italian okay for you?'

'I like pasta, Sir. Let's just get out of this snow before my face freezes and drops off.'

He took hold of her arm and guided her across the road.

Inside the *Signor Carlo Restaurant* they were seated near the window and were able to watch people struggling through the snowstorm. Parish ordered what he knew, which was a lasagne with garlic bread and a half glass of lager. Richards had shallow fried calamari with rocket and asparagus salad, and a glass of still water.

'She'll have no personality, Sir,' Richards said when the waiter had brought their drinks.

Parish's eyes creased up. 'What are you talking about, Richards?'

'Mr Chivers' secretary, she's all breasts and backside.'

'What makes you think I'm not a breasts and backside type of guy?'

'You're not, Sir.'

'I don't remember appointing you as my relationship advisor, Richards?'

'When you asked me to become your partner, Sir, you got more than an attractive woman with brains, you know.'

Parish laughed. 'So it would seem, Richards. Now, can we move away from my non-existent private life and discuss the case?'

'The email was a good idea, Sir.'

'I thought so as well. I was disappointed to hear about the case files though. I expected some answers today, but sometimes trying to find a viable clue is like pulling teeth.'

'Do you think there'll be more murders?'

'I certainly hope not, Richards, two is quite enough for me.'

'What do you want me to do whilst you're appearing on the television, Sir?'

'A necessary evil, Richards. I'll log you on to my computer and you can send the emails to Arvid Carlgren and Mr Chivers' secretary.'

Her eyes opened wide. 'You want me to compose the one requesting information about the tokens, Sir?'

'Can you do that?'

'I suppose so, Sir.'

'Do it in Notepad. Copy and paste the picture of the token into the document from the memory stick, ask if anyone knows anything about them, put the number of the station and my email address, and then attach it to the email.'

'I know how to do it, Sir.'

'Just helping. Oh, and print me a copy out.'

'Are you going to tell the press about the marlinspike and the tokens, Sir?'

'No, we don't want any copycats. The press can be useful sometimes, but they can also be a pain in the arse.'

'They're sure to find out about the tokens when the email is sent to all the people at the Council.'

'There's nothing we can do about that, but they won't know what connection the tokens have to the murders.'

He checked his watch. It was ten past one. 'Have you finished playing with your food, Richards?'

'Yes, it wasn't very nice.'

'It didn't look very nice either. Come on, I don't want to be late for my big break. There could be Hollywood scouts there, they could snap me up for the next Gladiator movie.'

'You have a weird imagination, Sir.'

If anything, the snowstorm had become worse. It was nearly a whiteout. Vehicles were creeping along the road with their windscreen wipers on full, but crossing was easy. 'Are you going to be okay driving in this, Richards?'

'I'll have to be, Sir, we wouldn't want to deprive Hollywood of the next Russell Crowe.'

'I see a bright future ahead of you, Richards.'

They arrived back at the station at five to two. It was a mad panic. Parish needed the toilet and to check in a mirror that he looked presentable before the press saw him. Richards forced him to sit down in a chair in the squad room whilst she combed his hair. The whole time he was wriggling for a pee.

'You'll be all right logging in on your own?' Parish asked her.

'You've given me your username and password, Sir. I've seen how the intelligent people use computers, I should be able to manage it.'

'Sarcasm doesn't suit you, Richards. You know…'

'…you're in the press briefing room, Sir. Yes, now go, I'll be all right.'

'And…'

'Kowalski's not even here, Sir.'

He couldn't stop himself from smiling. They were finishing each other's sentences like detectives who'd been working together for years.

The Chief appeared. 'Come on, Parish, you don't want to be late for your big break.' He started laughing, but it turned into a strangled cough. 'There might even be some Hollywood scouts there,' he said after he'd brought his breathing back under control.

'I need the toilet, Sir,' he said wishing he hadn't had a lager with his meal.

'Too late for that, Inspector. You'll have to grit you teeth and squeeze. Or you might consider getting a prostate like mine, and then you could have a catheter inserted and go all day without peeing.'

The twenty chairs in the press briefing room were taken, and there was some reporters stood at the back.

The bright light from the television camera shone right in his eyes, and he was beginning to sweat. It seemed that no one had connected the stabbing of Redbridge Council's Director of Social Services with Gregory Taylor's murder, but he knew they would soon enough, and then there would be trouble. Diane Flint was a high-profile death. People expected answers, and quickly.

He thought his bladder was going to burst and drench all the reporters, lighting crew, and cameramen in urine. His big break would be known as the big piss. It would be caught on camera for posterity. He'd have to resign, change his name, and go for plastic surgery to alter his appearance.

The Chief read out the press briefing, which he had prepared earlier, based on Parish's reports. He introduced Detective Inspector Parish as the lead detective on the case, and Parish nodded sombrely. Thankfully, there was no mention of the fact that he'd been promoted today. The Chief fielded all the questions at the end, and then miraculously Parish was leaning over the urinal holding onto the wall and trying not to faint. The relief was something he would savour forever, and he made a mental note to give himself ten minutes before the press briefing on Monday at eleven o'clock.

***

It was twenty past three when Brian Ridpath fell out of the *Two Brewers* public house on Lambourne Road in Chigwell, and turned left towards his council flat on Romford Road.

He had gone to the pub at eleven-fifteen and sat in his usual seat at the bar. Pat, the barman, began talking about the football fixtures on Saturday, especially the match between Chelsea and West Ham. They both agreed that West Ham didn't stand a chance of even scoring, never mind winning. It was about two o'clock that he started feeling sleepy, and then his head began nodding like a toy dog in a car rear window. Finally, his speech became slurred and he lost count of the number of beers he'd had, but that didn't stop him ordering one more for the road.

Local residents were used to seeing Brian Ridpath stagger home at this time of day. Often, he didn't reach his flat, but slid down one of the many walls along his route and slept until the early evening when he would turn around and go back to the *Two Brewers*.

Today, he needed to relieve himself and stumbled into Maypole Alley between the cardboard box factory and the container storage yard, and began pissing up the wall behind a dustbin.

It was in Maypole Alley at three fifty-five that a man dressed in black wearing a hood and carrying a marlinspike said, 'Time to die Mr Ridpath,' and then stabbed Brian Ridpath in the heart as he turned around still struggling to put his penis back in his trousers. Ridpath's mouth opened in a silent scream and he crumpled to the ground dead.

The man slipped a token, with the number 14 stamped on it, into the dead Mr Ridpath's mouth and said, 'For Liam Preston,' then walked away.

When the man reached his flat, he put a cross through the picture of Brian Ridpath. He wouldn't be able to kill the next one until Monday evening, but he had waited twenty-four years already what was another two days in the grand scheme of things?'

He lay down on the bed and stared at the ceiling until, much later, the nightmares took him.

***

'How did the press briefing go, Sir?'

'I didn't spot anyone from Paramount or Warner Brothers, Richards.'

'They're usually stood at the back smirking, Sir. You'll just have to be patient, I'm sure they'll invite you over to America for a screen test before too long.'

'Stop humouring me, Richards. Did you send…?'

She passed him copies of the two emails.

He looked at the attachment to Carrie requesting information on the token and muttered, 'Good.' Then he turned to the one sent to Arvid Carlgren. The metal content of both tokens was exactly the same, which he supposed meant that they were probably produced at the same time:

Diameter: 18 mm
Metal content: Copper 95%, Zinc and Tin 5%
Weight: 2.12 grams

'Well done, Richards. I suppose we'll just have to be patient now. Whilst we're waiting, we can look through the two files we acquired this morning, and try to unearth some more leads.'

'We've not got much to go on have we, Sir?'

'No, Richards, not much at all, but that doesn't prevent you from making me a coffee.'

Clucking, she stood up and headed towards the kitchen.

'Don't forget…'

'…four sugars. I know, Sir.'

'You're becoming a right know-it-all, Richards,' he shouted after her. 'I'll be in the incident room.'

First, he read Diane Flint's file and Richards rifled through Gregory Taylor's. Then they swapped.

'Nothing,' he said.

'I thought maybe it was me, Sir,' Richards said.

Parish stood up, went to the whiteboard at the end of the room and rubbed off the timeline of Gregory Taylor's life. 'Right, lets go over what we've got, and see where we go next.'

'We've got two murders,' Richards began. 'Gregory Taylor killed on 14th January on Ralston Road in Chigwell, and Diane Flint killed on the 16th January in the basement car park of Redbridge Council.'

Parish wrote the details on the board using a black marker pen.

'Both victims were killed by a marlinspike, which is a tool used in rope work. And both had an old token inserted into their mouths, Gregory Taylor's was number 27 and Diane Flint's was 32. Each token has a diameter of 18mm, weighs 2.12 grams, and was made from 95% copper and 5% zinc and tin.'

'What do the bloody numbers refer to?' he mumbled to himself. 'Keep going, Richards you're doing fine.'

'Both victims worked at Redbridge Council between 1982 and 1986. Diane Flint as a Social Worker, and Gregory Taylor as a Rent Advisor in the Housing Department.'

'Could it be just coincidence that they worked at the Council together during that period, Richards?'

'Well no, Sir. We have the tokens and the marlinspike as well. All three things can't be coincidence.'

'As you said earlier, the marlinspike and the tokens may simply be the killer's signature.'

Richards thought for a time then said, 'The marlinspike probably, but if the tokens were being used as part of the killer's signature wouldn't he use ones with the same number on, or consecutive numbers?'

'Maybe what he's using were the only ones he could get hold of.'

'Do you think he bought them, Sir? I mean, places where you can buy old tokens aren't exactly filling up the High Street?'

'The Internet, Richards, there are auctions and collectors on the Internet that sell tokens.'

'If he bought them in a shop or on the Internet, he would be traceable? I can't imagine why a killer would buy some old tokens to use as his signature, it's too far-fetched, Sir.'

'You're the one that suggested it, Richards.'

'I've changed my mind, Sir. I think that the tokens and the numbers have some specific meaning, we just don't know what it is yet.'

'Okay, so we're still convinced that to unlock the puzzle box we need to find out the connection between Taylor and Flint during 1982 to 1986 at Redbridge Council, and the numbered tokens.'

'Yes, Sir.'

'What now?'

'We're waiting for an email from that man Carlgren in Sweden about the tokens, and we've also asked Mr Chivers to send an email out to all the Council's employees in the hope that someone will remember the tokens.'

'And the dates?'

'We tried to find out what Taylor and Flint worked on during that period, but there are too many records, Sir.'

'Should we let that stop us, Richards?'

'We'd never be able to look through all those records, Sir. And even if we could there would be no guarantee we'd find what we needed.'

'So how else can we find out what they worked on during that period?'

'The tokens, Sir.'

'What about them?'

'Where would they have been used?'

'That's the problem, Richards, we don't know.'

'We could guess, Sir.'

'And then what?'

'Well, what I'm thinking is trying to connect Taylor and Flint with the tokens.'

Parish sat on the end of the large oval table that took up most of the room. 'And...?'

'Where might the tokens have been used that both Taylor and Flint would have come into contact with them?'

Rubbing the stubble on his chin Parish said, 'You might be on to something, Richards. Who were Diane Flint's clients between 1982 and 1986?'

'What do you mean, Sir?'

'Well, I was wondering if she worked with old people, children, or someone else? And its also just occurred to me that she must have worked with other social workers who might know what she was doing then that got her killed now, and they also might know about the tokens.'

Richards looked in Diane Flint's file. 'She worked in the children's team, Sir. And don't forget that Mr Taylor would have had work colleagues as well.'

'Yes, you're right, Richards, excellent. We now need to get back on to Mr Chivers and ask him to provide a list of people who worked with both Taylor and Flint between 1982 and 1986.'

'How would Mr Taylor be involved?'

'I don't know, Richards, but he clearly is.' Parish checked his watch. It was four-fifteen. 'I need the toilet,

let's take a break. Go and ring Mr Chivers and tell him what we need. Apologise that it's going-home-time on a Friday night, but tell him we'd like the information before the end of the day.'

'If they're still there, Sir. Councils usually finish early on a Friday.'

'Then we'll have to get him back. If he's not there, ring him at home.'

'Okay, Sir.'

Parish went to the toilet. When he came back, Richards was sat on the opposite side of his desk still talking on the phone so he checked his email account. There was one from Arvid Carlgren, which he sent to the networked printer on the other side of the room:

Inspector,

I have forty-five tokens in my collection with the same diameter, weight, and metal content as the two you have described. They are numbered 1 – 60, but numbers 4, 7, 14, 21, 23, 27, 32 35, 37, 38, 43, 49, 50, 55, and 59 are missing. I have heard rumours that the tokens were used at a school, but I cannot verify the information. Which school and what they were used for, I have no idea. Finally, I would be grateful if I could purchase the tokens from you when you have finished with them together with any information relating to them.

Arvid Carlgren
Token Specialist
Stora Herrestad

He sent a reply saying: Thanks, and he'd do what he could for him about the tokens. Then he collected the email from the printer, and put it in front of Richards when he got back to his desk.

She put the phone down and said, 'Mr Chivers is not at his office, Sir, and he's not at home. His wife said that he's at Heathrow airport boarding a plane to America. He's going to a Human Resources Conference in California.'

'I've a good mind to ring the Air Force and get that plane shot down, Richards. Bloody California! Surfing! And we're stuck here trying to solve a murder in ten feet of snow. Another Council fat cat we should throw excrement on.'

'Yes, Sir. What about Carrie, his secretary?'

Parish licked his lips. 'I'll ring her should I?'

'I'll do it, Sir. If you ring her, we might never find out the information.'

'Tell her I'll come into the Council offices to help her find the information we need.'

'I'll come with you, Sir.'

'Three's a crowd, Richards.'

'Then I'll go on my own, Sir.'

'Okay, Richards you do that. I've got to go to *Dirty Nelly's* anyway.'

'You did that on purpose didn't you?'

'You're becoming paranoid, Richards.'

She looked down and read the email. 'A school, Sir?'

'Maybe that's what connects Taylor, Flint and the tokens, Richards. Flint's clients were children, and Taylor became a teacher.'

'I hope there's not going to be another thirteen murders, Sir.'

'So do I.'

'We're getting close though, aren't we, Sir?'

'It feels like it. Are you sure you don't want me to go and rummage in Carrie's files, Richards?'

'I'll go, Sir, you celebrate your promotion.'
Just then, Parish's mobile rang. It was Doc Michelin.

ELEVEN

'Not another one, Doc?' Parish said leaning back in his chair.

'I'm afraid so, Sergeant.'

'I'm an Inspector today by the way.' He still couldn't get used to the idea of it.

'Congratulations, but you'd better get your newly promoted arse over to Lambourne Road in Chigwell. A Mr Brian Ridpath has been stabbed in the heart with a marlinspike, and the token in his mouth has the number 14 on it.'

'We're on our way, Doc.'

He put the phone down and glanced at the clock on the wall. It was ten to five. Crap! What a way to spend a Friday night. He could send Richards home and go to the crime scene by himself, but he knew she wouldn't go along with that. It wasn't fair to treat her any different than a real partner. She wasn't a detective, but what she lacked in experience she made up for in intelligence and enthusiasm.

'Come on, Parish,' Kowalski shouted as he bounded into the squad room. 'Let's get down to *Dirty Nelly's* and celebrate your admittance into the ranks of the exalted.'

It occurred to Parish as he went to meet Kowalski that the man was a loudmouth. 'I've got another murder in Chigwell,' he said taking his wallet out and handing over £50. 'Buy the drinks for me will you.'

'You're joking, Jed?'

'I wish I were. I could have done with a few drinks tonight, and then woken up with a weekend-destroying headache.'

'You don't have to take Richards with you do you? Let me escort her to the pub, I promise to get her home mostly in one piece.'

'You can ask her if you like, but I guarantee she won't go with you, Ray.'

'Richards,' Kowalski shouted. 'Let me take you away from all this. Come to the pub with me and we'll celebrate Parish's promotion *in absentia*?'

Richard's face turned serious. 'So you want me to go out drinking with you whilst my partner goes to a crime scene without any back-up?'

'Inspector Parish has to go, but you don't. He can look after himself.'

'You're being extremely mean, Sir. I'll be going with my partner, that's why they're called partners.'

'Another time then, Richards,' Kowalski said.

'I doubt it, Sir,' she said turning back to what she was doing.

Parish smiled. 'Tell everyone to have a good time on me, Ray.'

'Will do, Jed,' Kowalski said heading for the stairs. 'Have a good weekend, and thanks for the money.'

'You're welcome, Ray.'

'I've decided I don't like Inspector Kowalski, Sir.'

'Oh he's all right, Richards. Like most people, he can be an idiot sometimes.'

'Where's the murder this time, Sir?'

'Lambourne Road in Chigwell.' He told her what Doc Michelin had said as they walked out.

'What about Mr Chivers' secretary and the list of people who worked with Taylor and Flint?'

'We'll just have to contact her tomorrow and see if she's willing to give up her Saturday to help us.'

'Us, Sir?'

'As you said to Kowalski, Richards, we're partners.' He grinned at her. 'I couldn't let you go on your own, now could I?'

Parish thought that if snow were money he'd be rich. It had just stopped snowing as they walked out of the station. There was a fresh layer of white covering the black ice on the roads. Richards hadn't taken the pool car back, and he stood looking at it undecided about what to do.

'The pool car, Sir?'

'Yes, but seeing as you haven't taken it back tonight, you'll have to keep it all weekend now. I want to keep the driving to a minimum, so we'll leave our own cars here and you can drop me off at home when we've finished then pick me up in the morning.'

'What, you mean take the pool car home with me instead of leaving it here?'

'Yes, Richards, you may as well.'

'My mum will be impressed.'

'You can't use it for shopping trips and joy rides you know, Richards.'

'I know that, Sir.'

It took them forty-five minutes to drive the short distance to Lambourne Road in Chigwell. Toadstone had taped the area off and was rummaging in cardboard boxes and other rubbish next to a large silver dustbin on wheels. Parish assumed he was looking for evidence. An ambulance was parked up with its engine running and all the lights on. The paramedics were sat inside keeping warm. Neither of them looked like Richards' paramedic.

'You didn't have to finish your five-course meal and have another bottle of wine before you came out here, Parish,' Doc Michelin said stamping his feet and blowing into his hands. 'Its like living in the Gulag Archipelago with all this snow.'

'Sorry, Doc, but you do know the roads are lethal don't you? We're just lucky not to be lying on a slab in your Mortuary. And that's no reflection on Constable Richard's driving abilities.'

'Let's get on shall we, Inspector? I've wasted enough of my Friday evening here.'

'Okay, take me through it, Doc.'

The three of them walked along the alley. The corpse still lay on the concrete covered in a layer of snow.

Parish's forehead creased. 'Is that...?'

'Yes,' Doc Michelin said. 'Brian Ridpath was urinating against the wall behind the dustbin. As he turned round still fumbling to put his penis back in his trousers, he was stabbed in the heart. Needless to say, the penis never made it back into the warmth of his trousers.'

'That's disgusting, Sir,' Richards said screwing up her face.

'Death usually is, Constable,' Doc Michelin said.

'Who found him?'

The pathologist handed Parish a piece of paper. 'I didn't see the point in making him wait around in this weather. That's his address, but he said he'd be in the *Two Brewers* from six until eleven. If I was you, I'd interview him sooner rather than later he reeked of whiskey.'

Parish was thinking the same thing. 'Besides taking a leak, what was Ridpath doing here?'

'A man of habit apparently. Goes to the *Two Brewers* pub just up the road at approximately eleven o'clock every day until about three o'clock when he can hardly stand. Then he tries to walk home to his flat in Romford Road, but from what the man who found him said, he usually ends up sleeping it off somewhere between the pub and his flat.'

'The man who found Ridpath wasn't surprised to see him in the alley then?'

116

'No, he spotted Ridpath lying on his back and thought he'd check that he was all right. Obviously he wasn't, and that's when he called 999.'

'Much the same as the others then?' Parish said.

'Same murder weapon, similar token left in the mouth. Yes, apart from the location, Inspector, I would say much the same as the others.'

'Do we know anything about Mr Ridpath?'

'He's retired and spends his pension in the *Two Brewers*. More than that, I can't help you.'

'Have we got an address for his flat?'

'Number 62 Loftus Towers.' The Doc pointed to a tall high-rise towering above them. 'I would assume it's on the sixth floor.'

'What about a key?'

Toadstone came up and gave him a bunch of keys in a plastic evidence bag.

'Okay, lets wrap it up,' Parish said. 'What about you, Toadstone, anything for me?'

'Sorry, Sergeant. I'm just going through the motions here, but there's nothing of any interest.'

'It's Inspector now by the way. Have you drawn a blank on the other crime scenes as well?'

'There are some black fibres on the clothes embedded in the blood around each of the wounds, but there's nothing distinctive about them. I assume they come from a glove, but it's a cotton/polyester mix you can buy anywhere.'

'I thought forensics were meant to find evidence, Toadstone?'

'It's not through the want of trying, Sir.'

'Richards, go and tell the paramedics they can take the body away now.' Richards stomped over to the ambulance and banged on the bonnet. 'Shift your arses,' she shouted.

117

'I see you're training her well, Parish,' the Doc said smiling.

'That's Kowalski's influence, Doc, you know I'm not like that. When are you thinking of doing this post mortem?'

'Probably Monday now. I'm going to take Sunday off to spend with my wife and goldfish.'

'Goldfish?'

'Hey, don't knock the *Carassius auratus auratus* they have excellent memories and always welcome me home.'

As a foster child, Parish wasn't allowed to have a pet He'd wanted a puppy, but his foster parents wouldn't let him have one. At eighteen he'd left foster care to go to university, and then joined the police. Now, it wouldn't be fair to leave an animal in his flat alone all day – and night sometimes.

'We'll see you at ten-thirty tomorrow morning, Doc, and thanks for all your work tonight. Give the goldfish a hug from me.'

Doc Michelin chuckled. 'There's more chance of getting a hug from the goldfish than the wife that's for sure, goodnight Parish, goodnight Constable.'

***

'Do you want a drink whilst we're here, Richards? It is Friday night after all.' They were in the *Two Brewers* to talk to Larry Mogg before he became too drunk to interview. The whole place reeked of the past and had not been decorated since the smoking ban came into force. The ceiling was yellow, the parquet floor was sticky, and the pictures on the walls were old and faded.

'A cup of tea?'

'You could get arrested for enjoying yourself too much, but I'll ask.' Parish went up to the bar and asked for a tea, a coffee, and which one was Larry Mogg please? Larry Mogg was an anorexic-looking man in his mid-sixties with greasy hair, bat ears and a filthy donkey jacket. He stood leaning on the corner of the bar beneath a lopsided picture of the Queen Mother.

'You a copper?' Mogg asked.

Parish pulled out his warrant card. 'Detective Inspector Parish, Hoddesdon Police Station.'

'What about you, love?' he said to Richards.

'Yes, I'm a detective as well,' Richards lied.

'Have you got some identification then? You can't be too careful these days.'

Richards pulled out her warrant card and waved it in front of Mogg. '...Richards.' The word Constable was mumbled and distorted until it nearly sounded like Detective.

The barman brought their tea and coffee in two cups. Parish paid, passed Richards her tea and scooped four sugars from a sugar bowl into his cup.

'That's a sacrilege that is,' Mogg said. 'It's like pissing in church drinking tea in a pub.' He took a huge swallow of his beer in protest at what they were doing.

'We've not come here to talk about the merits of drinking tea or coffee in a pub, Mr Mogg. You were the one who found Mr Ridpath in the alley?'

'I was.' Mogg swallowed the last of his pint, moved the glass along the bar towards Parish and looked at it.

Parish realised what Mogg expected and signalled the barman to refill the pint glass.

'Yeah, I found him. Saw him lying on his back in the alley and didn't want him to choke on his own vomit, so I went to turn him on his side. We had a youngster in here not long ago who...'

'You turned Mr Ridpath on his side then?'

119

'No I did not, when I saw the state of him, I nearly shit myself. I had to come back here for a whiskey on the house, and to call you lot.'

'You didn't take anything off the body?'

'What do you take me for? I don't go around robbing dead bodies. Yeah, I did a bit of time for burglary once, but even criminals have a code of conduct, you know. We don't take stuff off dead bodies.' He finished his pint and slid the empty glass along the bar.

This was turning into an expensive night one way or another, Parish thought, and it wasn't as if he was getting any enjoyment out of it.

'Did you see anyone near the body, in the alley or walking away?'

'Not a soul, just Pete with his staring eyes and his dick hanging out. Whoever killed him could have waited 'till he'd put the mouse back in the house.' He took another long swallow of his beer. 'Can't get it out of my mind. Do you think I need counselling or something?'

'I'm sure you'll be fine in a few days, Mr Mogg,' Parish said. 'Do you happen to know what Mr Ridpath did for a living before he retired?'

Mogg's empty glass came sliding along the bar towards him again. Parish worked out that he was averaging three questions per beer.

'He told me once, said he worked for the Council as a caretaker.'

'Which Council?'

Mogg ran dirty fingers through his hair. 'No, don't recall.'

'Do you remember where he was a caretaker?'

'I suppose a school.'

'Which school?'

'It was a long time ago, and my memory isn't what it used to be.' The empty glass reappeared.

'Thanks very much for your help, and I hope we don't have to bother you again, Mr Mogg.' Parish gained some satisfaction from leaving the empty glass on the bar, but he still felt as though he'd been mugged.

Outside, Richards said, 'Do you think Ridpath will have worked for Redbridge Council, Sir?'

'I wouldn't like to bet against it. Let's go to Ridpath's flat, we should be able to find out more there.'

'Do we need a warrant, Sir?'

'You've been watching the Crime Channel again, haven't you, Richards?'

She turned her eyes away. 'No, Sir.'

He smiled. 'I bet. Well, we don't need a warrant because we've got a key. And let's face it, Mr Ridpath is hardly in a position to complain to the Police Complaints Commission is he?'

'I suppose not, Sir.'

TWELVE

The lifts were out of order in Loftus Towers. They had to walk up the six flights of graffiti-covered urine-smelling stairs to reach Brian Ridpath's flat.

Richards pressed a perfumed-drenched handkerchief over her nose and mouth with one hand, and held on to Parish's arm with the other.

On the sixth floor, they found number sixty-two and Parish unlocked the door. The stink from the flat was as bad as the foul-smelling stairs.

'You can stay out here if you want to, Richards?'

'That's very chivalrous of you, Sir,' Richards mumbled through the handkerchief, 'but I'll be all right.'

Parish switched the hall light on. There was cracked and broken linoleum on the floor, and mould climbing up the walls. In the living room – the first room on the left – a chocolate brown carpet that Parish was sure had never been cleaned or vacuumed covered the floor. In front of a threadbare easy chair sat a worn out oblong coffee table. A television stood in one corner, and in another there was a mountain of squashed beer cans.

'How can people live like this, Sir?' Richards said through the handkerchief.

'This is a five-star room compared to some of the places I've seen, Richards.'

'What are we looking for?'

'Pension book, bank statements, letters, anything that could tell us where he worked.'

'I'll look in here, Sir, I don't think I could face the bedroom.'

'Okay, I'll look in the other rooms.' He moved back into the hall. The next room on the left was the kitchen. An army of cockroaches ran for cover when he switched the light on. Pizza cartons, fish and chip wrappings, Chinese take-away boxes and other fast-food leftovers covered the floor. He switched the light off and carried on. At the end of the hall was the bathroom. The sink was heavily stained with green limescale from a dripping tap. Black mould was everywhere, and the bath had clearly never been cleaned. Parish saw no toothbrush, toothpaste, shampoo, soap, or towel, and he wondered how Ridpath had kept himself clean. He moved back up the hall to the last room – the bedroom. There was a double bed with urine-stained rags on it. A heap of assorted papers filled the gap between the right-hand wall and the bed. Parish picked up a handful and began to sift through them. A bank statement, dated a week ago, showed a balance of £129,567. Parish couldn't imagine someone living in a hovel like this, and having that amount of money. Maybe, besides his alcoholism, Brian Ridpath had mental health problems, he thought. He examined the bank statement further and discovered that at the beginning of the month, £2,000 was paid in from Redbridge Council. Apart from gas, electricity and the usual monthly bills, Ridpath had very few outgoings. Every couple of days Ridpath would take out a hundred pounds in cash, probably for his drink and the takeaways. Parish found another bank statement from November showing a similar pattern.

What a grim life, Parish thought.

'Hello, Sir?' a nervous Richards called from the hall.

'In here, Richards,' Parish said.

Richards came in and stood beside him. 'You've found something then?'

'And very interesting it is as well. Do you know that Mr Ridpath had a £130,000 in the bank?'

'You're joking, Sir?'

'Here, take a look for yourself.' He passed the bank statement to her.

She took it between thumb and forefinger. 'But, that doesn't make sense, Sir.'

'What doesn't make sense, Richards, is that a caretaker was being paid £2,000 each month by Redbridge Council.'

'It didn't do him much good did it, Sir?'

'That's another issue entirely, Richards.'

'It'll take us the rest of the night to go through all that paper.'

'I think we'll let Mr Toadstone from forensics take on that lovely job, Richards. One thing's for certain though, Redbridge Council is central to our investigation.'

They left the flat and locked the door.

'I'm glad that's over with, Sir,' Richards said as they walked down the stairs.

'I'm sure it wasn't the perfect Friday night you dreamt of, Richards.'

'Oh it was, Sir, but without the smell. I love being a detective. I wouldn't swap what we're doing now for all the tea in China.'

They stepped out of the concrete monstrosity into the freezing cold.

'We've not finished yet, Richards.'

'What are we going to do now, Sir?'

'Do you fancy a kebab?'

'You're trying to feed me up and then sell me to the carnival as the elephant woman, aren't you, Sir?'

'One kebab won't hurt you.'

'Not for me, Sir, and you shouldn't either. Kebabs are the absolute worst you can eat for saturated fats. Why aren't you married with children, Sir?'

'That's a rather personal question, Richards.'

'If you were married, you wouldn't be eating crap all day, well?'

'The only women I get chance to meet are victims, suspects, or coppers, Richards. That's why Carrie increased my heart rate.'

'Don't lie, Sir, that was lust.'

'I don't know what you mean, Richards.'

They reached the car and climbed in.

'Before we knock off for the night I want a kebab, and then whilst I'm eating it you can drive to Redbridge Council. There's a security guard on at night who will let us in. He'll have some emergency contact numbers. We need to ring Carrie and persuade her to come into the office tomorrow to provide us with the information we need.'

Richards drove to Chigwell town centre and parked up outside Ugar's Kebab House.

'Are you sure, Richards?'

'I'm sure, Sir.'

Once Parish had bought his kebab and climbed back into the car, Richards headed towards Redbridge Council offices.

He began munching the kebab, careful not to get the double extra chilli sauce on the front of his coat.

'That stinks, Sir.'

Parish slurped, licked his lips and said, 'I know.'

***

It was ten past nine when Parish banged on the glass entry doors of Redbridge Council. Paul Cummins arrived in his dark blue uniform and let them in.

'Hello, Inspector. Have we had another murder?'

'In a manner of speaking, Mr Cummins. I need the home contact number of Mr Chivers' secretary, Carrie.'

'You'd better come in then.'

He let them in and locked the doors. 'Follow me, I'll have a look for you.'

After looking through a variety of folders for five minutes, he shook his head. 'Sorry, there's not much call to contact a secretary from Personnel out of working hours, and they haven't provided her number in the list.'

'I really need to contact her tonight, Mr Cummins. Can we go up to her office and see if there's anything up there?'

'I'm sorry I can't do that, but it is time I did my rounds and if you were to follow me up to the Personnel Director's office, well…'

Parish smiled and nodded. 'You stay here, Richards,' he told her. 'Mr Cummins might hear two of us following him.'

'Make yourself a cup of tea if you want, Constable,' Cummins said.

They went up to the fifth floor in the lift, and Cummins let Parish in to Mr Chiver's office. He found Carrie's home number in a drawer of the mahogany desk, sat in the real leather executive chair and rang the number using the Director's telephone.

'Hello?'

'Carrie?'

'Who is this?'

'Detective Inspector Parish. I was…'

'Yes, I remember you. What do you want?'

'I need information. Is it possible you can come into the office tomorrow?'

'What type of information?'

'I need a list of people who worked with Mr Taylor and Mrs Flint between 1982 and 1986. We've also had another murder, a Mr Brian Ridpath who was retired, but previously employed by the Council as a School

126

Caretaker. I'd like some information on him if that's possible.'

'I'm sure I can provide that information. What time do you want me, Inspector?'

What jumped into his mind was not very professional, and if his imagination had been monitored they would have locked him up and thrown away the key. Instead, he redirected his thought patterns to providing Carrie with an answer. Diane Flint's post mortem was scheduled for ten-thirty. He didn't really want to start rushing about on a Saturday morning. 'What about two o'clock tomorrow afternoon?' he offered.

'My husband is away on business, so I'll have to bring my two children with me. I hope it doesn't take too long because they have the attention span of gnats.'

Husband! Two children! His bubble of her had burst. Richards would be happy. 'I hope so too. Thanks very much, Carrie and I'll see you at two tomorrow.'

The phone went dead.

'All sorted?' Cummins asked.

'Yes,' Parish said and smiled. 'All sorted.'

They thanked Paul Cummins for his help, and Richards drove Parish home.

When she pulled up outside his flat he said, 'Thanks, Richards. Pick me up at ten o'clock tomorrow morning.' He climbed out. 'Oh by the way, Carrie has a husband and two children.' He saw her smiling. 'Drive carefully, Richards.'

'Goodnight, Sir.'

***

Saturday, 18th January

He felt like shit. It was only four-thirty, but he got up anyway and took a shower. He'd been having a nightmare, and he woke up drenched in sweat. What the nightmare was about he had no idea, but his heart was still racing as he dried himself. If the Chief hadn't promoted him and kept him on the case, he'd have probably slept in and had a leisurely weekend. Instead, he was fighting unknown demons at four-thirty in the morning, and staring at a full day's work ahead of him.

Outside, it was still dark. From the glow of the orange streetlights he could see that it was snowing again. He put the heating on and made himself a coffee. In the fridge he had eggs, but the bread had gone off again. When you weren't hungry there was food everywhere, but when you were starving – as he was now – everything was either out-of-date or had fur on it. In the freezer there was a pizza, but he didn't fancy pizza at five in the morning. He placed four eggs in a pan of water, put it on the cooker, and began to boil them. From the middle of the sliced loaf, he managed to salvage three pieces of bread. He cut the furry edges off and put them in the toaster.

Whilst the eggs were boiling he took out a plate from the cupboard, but then realised he didn't have an eggcup. He looked around for an alternative, but couldn't find anything even remotely similar. Then he realised he didn't have any butter for the toast either. God, he hated living alone. His life had been like this for years, and he still hadn't mastered looking after himself. He ran the eggs under the cold water tap until he could peel the shells off, but he was no eggshell peeling expert and only one egg looked like an egg, the others looked diseased. He threw what he had left of the eggs on the plate, sprinkled salt over them, and began to eat them with a spoon at the same time as biting into the dry toast. He decided when he'd finished that it was the worst breakfast he had ever eaten bar none.

At five-thirty he logged on to FindLove.com. He wanted a woman who liked cooking, cleaning and having sex, but not necessarily in that order or one after the other. Up to now he hadn't found any women like that on the site. There were twenty-four messages waiting for him, and he opened and read each one in chronological order. He deleted all those with children, which left thirteen. He deleted all those that had strange predilections such as sadomasochism, which left one – Jenny Rennie.

Jennie Rennie was thirty-one and looking for Mr Right. He wondered whether he was Mr Right, and if her name was a pseudonym like Brad Russell. He sent her a message:

Dear Jenny: I'm looking for Miss Right, are you her? What about meeting? Brad.

It wasn't even six o'clock and he was bored. He'd forgotten to write his report for the Chief last night, so he composed one.

I have three murders now: Taylor, Flint and Ridpath. They all worked for Redbridge Council between 1982 and 1986 (Did Ridpath? I'd have to check that out with Carrie). Taylor was a Rent Advisor, Flint a Social Worker, and Ridpath a School Caretaker (to be confirmed). They were all killed by the same person, the same weapon, and in the same way. All had a token with a different number stamped on it inserted into their mouths. Taylor was number 27, Flint 32, and Ridpath 14. If the killer has the remaining twelve tokens will there be another twelve murders? Besides these similarities, what connects all three victims? Were they all involved in something between 1982 and 1986 that is getting them killed now? Who is killing them? What do the tokens mean? Why have Redbridge Council been paying Brian Ridpath £2,000 each month? Are they paying anyone else? Is there a cover up?

When he read the report back, he realised it had been written by someone with dementia. There were so many questions left unanswered. Well, today he'd better get some of those questions answered. It had been three days since Gregory Taylor was murdered outside number 29 Ralston Drive, and they had no suspects – not even the hint of one. He left the report as it was, but added that he and Richards were going to attend Diane Flint's post mortem at ten-thirty today, and then search for some answers from Carrie at Redbridge Council. He pressed send. All he could do was his best. A determined killer was always going to be two steps ahead of the police, and this seemed to be a very determined killer.

THIRTEEN

He heard Richards beep the Mondeo's horn. The trouble was, he still had his dressing gown on. Crap, he must have dozed off. He ran into the bedroom and threw a pair of jeans, a T-shirt, and a jumper on. Whilst he was tying his shoes he took deep breaths to slow his heart rate down. What was he doing? Did he need to take anything with him? Was everything switched off? Locked? He picked up his keys, put his coat on and ran out of the door.

'You're late, Richards,' he said as he climbed into the car and clicked the seat belt.

'Did you lose your razor and comb, Sir?'

He pulled the sun visor down and looked at his reflection in the vanity mirror. The five o'clock shadow didn't look too bad, but he was clearly having a bad-hair day. Waking up so early and having a shower, then nodding off again had completely disoriented him. He'd need a map and a compass to navigate his way through the day. 'Its Saturday, I'm slumming it.'

'The Mortuary?'

'Are you insinuating something, Richards?'

'But...'

'Just drive.' He put the seat back and closed his eyes. He needed to get his bearings before they reached the hospital. His head was still stuck in the nightmare he'd been having when Richards had beeped her horn. Drowsiness clouded his brain, but he recalled being dragged along dark corridors to a place that filled him with dread.

They arrived at the hospital at ten twenty-five. It was snowing as if it couldn't be bothered, and the icy wind made them shiver.

'I need a coffee, Richards.'

'We'll be late, Sir.'

'Its not as if we're going to miss anything important is it, a few slashes with a scalpel, the removal of every organ, the stench of death and formaldehyde, and Doc Michelin eating his donuts? All we want is the end result. We don't really need to see the dissection being performed.'

They went up in the lift to the cafeteria. Parish had four pieces of buttered toast as well as a mug of coffee with four sugars. It was at the till that he realised he'd left his wallet and warrant card on the dressing table in the bedroom.

'You'll have to pay today, Richards, I've forgotten my wallet.' He left her paying whilst he found a table in the busy restaurant.

When she joined him with her herbal tea she said, 'Is there something wrong this morning, Sir?'

'What makes you ask that?'

'You're not your usual happy self.'

'Don't think I can't recognise sarcasm when I hear it, Richards.' He told her about waking up, showering, and dozing off again. 'In the end I had to rush to get ready, and I hate having to do that.'

'I hope you're not going to be grumpy all day, Sir?'

'Grumpy? He was one of the Seven Dwarves wasn't he?'

***

It was five to eleven when they walked into the Mortuary. Doc Michelin looked up from the nearly empty torso of Diane Flint.

'Tardiness is becoming a bit of a habit lately, Inspector.'

'I was mugged, Doc, they took my wallet. Constable Richards had to pay for the coffee and toast in the cafeteria whilst we were recuperating.'

'You certainly look as though you've been mugged, Parish, but I'd say they took your razor and hair brush as well as your wallet.'

'Never mind the flattery, Doc. Have you got anything for me?'

'As you can see, I am part way through the post mortem. Be kind enough to wait until I've concluded it.'

They waited twenty minutes whilst Doc Michelin removed the remaining organs, mumbled into an overhead microphone, took photographs, and then closed up the Y-shaped cut he'd made with a 5" curved suture needle and twine. It certainly wasn't a cosmetic closure, Parish thought.

'Well?' Parish said when the Doc looked up.

'What do you want me to say, Parish? Diane Flint was fifty-three years old, in the early stages of undiagnosed cervical cancer, and suffered from lower back pain. The murderer stabbed her once in the heart with the same weapon he used on Gregory Taylor.'

'You could have rung me and told me that, Doc.'

'That wouldn't have been nearly as much fun, now would it, Inspector?'

'Thanks anyway.'

'You're welcome, Parish. I'll get the PM report to you by Monday afternoon. Are you going to be here for Peter Ridpath's post mortem on Monday morning?'

'Is there much point? I mean, we know how he died, and its not as if watching post mortems is one of my favourite pastimes.' Then he remembered the press briefing. 'Sorry, Doc, the Chief arranged a press briefing for eleven o'clock on Monday, so I won't be able to make it anyway.'

'Up to you, Inspector. If you're not here, and I discover something unexpected I'll give you a ring. Otherwise, you'll get the report Wednesday morning at the latest.'

'Thanks, Doc. Have a good Sunday, and say hello to your wife and the goldfish for me.'

Doc Michelin waved as Parish and Richards headed for the swing doors of the Mortuary.

***

'What now, Sir?'

Parish checked his watch, but it wasn't there. 'What time is it?'

'You forgot your watch as well, Sir?'

'I wouldn't be asking you for the time if I hadn't. Well?'

'Quarter to twelve.'

'What do you want to do, Richards? We can go back to my flat so that I can recover the pieces of my life I left behind this morning, and then we can go and have some lunch with me paying, or we can go directly to lunch and you pay the bill, your choice?'

'I don't mind paying, Sir, but I'll take you back to your flat because you need to do something with your hair. I'm embarrassed about being seen with you.'

'Thanks very much, Richards. I could go and get it cut. I've been meaning to for ages.'

They reached the car and climbed in.

'That's a good idea, Sir, before my mum sees you tomorrow.'

'What's that got to do with anything?'

'Nothing, but I don't want my mum thinking I work for a scruffy boss.'

'Scruffy, Richards?'

134

'You know what I mean, Sir.'

'I have no idea, but you'd better take me to the barbers anyway. Go towards my flat, there's a barbers close by. You'll have to pay, but I'll give it you back.'

'What type of haircut are you going to have, Sir?'

'What do you mean, what type? A normal type with a parting on the left.'

'That's a bit old-fashioned, Sir.'

'You've probably noticed that I'm not a teenager, Richards.'

'No, but I was thinking layered and spiked.'

'I'm a Detective Inspector, Richards not a fashion icon. I have a certain image to uphold.'

'It doesn't mean you have to look like a boring old man, Sir.'

'Are you saying I look like a boring old man?'

'Not this morning, Sir. If I said what you looked like this morning, you'd sack me.'

'All right, Richards, I'll get a trendy haircut, but if I end up looking stupid, you will get the sack.'

They reached the barbers, Richards parked up, and they both went in. There were three people in the queue and two people in the chairs, so they sat down to wait. Richards sat with him and they skimmed the magazines. After thirty minutes it was his turn.

'Usual, Jed?' Wally the barber asked. Wally had been his barber for fifteen years, but Wally was seventy now and long past the age of retirement. He wore glasses like milk-bottom bottoms, and everyone was sure that he was blind and cut people's hair based on experience and intuition rather than sight.

'Something different today, Wally. My new partner thinks I look like a boring old man, she suggests layered and spiked.'

Richards came up to the chair. He could see her smile and sparkling brown eyes in the mirror. 'I was thinking about an inch long on top and tapered downwards,' she said to Wally. 'And if I'm paying, give him a shave as well.'

Wally nodded. 'She seems to know what you want, Jed.'

'So it would seem. I'm not going to look stupid am I, Wally?'

'Nah, it'll take ten years off you.'

'Okay, if you say so.'

Wally gave him a shave first. Parish closed his eyes and dozed off, but the image of being dragged along a dark corridor made him jerk awake.'

'Whoa,' Wally said holding the cut-throat razor in the air. 'You nearly ended up in the cellar where Mrs Lovett is making her lovely pie fillings.'

'Sorry, Wally. I drifted off for a moment.'

After Wally had shaved him, he washed Parish's hair. He tried not to look as Wally began cutting. He felt as though he was undergoing surgery, and thought he should have asked for a general anaesthetic. He closed his eyes and thought about Carrie taking off her clothes, so that he wouldn't get dragged down that dark tunnel again.

'There you are, Jed.' Wally rubbed something in his hair and began moulding it into spikes. 'You'll need to put gel on it every morning otherwise it'll just lay flat.' He turned to Richards. 'What do you think, Miss?'

Richards came up to stand at the back of the chair again. 'A hundred percent better. I could fancy you myself if you weren't so old, Sir.'

'You really know how to make a guy feel special, Richards. Pay the man, and let's go and get some lunch whilst there's still time.'

As they walked to the car, he felt the cold wind circling round his head. It was as if Wally had cut his hat and scarf off. Before they reached the car, he saw a photo booth in the 24-hour Mart out of the corner of his eye.

'Seeing as I've got a new haircut and I'm now a DI, I need a photograph, Richards.'

'My mum's got one of those digital cameras at home, and I've got a camera on my phone.'

He pointed towards the Mart. 'A passport photograph for my new warrant card, Richards, not a holiday snap to throw darts at.'

'Oh, okay Sir.' She suddenly smiled. 'We can have some taken together.'

'Don't be childish, Richards.'

'Come on, Sir. You're my first partner. I'll be able to put them in my album and tell my grandchildren about us when I'm old and wrinkled. Please, Sir, pretty please...'

He couldn't stop himself from smiling. 'If you pull faces, Richards...'

She jumped up and hugged him. 'I won't, Sir, I promise.'

He went first to obtain the serious photograph he needed for his warrant card. Whilst he was waiting for the results to drop into the slot, Richards put her three pounds in, squeezed into the booth and sat on his knee.

'Are you mad, Richards?'

'Wind the stool down, Sir, so we can both get our heads in the window.'

When she was happy with her position she said, 'Ready, Sir?'

'Come on, Richards, let's get it over with...'

FLASH

'You didn't tell me you'd pressed the...'

FLASH

'I'm going to look a right...'

137

FLASH

'I'd shut up if I were you, Sir.'

'I think...'

FLASH

They had to wait two minutes for his serious photographs, which Richards pounced on before he'd noticed they'd arrived.

She laughed. 'You look like you're in shock, Sir.'

He snatched them off her. 'Give them here, Richards, photographs are confidential.'

Another five minutes passed before the second lot of photographs arrived.

Richards snapped them up again and squealed with delight. 'Ha, you don't want to see these, Sir.'

'Come on, Richards, I'm on them as well.'

She handed them over. He had his eyes closed in the first and third ones, and his mouth had morphed into something from a horror movie in the second and fourth pictures. In all of them Richards looked beautiful with her sparkling eyes and radiant smile, but she had used the hand of the arm wrapped around his shoulder to give him Indian feathers, an extra ear, and a five-fingered splay.

'I've never been very photogenic,' he said passing the photographs back to her.

'Do you want two of them, Sir?'

'I don't think so, Richards. You keep them all, but don't let anyone at the station see them.'

'I'll try not to, Sir.'

'Right, lets go to my flat, I'll get my wallet, warrant card and watch, and then we can go to lunch. Where do you want to eat, Richards, my treat?'

'We could go to that Italian restaurant opposite Redbridge Council. That way, we'll already be there at two o'clock.'

'Good idea, what time is it now?'

'Five to one, Sir.'

She drove to his flat. He rushed in, collected the fragments of his life, and rushed out.

They reached the *Signor Carlo Restaurant* at one-twenty. Parish was feeling adventurous and asked for a Ragu Bolognese. He had no idea what it was, but he thought what the hell, it wasn't as if they were going to poison him. Richards ordered Risotto with Chicken livers. They'd only just come out of a post mortem for goodness sake. He knew he had no press briefing today so he got the waiter to bring him a lager. When the food came, Parish was surprised to find that his meal was Spaghetti Bolognese with an Italian name. He stared at Richards' meal, but the chef had obviously done a good job in hiding the Chicken livers.

***

They'd finished lunch and were walking across the road at exactly two o'clock. Carrie stood waiting for them at the top of the Council steps with two young children, a girl of about five and a boy of about eight. Parish was surprised at how fantastic she looked in a green plaid knee-length skirt with brown boots. Underneath her dark green coat she had on a light green blouse and jumper, and covering her blonde hair she wore a green knitted hat worn like a beret. Maybe he wasn't a breasts and backside type of guy, but...

'Thanks for coming, Carrie. Hopefully, we can get some things cleared up this afternoon.'

'You've had your hair cut, Inspector. It makes you look ten years younger.'

'Thanks.' He smiled, surprised that she'd noticed. Richards nudged his arm.

He banged on the door and a security guard appeared. Parish pressed his warrant card to the glass. After a question and answer session they were in the lift on their way up to the fifth floor.

Once they were ensconced in the Personnel Department, Carrie took off her coat and hat, and sat her children down in the waiting area with strict instructions to behave themselves. The girl had a colouring book and pencils, while the boy couldn't take his eyes off a small hand-held computer console. Parish had never had time to play computer games and had no idea what games were available for children, but given the choice he would much rather have read a decent book.

It took Carrie twenty minutes to produce two lists of people with addresses and telephone numbers who had worked with Gregory Taylor and Diane Flint during the period 1982 to 1986. There were only thirteen who had worked with Gregory Taylor and four of those were dead, which left nine to contact. The turnover in the Social Services Department proved to be very different. Over the four years there had been seventy-four people who had worked with Diane Flint, and only seven were dead.

'There's nothing on the database about Brian Ridpath,' Carrie announced. 'Do you know when he stopped working for the Council?'

'We know very little about him,' Parish said.

'Then we'll have to go down to the lower basement and look in the archives. Its really spooky down there, will you come with me, Inspector?'

Parish felt his heart rate increase, and saw Richards throw Carrie a look of disgust. 'Of course,' he said to her.

'Richards, you stay here. Start phoning the people on the lists, and keep an eye on those kids. You need to ask whether they know anything about the tokens, or whether

Taylor/Flint were involved with a school of any kind. If so, which one. Clear?'

'Yes, Sir, but...'

'Good. We'll be back up as soon as we can.'

He knew Richards had tried to keep him away from Carrie, and wondered why. Anybody would think that Carrie Holden was the reincarnation of Lucretia Borgia. With a husband and two kids she was hardly going to be interested in a worn out copper like him.

The lift doors opened in the lower basement. Carrie stepped out and led him along a dark corridor towards a metal door. Parish silently agreed with her that the lower basement was spooky, and he was reminded of his nightmare again. She opened the metal door and switched the light on. It smelled musty. Filing cabinets and other furniture filled the long room. She shut the door and locked it.

As he stared at the locked door in confusion, Carrie pounced on him. In a tangle of arms, legs and lips he was propelled backwards until he fell across a table. She sat astride him.

'What...'

'Don't talk, words are meaningless.'

She tore at his jeans and exposed him. He was as hard as Nelson's Column in Trafalgar Square. She pulled her panties sideways and slid him into her. Before he knew what had happened she screamed, he ejaculated, and then they were looking for Brian Ridpath's file in the filing cabinets as if he'd imagined it all. They didn't find the file. What they found instead was an empty space where the file should have been. Someone had removed it. But it did at least confirm that Brian Ridpath worked for Redbridge Council.

Parish leaned against a cabinet and looked at Carrie. 'What...'

141

'My husband is having an affair with a young bimbo,' she said anticipating his question. 'I wanted to get back at him, and I quite fancied you.'

Parish didn't know whether he objected to being used for sexual revenge or not, but found it hard to believe that her husband would want another woman when he had Carrie. 'All I can say is, your husband must be a blind and very stupid man.'

'You're just saying that because…'

'I'm saying it because it's true, Carrie. You're beautiful, and if you were my wife I'd never look at another woman.'

'I have every right to begin an affair of my own,' she said looking into his eyes. 'Do you want to make love to me every day?'

He had an erection at the very idea of it. 'I can't think of anything I'd like more,' he said, 'but you know it will end in disaster.'

'Not if we're careful.'

He knew they would make mistakes. Her husband would find out, Jed Parish would be named in a messy divorce, there would be wrangling over the children, the money, the house, and the hamster. It was as if he could suddenly predict the future, but he didn't care. Carrie was someone he was willing to fight the monsters for.

'Okay.' He wrote his mobile number, email, and address on the back of one of his cards and gave it to her. 'We can use my flat for now until we get organised if that's okay with you, and the sooner you commit what's on that card to memory the better.'

They kissed.

'What about tomorrow?' she said.

'I'm having lunch with Richards and her mum, but I'll be home for about four o'clock. Are you sure you can get away? We don't want to mess it up right at the start.'

142

'The cheating bastard's away until Wednesday, and he's probably got her with him. I can get my mother to look after the children for a couple of hours.'

'Let's do it then, if you're sure?'

'I'm sure,' she said looking away. 'It's been a long time since a man appreciated me.'

'We'd better go back up before Richards sends a search party down for me.'

'Your partner doesn't like me much, does she?'

'Richards is a bit over-protective that's all.'

'She wants you for herself.'

'No, it's not that. We've only known each other for four days. It's something else. I think she's trying to save me for her mother.'

Carrie laughed. 'Her mother! Do you like old women?'

'There's no need to be bitchy.'

They'd been gone twenty-five minutes. Richards gave him a strange look as he walked towards her, but said nothing.

'How are the phone calls going, Richards?'

'Of the few people that I've been able to talk to, Sir, I've got nothing. No one knows anything about any tokens, or a school. What about you, did you get what you wanted?'

Scrutinising Richards' face, he decided to take the question at face value. 'No, somebody had removed Ridpath's file.'

'There's definitely something going on here, isn't there, Sir?'

'Yes, Richards, there is.' He turned to Carrie. 'You don't have access to any financial records do you?'

'No I don't, and only Martin Squires the Financial Director has the authority to give you access to the financial records.'

143

'Okay, we'll be back first thing on Monday morning to speak to Mr Squires. Thanks for your help, Carrie. Come on Richards, let's call it a day.'

FOURTEEN

Sunday 19th January

He woke up in a panic at some ungodly hour, but managed to slow his heart rate down and get back to sleep. Now, staring at the snow-reflected fingers of light piercing the gaps in the curtains, he wondered if what had happened with Carrie was a figment of his warped imagination. It was six-fifteen. He decided he'd lie in bed and run things through his mind, but the more he tried to focus on the case, or the lunch with Richards and her mum, the more he kept thinking of Carrie. He thought about what had happened between them and what was going to happen later. He recalled her softness, the smell and the taste of her. He was a Detective Inspector now, should he have agreed to an affair with a married woman who was the mother of two children? Surely he was expected to be better than that? Wasn't he letting the Chief down? Wasn't he letting himself down? If Richards found out she'd be disappointed in him, but didn't he have a right to a life? Didn't he have the right to love and be loved? He drifted off to sleep again with his jaw set hard.

It was ten past eight when he woke up. He climbed out of bed and made himself a coffee and four pieces of buttered toast from the provisions he'd bought on his way home yesterday afternoon. Whilst he was crunching through the toast, he logged on to FindLove.com. Jenny Rennie had sent him a message and there were another seven hopefuls languishing in his intray.

Hi Brad. I could be your Miss Right if you let me. Let's meet in Redbridge at the Hairy Lemon pub tomorrow night at eight? I'll have a red carnation in my hair, Jenny.

She'd written that last night, so she meant tonight. Carrie was going to be here from four until probably six. If he met Jenny wasn't he betraying Carrie? Didn't he say he'd never look at another woman? He didn't really mean that he'd never look at another woman, but both of them knew what he meant. Yet, here he was contemplating meeting another woman only two hours after he would probably have had sex with Carrie. It was clear what he had to do.

Hi Jenny. I've met someone, and I'm not a guy that cheats on women, so unfortunately I'll have to decline your invitation. If the relationship breaks down, I'll contact you if you're still interested? Brad.

He deleted the seven hopefuls from his intray as well, and felt much better for having done so. It had been a very long time since he'd had any kind of social life, but suddenly it was becoming complicated. What a difference a day makes, he thought. He switched to his emails and pulled up the one he'd sent to the Chief last night.

Hi Chief! Hope you're feeling okay? Diane Flint's PM didn't produce anything of interest. Doc Michelin is doing Brian Ridpath's on Monday at 1030, but I'm not optimistic that it will give us anything more than we've already got. Richards and I went to Redbridge Council this afternoon and the Personnel Director's secretary met us there. She produced two lists of people who worked with Taylor and Flint between 1982 and 1986. Richards started to contact them, but up to now she's had no luck. There was no record of Brian Ridpath in the Council's computer database so we looked in the archives. Brian Ridpath's name was there, but someone had taken his file. Whatever is going on, Redbridge Council is at the centre of it. Richards and I will be there first thing Monday morning to quiz the Finance Director, and I'll see you when I come back. If they were paying Ridpath £2,000 a month, there must be some record of it, and someone must also know why he was being paid that amount. PS. I've not forgotten about the press briefing at eleven o'clock. I'm taking a day off tomorrow, so I'll see you on Monday at about 10:30. DI Parish.

It was a good email. He'd had time to compose it properly last night instead of the rushed disjointed ones he usually sent.

Was that all he could do to find out about Brian Ridpath? He was also expecting an analysis of the paperwork in Ridpath's flat from Toadstone tomorrow morning, which might tell him which school Ridpath worked at. Carrie had sent the email to the Council's employees late on Friday, so he should start getting some replies tomorrow when the staff came in and read it. Maybe he needed to get a team of forensic accountants to burrow into the Council's finances. The Finance Director might be involved in any cover-up. He'd give Squires one chance to come clean. If he didn't deliver, then Parish would happily send in the accountants to find the dirty laundry. If he did that though, the press would be all over the case like limpets.

What was he going to tell the press? One or more of the eager reporters might have fitted the pieces together and realised the victims were all killed by the same person, but what more could they find out? He doubted they would discover the link to Redbridge Council. On the outside, it was merely three random knifings over five days – a teacher, a Director of Social Services, and a drunk. There was no reason to give the murders any more importance than that. Unlike the press, he knew about the marlinspike, the tokens, and the connection to Redbridge Council, but he was still struggling to complete the jigsaw. Without the key pieces, what chance did the press have of discovering the truth? He began to type up the press briefing. Yes, there had been three unconnected knifings in the local area, and investigations were ongoing. No, there were no suspects as yet, but leads were being pursued. What more could he say without creating a rod for his own back?

He set the alarm for twelve-thirty and dozed off again. When he woke, he wondered why Carrie had been dragging him naked along a dark corridor.

***

Parish arrived outside 38 Puck Road at exactly quarter to two. The three bedroom semi-detached house in Chigwell was buried deep within an anonymous road where the houses all looked the same. Snow lay like a blanket over everything, except the path leading to the house, which had been cleared. A snowman with a grin stood next to the front door. It held a board with 'WELCOME INSPECTOR' written on it in bold black lettering. He smiled, knowing that Richards had spent some of her morning building it.

As he climbed out of his car, he felt unusually nervous. Although he was looking forward to a home-cooked Sunday roast and a conversation with real people, he knew Richards was matchmaking and hoped her mum wasn't going to be disappointed when he didn't play along. He took the bunch of flowers and a box of chocolates he'd bought from the back seat of his car and walked slowly down the path to the front door as if he were going to his execution. He'd had no idea what to wear, had forgotten to ask Richards, and had tried on every stitch of clothing he possessed including his suits until he eventually decided on a pair of slacks and a loose-fitting shirt. Now, he felt underdressed and wondered whether he should rush back home and put a suit on.

The door opened before he had a chance to knock. Richards stood there bare-footed in a pair of jeans and a T-shirt with *Chastity is curable, if detected early* printed across her firm well-rounded breasts. Her long dark hair fell about her shoulders, and he knew that if he'd been ten years younger, and she wasn't his partner, he'd have asked her out on a date.

'Nice T-shirt, Richards.'

'Thanks Sir.'

'Is your boyfriend here today, as well?'

'I don't have a boyfriend, Sir.'

'What about that paramedic you gave your number to?'

'He rang up and told me what a creep he was, Sir.'

'Should we arrest him and give him a tour of the dungeon, Richards?'

'He's not worth it, Sir.'

'Your call. I like your snowman by the way.'

She grinned. 'I built it this morning. It's not a shabby one either. Do you want to come in, or do you want to have lunch served on the doorstep?'

He stepped inside.

'Before my mum comes, I finished calling those people on the list and none of them remember anything about a school or know anything about the tokens.'

'It was a long shot anyway, Richards. I hope you used your work mobile and not your home phone?'

149

'Yes, Sir.'

Another woman, who looked like Richards' younger sister, walked down the hall to meet him. She wore a smile and a green velvet dress that emphasised her hourglass figure and perfect breasts.

'You didn't say you had a younger sister, Richards.'

Both women laughed. 'This is my mum, Sir. People always think we're sisters.'

Parish stood in the hallway holding the flowers and chocolates with his mouth open like the jaws of a Venus flytrap. Time clearly had not affected Angela Richards. She was beautiful. Her dark crinkled hair cascaded over her shoulders framing a face, which would not have looked out of place in a montage of the ten most beautiful women in the world. She was taller than her daughter Mary, and the bottomless brown of her eyes were level with his mouth.

'Hello, Inspector,' Angela Richards said. 'Can I take your coat?'

He was going to kill Richards. She should have prepared him, told him her mum was a goddess living on earth.

'Should I take them, Sir?' Richards said holding out her hands.

He passed the flowers and the chocolates to her, but then said, 'There for your younger sister you know, Richards.'

Richards smiled, 'They always are, Sir.'

He shrugged out of his coat, and Angela hung it in a closet.

'Come through, Inspector. Would you like a lager, or something else?'

He followed the two women into a living room that oozed femininity. There were no males living in this house. The curtains were white with barely noticeable

150

pink flowers. The three-piece suite was soft white leather with a mountain of cushions in the same material as the curtains. The carpet was white with a hint of pink. There were antique looking ornaments in strategic positions around the room. 'Well, I'd like you to call me Jed for one thing, and yes, a lager would be good, thanks.'

'Okay, Jed, you can call me Angie.' She took the chocolates and flowers off her daughter and said, 'Thank you.'

'What about me, Sir?'

'What about you, Richards?'

'Can I call you, Jed?'

'No.'

'Oh.'

'I'm angry with you anyway, Richards. You should have told me you had an angel masquerading as your mother.'

Angie Richards came back into the living room with a tall glass of lager and a smile. She passed him the lager and said to her daughter, 'You're right, Mary, he's a smooth-talker all right. Please sit down, Jed.'

The corners of his mouth twitched as he sat on the sofa. 'Should I take my shoes off?' he asked.

'You can if you want to, but it's not really necessary.'

He kept them on just in case his feet smelled. He didn't want to put anyone off the meal, and he couldn't remember what the socks he had on looked like.

Angie sat on the sofa next to him. 'Thank you for taking Mary under your wing, Jed.'

'I needed some help. Mary was there.'

'She thinks you're wonderful.'

He wasn't used to praise and felt uncomfortable.

'Mum,' Richards said. 'Haven't you got things to do in the kitchen?'

Angie smiled. 'Take Jed into the dining room, Mary, the meal will be ready soon.'

They made him cut the beef joint. He had no idea what he was doing, but he produced passable slices of meat. Everything about the meal was perfect. The talk and the laughter were easy, and Parish realised how much he wanted to be part of a real family. He thought of Carrie, and knew that he had made a big mistake. Their relationship was already doomed. Again Richards was right, it was lust.

It hardly surprised Parish that Angie Richards had been out with many men. What did surprise him was that she was still single. That there were no suitors camped outside her door whilst she wove a tapestry depicting the Trojan War.

'In the end,' Angie said, 'none of them measured up. Mary keeps my feet firmly on the ground. If Mary doesn't like them, they don't get past the front door.'

He had an idea what she meant about not measuring up. At the moment he felt he didn't measure up, and wondered what he was going to do about Carrie.

As much as he would like to have stayed in the warmth and laughter, he excused himself at twenty to four and drove back to his flat.

***

Carrie was waiting for him outside his door when he arrived at five to four. He could smell her perfume as he walked up the stairs. She looked vulnerable. He thought that maybe he should get her a key cut so that she could let herself in, but then he began thinking of the implications if he did. He'd never done anything like this before and had to give serious thought to each move he was going to make. If he gave her a key what message would it send? Would she let herself in and start rummaging through his things, organising his life, and trying to turn him into someone else?

He was embarrassed. What should he say to her? Up to now they had hardly spoken. He knew nothing about her really. Who was Carrie Holden? A Personnel Director's secretary, a betrayed wife, a mother of two children, and a beautiful woman seeking revenge. Was this going to be a shallow relationship consisting simply of sex, or was she more than that? Was he more than that? He'd decided on the way home to give them a chance. Maybe their relationship would blossom into something more than snatched moments and sexual fluids.

She smiled nervously.

He held her face in his hands and kissed her on the lips.

'Open the door.' Her voice was hoarse.

He complied.

Even before the door had shut she was pulling at his clothes. He had no chance to switch the light on before he crumpled to the floor with his trousers round his ankles. The sex was hurried and unsatisfying, and the carpet burns on his knees hurt like hell.

Afterwards, they made love more slowly in the shower, and he told her that he was too old for carpet burns.

'Since my husband met his floozy,' she said as she dried his back, 'he doesn't make love to me anymore.'

Was that all he was, a replacement penis? Would her husband squeeze between them each time they made love like a non-permeable membrane?

They sat at the kitchen table wrapped in towels and had a cup of tea. He asked her to tell him about herself.

'There's nothing to tell really. I left school after doing my 'A' Levels. I met Paul and we got married. We were saving for a place of our own, so we decided I shouldn't go to university. I got a job as a secretary instead. Paul already had his degree. I fell pregnant with Tom after a year, and for the next five years I was a housewife until I got the job I'm doing now, all very boring and predictable.'

'Until I came along? Now you're screwing with the law.'

They both laughed, but it was hollow laughter.

'I could have been so much more, Jed.'

She got dressed in the bedroom, and they both knew that she would not come to his flat again. Under different circumstances they might have shared something special, but there was no future in what they had now. The lust was still there, but now it was mixed with pity. He hoped she would find what she wanted.

He showed her to the door. She kissed his cheek and whispered, 'Goodbye.'

'Goodbye Carrie,' he said. 'Drive carefully.'

The phone rang as he shut the door. He hoped it was a wrong number, a long-lost relative, or an idiot selling double-glazing. He prayed it wasn't someone from the station informing him that there'd been another murder.

'Jed Parish?' He thought he sounded tired.

'Hello, Jed. Is it a bad time?'

His heart skipped a beat. It was Angie Richards.

'Hello, Angie. What's the matter, did I forget something?'

'Yes, you forgot to ring and ask me out.'

The towel unravelled and fell in a heap on the floor. If he was unsure before about not seeing Carrie again, he was now certain. 'My memory is terrible. Does Mary know you're ringing me?'

154

'No.'

'If we're going to see each other, Mary mustn't know. If she finds out it will change the nature of our working relationship and I'll have to let her go.'

'Oh, I wouldn't want anything to spoil Mary's job. Maybe we shouldn't see each other then?'

'I didn't say that, Angie. We simply have to make sure she doesn't find out.'

'She'll find out, Jed, that's why she'll make a good detective.'

'Yes, but not yet, not until our relationship has had a chance to either sink or swim without her interference.'

'All right, I'll keep it from her for as long as I can, but she'll drive me crazy. You don't have to live with her.'

'No, but I have to work with her. If she knew about us, she'd drive me crazy as well. Anyway, enough about Mary, let's talk about us.'

They arranged to meet in the *Gooseberry Restaurant* in Chigwell at eight o'clock the following night. She understood that sometimes his private life came a poor second, but he told her he would ring her if something came up.

FIFTEEN

Monday, 20th January

He was stamping his frozen feet outside the station with his hands stuffed in his pockets when Richards turned up in the pool car at eight thirty. The snow on the ground had turned to ice over the weekend, and the snowman Richards had built behind her car looked pleased with the exceptionally large penis someone had kindly given him.

'Good morning, Richards,' he said climbing into the warmth of the Mondeo and making sure the hot air was blowing on his frost-bitten feet. 'Thanks for inviting me to lunch yesterday, I had a great time.'

She pulled out into the slow-moving traffic towards Redbridge. 'Did you like my mum, Sir?'

Richards was like a Rottweiler with a bone. 'I thought your mum was very nice.'

'Very nice? Is that very nice as in the chocolate cake was very nice, or the hat you're wearing is very nice?'

'You know what I mean, Richards?'

'Yesterday, you said she was an angel.'

'She still is.'

'Then why didn't you ask her to go out on a date, Sir?'

'Because of this, Richards.'

'What?'

'You.'

'I haven't done anything.'

'Do you want to carry on working with me?'

'Of course I do, Sir.'

'If I went out with your mum I'd have to get another partner, or move to another country.'

'Oh.'

She said nothing for some time then, 'All right, Sir.'

'All right, what?'

'You can find another partner if that's what it takes.'

'I don't want another partner, Richards, I like the one I've got.'

'My mum deserves some happiness, and I think you'll make her happy, Sir.'

'I'm sure she does, and thanks for the vote of confidence, but we're in the middle of a murder investigation, and I'm not swapping partners to go out with a woman I hardly know, regardless of how angelic she is. Can you imagine what the Chief would say after he's gone out of his way to help you, Richards? Now, concentrate on getting us to Redbridge in one piece and stop asking questions about my private life.'

'What private life, Sir?'

'Stop talking, Richards.'

***

As they were asking to see Martin Squires, the Finance Director, he walked into the Reception. Cindy, the middle-aged receptionist, called out his name and moved round the counter to speak to him. Parish could see the conversation she was having with him was not going well, so he stepped forward with his warrant card.

'Detective Inspector Parish and Constable Richards. Mr Squires, we'd like to ask you some questions.' Cindy backed away.

He looked agitated. 'I'm sorry, Inspector, but now is not a convenient time.'

'Would it be more convenient if I took all your accounts away and gave them to our forensic accountants?'

'Excuse me?'

'I'm conducting a triple murder investigation, Mr Squires. I expect a degree of co-operation.'

Squires relented. 'Please follow me, Inspector.'

'They followed Martin Squires into the lift. On the sixth floor, they walked along a corridor and into his office. Finance Directors were obviously closer to God than Personnel or Education Directors.

His secretary, a middle-aged woman with hairs on her chin like an oasis in a parched desert of makeup, stood up as Squires strode through her office. She was slightly confused that he had people with him. 'Your nine o'clock is here, Sir?'

'Cancel it, Deirdre, something has cropped up.'

'But...'

He stopped at the door to his office and stared at her. 'Did I not make myself abundantly clear?'

'Yes, Sir,' Deirdre said, her bottom lip trembling. She sat down and picked up the phone.

Parish decided that he didn't like Martin Squires, and just knew this was the man who had removed Brian Ridpath's file from the archives. What he didn't know was why.

Squires put his briefcase down next to his desk and threw his coat and scarf onto an easy chair. He shrugged out of his jacket and hung it on a hangar at the back of the door. 'What is it you want, Inspector?'

They clearly weren't going to be offered coffee. 'A man called Brian Ridpath was being paid £2,000 at the beginning of each month,' he said to Squires. 'I want to know why?'

'I'm afraid employee financial information is confidential.'

Parish noticed that Squires didn't ask who Ridpath was. 'I can easily get a search warrant, Mr Squires. And as I've said, I'll remove all of your financial records, and you

158

won't be able to access them for a long period of time whilst we examine them in detail. It would be in your best interests to co-operate with us.'

He was surprised when Squires said, 'I'm sorry, Inspector, you will need a warrant.'

Parish's jaw set hard. 'When I do come back with a warrant, Mr Squires, I'm going to take a very close look at you as well. The only reason that you would require me to get a search warrant is if you had something to hide. I promise you, I'll find out what that is.'

Squires looked at him, but said nothing.

'Let's go and get a warrant, Richards.' To Squires he said, 'We'll be back before lunch, Mr Squires.'

In the lift Richards said, 'He wants time to destroy the evidence doesn't he, Sir?'

'That's my guess, but we're powerless to stop him.'

'We could arrest him?'

'For what?'

'Perverting the course of justice?'

'I'm going to speak to your mother about you watching the Crime Channel, Richards.'

'When, Sir?'

'When what?'

'When will you speak to her?'

The lift doors opened, but Parish didn't move.

'We're here, Sir.'

'I've had an idea, Richards.' He strode over to the reception desk.

'Hello, Inspector,' Cindy said. 'You didn't arrest Mr Squires then?'

'Tell me, Cindy, who is in charge of the Council?'

'You mean the Mayoress, Sir?'

'Is she here now?'

'No, she doesn't have an office here, Sir.'

'Well, who's in charge here?'

'Ah, I think you mean the Town Clerk, Inspector. He's in charge of the day-to-day running of the Council.'

'Is he in? It's urgent I speak to him.'

Cindy picked up the phone. 'I'll find out for you.'

After a short conversation she put the phone down and said, 'Mr Traynor is in. If you go up to the seventh floor he'll see you now.'

'Excellent, thank you for your help, Cindy.'

'You're welcome, Inspector.'

They went back up in the lift to the seventh floor, which contained a number of meeting rooms, the Town Clerk's large office, and his secretary's office.

A man, in his early forties with steel grey hair, came out of the Town Clerk's office to meet them. He dwarfed Parish by at least four inches. Shaking hands with both Parish and Richards he introduced himself as Paul Traynor. He ushered them into his office, and asked his homely secretary for a tray of refreshments.

They sat in easy chairs around a glass-topped coffee table. Mr Traynor smiled then said, 'How can I assist the police with their enquiries, Inspector Parish?'

Parish got that all the time. He told the Town Clerk what had transpired in the Finance Director's office. 'What we're concerned about,' he said, 'is that evidence may be destroyed.'

Traynor looked thoughtful. 'I can't imagine Martin Squires doing anything like that.' He stood up and went to his desk. 'Clare,' he said into the intercom system, 'please ask Martin Squires to come up and see me.'

He came back to his easy chair. 'We'll get this mess sorted out. Who exactly was this Brian Ridpath?'

'As far as we know, he was a School Caretaker.'

'A School Caretaker being paid £2,000 a month, there must be some logical explanation.'

The office door opened and Mr Traynor's secretary, Clare came in with the tray of refreshments.

Traynor stood up, took the heavy tray off her and placed it on the table.

'I'm sorry, Sir,' Clare said, 'but no one seems to know where Mr Squires is. His secretary said he left his office shortly after the police went.'

Getting up, Mr Traynor said, 'Let's walk down to his office, Inspector,' and led the way.

They took the stairs and were soon stood in Martin Squires' office. His coat and briefcase were on the chair where he'd dropped them so it was unlikely he'd left the building.

'Has he got his mobile phone on him?' Richards suggested.

'Good thinking, Constable.' Mr Traynor pulled out his own mobile and found Mr Squires in his contact list. He called the number and held it up to his ear, but didn't speak. 'Mrs Wilson,' he said to Mr Squires' secretary, 'call Security and ask them to see if they can locate him.'

Parish looked at his watch, conscious that he was expected to be in the Chief's office at ten-thirty and also had a press briefing at eleven o'clock. It was quarter to ten. He'd give it another fifteen minutes and then he would have to leave.

'We may as well wait in my office,' Mr Traynor said. 'At least there's a cup of tea and some biscuits to keep us company.'

At five to ten Clare knocked and came in. She whispered something in Mr Traynor's ear. He thanked her and she left.

'Security has found Mr Squires in the lower basement. He appears to have hung himself. I've told someone from Security to stay with the body, and not to touch anything. First Diane, and now Martin. What the hell is going on here, Inspector?'

'I wish I knew, Mr Traynor.' Parish called Doc Michelin and asked him to send someone for the body of Martin Squires. He then phoned the Chief, told him what had happened and asked him if he'd take the press briefing, and Parish would catch up with him later. The Chief agreed, and Parish read off the short statement he'd devised. He then phoned forensics and asked them to send a team of forensic accountants. He wanted answers, and he wanted them today. There had been too many deaths with this case already. 'I apologise if I sound insensitive, Mr Traynor, but in the absence of Mr Squires is there someone else who could provide us with financial information.'

Mr Traynor went out and spoke to his secretary, then returned. 'I've told Clare to ask Susan Tollhurst, the Finance Manager, to come up. She'll give you all the information you require.'

'Thank you, Mr Traynor. You should also know that a team of forensic accountants are on their way. Unfortunately, they'll close the Finance Department until we've got to the bottom of what's been happening. If you're lucky, it might only be for a couple of days, but I have the feeling this is a large can of worms.'

'I understand, Inspector. I'll have to call an emergency Council Meeting. The Members will need to prepare their armour, and get ready to pull up the drawbridge. It'll only be a matter of time before the piranha begin circling in the moat outside, and the enemy set up camp on the opposite bank.'

Parish thought the Town Clerk was being a bit over-dramatic, but then what did he know? He did know what the press was like, and piranha was probably an apt description. Not only would the Council be put under the microscope, so would he. He was on borrowed time now.

There was a knock on the door. A thin woman with lank black hair, a pasty complexion and nervous eyes opened the door and stuck her head through the gap.

'Ah, Susan, please come in. This is Detective Inspector Parish and Constable Richards.'

Parish nodded in greeting.

The Town Clerk's voice dropped an octave lower. 'You've heard about Martin?'

'Yes, Sir.'

Parish thought she didn't look too upset.

'I know this will be a difficult time for everyone, but I'd like you to co-operate fully with Inspector Parish. You have my authority to show him whatever financial information he wants to see.'

She raised an eyebrow. 'Anything, Sir?'

'Anything,' he reiterated.

Parish stood up and extended his hand. 'Thank you for your help, Mr Traynor.'

'You're welcome, Inspector. I hope this doesn't turn out to be as bad as you forecast.'

They followed Susan Tollhurst out and into the lift. She pressed for the second floor.

'What is it you want, Inspector?' she asked.

Parish had a feeling of déjà vu. 'A man who is now dead called Brian Ridpath was paid £2,000 at the beginning of each month. I want to know why. He used to work for the Council as a school caretaker, but then he retired.'

'£2,000?'

'Yes.'

'And we pay it to him? Are you sure it isn't the Local Government Pension Scheme?'

'It had Redbridge Council on his bank statement.'

163

'Oh.'

The lift doors opened on the second floor. They stepped out and went through an access-controlled security door. Once inside the Finance Department, Susan told three people with worried expressions who were waiting for her that she'd see them later, then directed Parish and Richards into two easy chairs in her office.

'Right,' she said sitting behind her desk, 'lets see what's going on.'

Susan Tollhurst typed in her password, then her pasty face began to turn ghostly white. 'Oh no!'

Parish shuffled forward in his chair. 'What's wrong?'

'I suspect that Mr bloody Squires has activated the self-destruct button.'

'What do you mean?'

'All the Council's accounts are being deleted.'

'Can't you stop it?'

She banged various keys on her keyboard. 'Apparently not, the program wants a password.'

Parish felt as though he was a horse racing in the Grand National, and Becher's Brook had just claimed another victim. After falling at every fence, and picking himself up to carry on, he now realised that the fences had all been sabotaged.

'Backup?' he asked.

Susan's eyes lit up. 'Yes.' Then they clouded over again. 'Oh!'

'What?'

'The back-up server is kept in Mr Squires' office. He maintained a week's worth of backup tapes there, which is far enough from here to be safe.' She stood up. 'I won't be long.'

'This isn't going very well is it, Sir?' Richards said once Susan Tollhurst had left the room.

'That's an understatement, Richards.'

'What do forensic accountants do, Sir?'

'They follow the money, Richards.'

'Is everything on computer, or do they keep paper records as well?'

'I don't know, but examining paper-based accounts is bound to be more time-consuming than looking at computer-based accounts. We won't get any quick answers, and I expect there'll be another murder soon.'

Susan Tollhurst returned. 'No back-up tapes. Mr Squires took them down to the basement, put them in a waste paper bin and set fire to them.'

'Is that it then?' Parish asked disgusted that evidence could be destroyed so easily.

Susan smiled for the first time, and then started tapping her keyboard again. 'Off-site back-up,' she said. 'Every night, all our computer accounts data is transferred to a massive storage facility in the Nevada… I don't understand…'

'What now?' Parish asked expecting the worst.

'According to this, we have no account with them.' She threw herself back in her chair. 'He was a bastard right to the end. He's deleted our account. We have no live data, and we have no backup either.'

'Surely you have paper records?'

'Yes, but it will take months to reconstruct the accounts. We're two months from the end of the financial year. It's a disaster of epic proportions.'

'We have computer specialists,' Parish said. 'Maybe they'll be able to recover the live accounts.' He took out his mobile and phoned forensics. 'Toadstone, just the very man.'

'You're not my favourite person at the moment, Inspector. That flat was heaving. I'm sure I've got fleas or something.'

'Yeah, sorry about that, Toadstone, but it needed doing. On that, have you sifted through all that paper yet and summarised it for me?'

'You've obviously not picked up your emails yet?'

'I've been rather busy this morning. Listen, I'm at Redbridge Council and there's a team of forensic accountants on their way here.'

'Yeah, I heard you'd requested the 'A' team... 'A' Accountants.'

'Very droll. Well, as I was saying, the Finance Director committed suicide earlier, but before he departed the world he deleted the live accounts and all the backups. Have you got anyone there that can recover deleted data?'

'Pocahontas.'

'I'm sorry?'

'That's her online ID. She thinks she's the reincarnation of a virgin Indian princess called Pocahontas. Personally, I have my doubts.'

'Whether she's a virgin, or an Indian princess?'

Toadstone chuckled. 'Both.'

'I can imagine. Is she available now?'

'Just a mo...' The phone went quiet for about a minute, 'Yeah. She's on her way. Should be there in about thirty minutes.'

'Thanks Toadstone, and for the email.'

'I won't say it was a pleasure, but hey, that's what I'm here for. Oh, and whilst I've got your attention, I've sent you an email about the security disc from the Flint murder. You wanted us to magic up a face. Our techie did what he could, but the face is completely in shadow. Seems your killer knew what he was doing.'

'Another dead end. Thank your techie for trying anyway.'

'Will do.'

Parish disconnected the call. He'd thought for a long time that people in forensics were educated idiots, but maybe he was being unkind. He went back into the office and interrupted a conversation about shoes.

'Susan, I've got someone from our forensics department, who specialises in recovering deleted data from hard drives, coming over.' He realised then that he'd forgotten to ask Toadstone what Pocahontas' proper name was. 'Because she works for the government on top secret missions she's only known as Pocahontas.'

'Really, Sir?' Richards said.

'No, Richards, I just don't know what her real name is.'

Susan picked up her phone. 'I'll let reception know to expect an American Indian in a dress then, Inspector.'

'Good idea. I would also suggest you stop people from trying to use the financial software, if there's anything left of it.'

She made the phone call to reception, then stood up.

'Whilst you're out there, can I access my email account on your computer?'

'Of course.'

'He sat in her warm seat, logged on to Yahoo and his email account. He had forty-three new emails, but was only interested in Toadstone's analysis of Brian Ridpath's paperwork. He printed two copies off and gave one to Richards.

SIXTEEN

'I've never heard of Beech Tree Orphanage, Sir,' Richards said.

Toadstone had been efficient. The papers in Brian Ridpath's flat contained 70% junk mail and 30% other. A summary of the 'other' paperwork was mostly about financial matters. It seems that, not only did he have £130,000 in the bank, but he also had savings of £50,000 in the form of a Building Society Account, and within the papers themselves £20,000 in cash. There was a letter from a cousin in Australia asking him if he wanted to be a partner in a sheep ranch; and the deeds to a detached house in Surrey that had been left to him by a childless sister two years ago. Hidden amongst all the paper was one mention of a place called Beech Tree Orphanage. Reference to the orphanage was contained in a letter addressed to Mr Ridpath from a Mr Henry Easterby of the Council asking him if he would like to claim personal items from his locker in the Caretaker's lodge before they were disposed of.

'I haven't either, but it would seem that despite efforts to keep it from us, we've found Mr Ridpath's place of employment.'

Susan Tollhurst returned to her office. 'I've sent the finance staff home until tomorrow. If forensic accountants are going to take possession of the paper records, and the computer records are under repair, then there's no point in keeping them here. I'll stay though, to answer any questions the accountants might have.'

'Have you ever heard of Beech Tree Orphanage?' Parish asked her.

'No. You might want to try Social Services on the third floor, they would probably have some record of it.'

Yes, of course, Parish thought, Diane Flint. 'What about Henry Easterby?'

'I think he was an administrator in Social Services, but he died years ago.'

They waited until the accountants breezed in like removal men and began putting the files into large boxes for transportation to a secret destination. Then an anorexic looking girl, dressed like a Siberian deportee in a fur hat and coat and with the complexion of an ice maiden, appeared in the door to Susan's office.

'Where do you want me?' she said to no one in particular.

'Pocahontas?' Parish guessed.

'I suppose.'

Susan Tollhurst took charge. 'Do you want something to eat first?'

'Got any chips?'

'We can get some.'

'And bread, and ketchup, and beef and onion pie?'

'I'll arrange…'

'And chocolate cake, and coke – not that diet crap though – and…'

Parish stood up. 'Come on, Richards, we're no longer needed here.'

They left the forensic accountants putting files in boxes, and Susan Tollhurst taking Pocahontas' food order like a waitress in a café.

'Whose day are we going to wreck now, Sir?'

Parish grinned. 'Good one, Richards.' He looked at his watch. It was eleven twenty. 'I need to go back to the station to update the Chief, but first we should go and take a look in Martin Squires' office to see if there's anything in there that will give us some answers. We'll find out where he lives, help ourselves to his house keys and have a look in his house later this afternoon. After we've been up to Squires' office we'll go and see someone in Social Services about Beech Tree Orphanage, and then we can get some food before I die of starvation.'

'Are we allowed to take Mr Squires' keys and search his house without a search warrant, Sir?'

'You asked me the same thing about Brian Ridpath's flat, Richards. Martin Squires isn't here to complain is he?'

'No, but Brian Ridpath was an old drunk, and Martin Squires was a Director of Finance.'

'Are you suggesting that the rich and the poor should be treated differently, Richards? Have you abandoned your policy of fairness for all already?'

'I was thinking that we're more likely to get found out going into Squires' house without permission than Ridpath's dirty flat.'

'When we get to Squires' house we will of course knock on the door and request access if he has a wife or a partner. If he doesn't, we'll use the key and rummage around in what was once his life to try and find out why he killed himself and why he destroyed the Council's financial data.'

'You're the Inspector, Sir.'

'Yes I am, Richards, and don't you forget it. Now let's go up and search Squires' office. The sooner we do what we have to do the sooner I can eat. My stomach thinks you've put me on a diet.'

They stepped into the lift and Richards pressed the button for the sixth floor.

'You need a good woman who will give you wholesome balanced meals, Sir. Have I mentioned that my mum is a good cook?'

'Will you stop trying to fix me up with your mum, Richards, and stay away from my menu.'

'I'm only trying to help, Sir.'

'You're trying to change me, Richards. Stop it.'

'Sorry, Sir.'

The hairy Mrs Deirdre Wilson sat at her desk staring into space.

'Are you sure you should be here, Mrs Wilson?' Richards said putting an arm around her shoulders.

'I'm not sure of anything anymore, dear.' Tears burst from her eyes and dripped onto the desk. 'Why did he do it? I know he was a difficult man to work for, but he could be lovely sometimes. I just don't understand. First Mrs Flint, and now Mr Squires. We've all been cursed, haven't we? I know some of the Council staff are organising a séance after work to try and expunge the evil spirits from the building. There's a secretary on the second floor who has had some experience of fighting the forces of darkness.'

Richards looked at Parish, who screwed up his eyes. 'I think you're in shock, Mrs Wilson,' Richards said. 'You should go home until you're fully recovered.'

'Before you go,' Parish said. 'Was Mr Squires married?'

'No, he said he was too selfish to share his life with someone else. I would have married him if he'd asked.'

Richards and Parish looked at each other. 'Do you have his home address?' Parish said.

'Yes, but… Oh, he's dead, isn't he? He won't mind now if I give you his address.'

Richards made soothing sounds as Mrs Wilson pulled out an address book from her bag and wrote down 5 Willow Close, Abridge.

'I went there once, you know, to drop off some papers. He has a lovely thatched cottage. It backs onto the River Roding. He said he liked how it was so secluded. He also used to fly for a hobby, and it's close to Stapleford Aerodrome where he kept his plane.'

'You go home now,' Richards said in her melting chocolate voice. 'You need time to grieve.'

'Yes, thank you dear. Now that Martin's gone, there's nothing left for me here.'

Richards went with Mrs Wilson to the lift.

'I thought we were never going to get rid of her,' Parish said when Richards came back. 'And you didn't help matters by acting like a bereavement counsellor.'

'That's not very nice, Sir. She was just upset.'

Parish let himself into Martin Squires' office. 'I'm not very nice, Richards, especially when I have multiple murders to solve. You take the left, I'll take the right, and we'll meet in the middle.'

They began searching the office. Parish went straight to Squires' jacket hung up behind the door. In the pockets he found Squires' keys and wallet, some change, and a pen. He put the keys in his own pocket and then went and sat in Martin Squires' chair. He emptied the contents of the wallet onto the desk: There was two hundred and fifty pounds in cash; membership cards for the Institute of Chartered Accountants, the Chartered Institute of Taxation, and Local Government Finance Professionals (Finpro); a mobile top-up card, a Visa card; an American Express card; a photograph of a young boy with the name Billy written on the back; an NHS card; and one of the old paper driving licences that had seen better days.

Next, he felt in the pockets of the overcoat, but found nothing of interest. Then he picked up the briefcase, but it had two combination locks. There was a letter opener on the desk, which he used to prise them open.

'Well, well,' Parish said.

Richards stopped searching the books in the bookcase and turned to look at him. 'What, Sir?'

'Ridpath's file,' he said holding it up. 'I had the feeling Squires had taken it when I first saw him this morning. It also proves that Martin Squires knew about the money being paid to Brian Ridpath, and that there's a lot more to this than £2,000 a month.'

'What does the file say, Sir?'

Parish held the file up to his ear. 'It says we're still searching, Richards, and that it is happy to wait until we've finished what we're doing.'

'My mum says that men aren't very good at multitasking.'

'I think I could manage to sack you whilst I'm searching, Richards.'

'Stop being mean, Sir.'

Inside the briefcase he also found Martin Squires' diary, which he put on top of Ridpath's file. He would need time to examine both items properly.

Parish rifled through Squires' desk drawers, but found nothing else of interest, and Richards came up empty-handed as well.

'Right, let's go down to the Social Services department and see what they can tell us, Richards.'

'Do you want me to carry Ridpath's file and Mr Squires' diary, Sir?'

'You must think I'm stupid, Richards. I know you want to read them whilst we're travelling down to Social Services, and thus prove your mum right. I'll carry them, thank you.'

***

The Social Services department was on the third floor. A receptionist, visible through a small bullet-proof window, said they could come in and speak to the agency Manager Mr Tom Walters. She buzzed them in. Yes, they'd heard rumours of Beech Tree Orphanage, but no one knew if it still existed or where it was. Someone had heard a rumour that it had been demolished and turned into a multistory car park, a shopping mall, and a theme park even though there were no theme parks in the local area.

Parish thanked them for their help and left. 'Now I need food, Richards.'

'We could go to my house, Sir. My mum will be there and she'll have some roast beef left.'

'Still trying to play matchmaker, Richards?'

'Who me, Sir? I was thinking more of you eating a healthy meal.'

'I'll bet. All that talk of pie and chips has made my mouth water. Let's go and find the nearest fish and chip shop.'

'Sirrr?'

'A man has needs, Richards, and fish and chips drenched in salt and vinegar is one of those needs.'

They left Redbridge Council offices and walked along the road until they found the *Friary*. Richards didn't want the car stinking of fish and chips so Parish was forced to sit at one of the three tables by the wall opposite the counter and eat his fish, chips and mushy peas with two slices of bread and a mug of tea. Richards sat with her chin in her hands and watched him devour the meal like a homeless man who hadn't eaten for a month.

'I've decided that cooking a lovely meal for a man is a waste of time, Sir. My mum and me cooked that fantastic roast dinner for you yesterday, but you'd have been just as happy with a Chinese takeaway.

'Mmmm, I love Chinese takeaways, Richards. Number 55 with egg fried rice and prawn crackers is my favourite.'

'Men are so coarse.'

'Just because that paramedic is an idiot, Richards does not mean that all men should be lumped in the same category. You're a beautiful woman with a personality to match. The man who gets you will think he's died and gone to heaven.'

'Ah, thank you, Sir.'

'For what?'

'For what you just said.'

'I don't know who you've been talking to, Richards, but I've been eating my chip butties.'

'If you say so, Sir.'

'I do say so, Richards and I'm the Inspector, remember?'

He passed her the file and diary. 'Occupy yourself by reading those instead of watching me poison myself.'

'So, you admit it, Sir?'

'I'm admitting nothing without my lawyer present, Richards. Now read.'

Parish finished his meal and washed it down with sweet tea whilst he waited for Richards to finish skimming. Eventually, she closed the diary.

'Ridpath's file confirms he worked at Beech Tree Orphanage between 1979 and 1986 as the Caretaker, Sir. Before that he was a school caretaker. He had no disciplinary problems.'

'And the diary?'

'Mr Squires had only just started it, Sir. There was to do lists, appointments with people, and committee meetings listed on the working days of this month. He also had a contact list with telephone numbers against people's names. I think it's just a work diary. If he had anything to hide, I don't think he would hide it in his diary.'

'Hiding things in plain sight can sometimes be a good strategy, Richards.'

'Okay, Sir.'

***

Colin Jackson emptied the food waste into a dustbin in the alley behind the *Pepper Pot* café in Redbridge. He'd been employed as an assistant chef on a trial basis two weeks ago. He hated the job. If it hadn't been for the government threatening to withdraw his Jobseeker's Allowance, he'd be in the *Anchor* now having a pint. He lit a cigarette and took a long drag. Bloody country was going to the dogs. He was sixty years old for God's sake, they should let him retire gracefully and enjoy what was left of his life. Since the orphanage had closed down in 1986 he had hopped from job to job. He'd been one of the four cooks at the orphanage, holding a position of importance with lots of fiddles. The fiddles on the side kept him in beers, but were nothing compared to his membership of the exclusive after-hours club organised by the manager. It was a great shame that someone bought the orphanage and closed it down, because his life had been shit ever since.

He'd made a mistake in 1992, and got ten years in the Scrubs. He was lucky to get out of there with his life, and had spent most of the time in protective custody. When he came out in 2000, after eight years of hell, Evan Hughes had become a liability so he'd paid an acquaintance to change his identity to Colin Jackson.

He saw the small thin man dressed all in black walk towards him, but paid no attention until he stopped in front of him. The man had a hood covering his face, but a cigarette protruded from his mouth.

'Got a light?' the man asked him. Colin was sure he'd seen him in the café earlier.

'Yeah sure.' He went to retrieve the plastic lighter from his trouser pocket, but there was a massive pain in his chest. He looked into the man's dark eyes as he crumpled to the snow, and thought he recognised something he had seen a long time ago. The thought did not have time or momentum to solidify. Colin Jackson's heart stopped pumping. Oxygen ceased to travel to his brain. In effect, the man who called himself Colin Jackson, but who was born Evan Hughes, died.

The man in black slipped a token in Evan Hughes' mouth with the number 4 on it and said, 'For Frank Landon.' Then he walked out of the alley.

***

He'd eaten his lunch in the *Pepper Pot* café in Chigwell. Thought he caught a glimpse of Evan Hughes through the plastic curtain leading into the kitchen, but he wasn't sure. It was a long way to come for lunch and he would probably be late back to work, but he could devise some excuse during the return journey. It wasn't as if his time-keeping was generally poor. Ollie was an okay guy and would believe him.

Waiting at the corner of Bichard Street and Twopenny Alley behind the *Pepper Pot*, he saw Evan Hughes enter the alley via the back door of the café, empty waste into a dustbin and light up a cigarette. Terry Reynolds walked towards him with a cigarette in his mouth, had asked him for a light even though he didn't smoke. Had killed Evan Hughes, who had stolen many things, but more recently, the identity of someone called Colin Jackson. After putting token number 4 in Evan Hughes' mouth, Terry Reynolds walked to the deserted bus stop on Cranbrook Road.

The bus back to Redbridge came along within ten minutes. Yes, he would be a couple of minutes late clocking back in. Ollie Townsend, the Head of Security, wouldn't say much, he'd know that Terry Reynolds was a good worker and usually on time.

Terry Reynolds would tell him his mother was sick, had to travel to Goodmayes on the bus to visit her, make sure she had her medicine, food and so forth, and that the heating in her house was working. It was a mission of mercy. And once he had got back to Redbridge Council offices and changed back into his security uniform, Ollie was sympathetic when he heard about Terry's poor old mum. 'Take as much time as you need,' Ollie had said and that was the end of it. Of course, mums were special, if you needed time off to look after your mum then hell, just say the word, Terry. Trouble was, Terry didn't have a mum, had never had a mum. His mum had died giving birth to him.

He was looking forward to getting back to his flat when his shift ended. Always enjoyed putting a cross through their faces once he had killed them. It changed nothing, but there was a vague sense of closure. He always had a feeling of satisfaction when he crossed one more off his 'To Kill List'.

***

Parish knocked on the Chief's door at one-fifteen.

'Come in, Parish.'

Parish pushed Richards in first. 'How did you know it was me knocking, Sir?'

'You have a distinctive knock. I know everyone's knock in the squad room. So, this is Constable Richards?' He moved from behind his desk with his arm extended. 'Welcome to Hoddesdon Police Station, Constable.'

'Thank you, Sir.'

'How are you liking it so far?'

'I love it, Sir. Thanks very much for letting me work with DI Parish.'

'I felt sorry for him, Richards. He needs a woman in his life, even if it is only as a partner.'

He pointed for them to sit down in the easy chairs and came to join them. 'Tell me what's going on, Parish?'

Parish explained all that had happened at Redbridge Council that morning.

'How did Paul Traynor take it?'

'Do you know the Town Clerk, Sir?'

'Of course I do, there's not many people of importance in the area that I don't know, Parish.'

'He took it well, Sir. Whatever happened, I think it was before his time. He just wants to get to the truth.'

The Chief nodded as if he didn't expect any other answer. 'I've been keeping the Chief Constable in the loop, Parish,' he said, 'and he's very pleased with your progress.'

Parish felt uncomfortable. He'd never been any good at accepting praise. 'Even though there's four dead bodies and no suspects, Sir?'

'You say that as though someone more senior would have already solved the case. I can tell you they wouldn't, Parish. You're doing a good job with what's available and that's all anyone can ask. And as you're a newly promoted DI, the Chief Constable will have an experienced DCI shadowing you. So, if he says you're doing a good job, you can put it in the bank.'

'Okay, thanks, Sir. Mr Toadstone from forensics also did a good job in Brian Ridpath's flat. He found Ridpath's place of employment, which is what we've been looking for, and what Martin Squires tried to keep from us.'

'So, do you think this Beech Tree Orphanage is the key?'

'I'm hoping so, Sir.'

'What's your next move then, Parish?'

'Richards and I are going to take a look in Martin Squires' house in Abridge this afternoon, and then come back to consolidate what we've got, tie up the loose ends. Tomorrow, we'll go and find this Beech Tree Orphanage if it still exists.'

'I'll look forward to reading your report, Parish.'

'What happened at the press briefing, Sir?'

'Oh yes. Well, they weren't happy with the sparseness of information you provided.'

'Have any of them fitted the pieces together?'

'If they have, it wasn't apparent.'

'I'm sure they will today, Sir. The Town Clerk was preparing for a siege.'

'Yes, now that two of the Council's Directors have died, and accountants are removing boxes of files out of the front door, I think some of the more intelligent reporters might start connecting the dots.'

'When's the next briefing, Sir?'

'Tomorrow at nine.' He smiled. 'I thought you could get it out of the way before you go out, and then ring me up with an excuse about why you can't get back.'

'Yeah, sorry about that, Sir.'

'Right, get back to work, Parish, and stop procrastinating in here.'

Parish stood up and headed for the door.

'Good to meet you, Richards,' the Chief said.

'And you, Sir,' she said. Outside she whispered, 'The Chief doesn't look well, Sir.'

'Prostate cancer. He's having chemo- and radiotherapy.'

'He's such a nice man as well.'

'Unfortunately, Richards, cancer doesn't take niceness into account when it's looking for a victim.'

'

SEVENTEEN

It was ten to two. Kowalski and Gorman, an overweight detective in his forties with a combover, were having a game of darts at the far end of the squad room. All the others had their heads down working.

'Come and have a game with us, Parish,' Kowalski shouted. 'Ten pounds says Gorman and me can beat you and Richards at a game of three-o-one?'

'I'm good at darts, Sir,' Richards said flexing her throwing arm. 'If you want to take them on I'm ready and willing.'

'I don't, Richards. We've got three murders and a suicide to solve remember?'

'Sorry, Sir.'

'Glad you've got time on your hands, Kowalski,' Parish said, 'but we're up to our eyeballs.'

'Up to your eyeballs in bodies, Parish.' Kowalski's laughter broke the sound barrier.

'Ignore him, Sir,' Richards said. 'He's a moron.'

Parish sat down at his desk, logged on to the network and accessed his emails again. There were now forty-seven unopened emails. He began ticking those he was going to delete without opening them.

Richards sat in the chair in front of his desk. 'What do you want me to do, Sir?'

He passed her the post mortem reports of Diane Flint and Brian Ridpath, which were sitting on top of his intray. 'Read.'

She opened Diane Flint's report and began reading.

Parish noticed an email with TOKENS in the subject heading. It was a response to his email that Carrie had sent to all Council employees. He opened it:

Inspector,

I recall seeing a token like the one below in Beech Tree Orphanage. I'm a Social Worker, and I was visiting the orphanage when I saw the token on the Manager's desk. I remember it because I thought at the time how unusual it was. I never visited the orphanage again, or saw another token.

Beth Masters

The email confirmed what he'd been thinking after reading Toadstone's email. He typed a reply back:

Beth,

Thank you for your email it was very helpful in confirming what we already suspected. Do you have a location for Beech Tree Orphanage?

DI Parish

He continued ticking the emails, and had reached thirty-two when his mobile rang.

'Parish?'

'Are you ever going to solve this case, Inspector?' Doc Michelin asked. 'I'm stood in an alley at the back of the *Pepper Pot* café in Redbridge freezing my nuts off. Colin Jackson is with me, but he's already dead from a marlinspike inserted into his heart. I have also retrieved a token from his mouth with the number 4 stamped on it.'

'We're on our way, Doc.'

'Not another murder, Sir?'

'Yes, it looks as though Martin Squires' house will have to wait until tomorrow.'

'You said there would be another one didn't you, Sir?'

'I would preferred to have been wrong, Richards. Go and get the car warmed up, I'll let the Chief know our plans have changed.'

***

It was five past four when they arrived at the crime scene. As usual, everyone else was there waiting for him. He noticed the paramedic from the Taylor murder and saw that Richards had spotted him as well. Toadstone was on his hands and knees examining the ground around the corpse.

'Hi, Doc.'

'To keep warm, I've been doing your job, Parish. I went into the café for a coffee and the people in there saw nothing. Betty, the owner, said Mr Jackson was employed on a trial basis and has worked for her as an Assistant Cook for two weeks. He lives at 15 Buckingham Road here in Redbridge, and his National Insurance number is NJ4756899Q. There's nothing more I've got to tell you, so I'm going to sit in my car with the heating on now. When you're finished, let me know so I can go home.'

'Okay, Doc, keep warm.'

'Huh.'

The corpse had on a pair of blue and white checked trousers and a white jacket with the sleeves rolled up to the elbows. A crimson mark over the heart looked like a flower in bloom. Parish squatted and looked into the victim's surprised face. What did you do Mr Jackson that brought a killer after you?

He stood up and noticed that night had replaced day. The orange streetlights were on, but he still felt as though he was thrashing about in the dark.

'What do we know, Richards?'

'We have four victims that have all been killed in the same way, Sir. The killer has put a token in their mouths with different numbers on.'

'And this crime scene, what does it tell us?'

Richards screwed up her eyes. 'It doesn't tell us anything, Sir.'

'Think of the other crime scenes. Where were they?'

'The first murder was in Ralston Drive. That's where you saw me, Sir and...'

'Keep focused, Richards.'

'Sorry, Sir. Then Diane Flint was killed in Redbridge Council car park, Brian Ridpath in an alley, and... They're all isolated locations.'

'Meaning?'

'He's picked them, Sir. He must have been watching them to know where to attack without being seen.'

'So the crime scenes do tell us something then?'

Richards turned sheepish. 'I suppose so, Sir.'

'Do you suppose that all the victims are connected in some way?'

'Oh yes, Sir. For one thing, we know that Redbridge Council employed them all. Well... we don't know about Mr Jackson, but I bet he worked for them as well.'

'And the tokens?'

'We know the tokens might have been used in a school, but it could be an orphanage.'

'I forgot to tell you something in the rush to get here, Richards. I received an email from a Social Worker in response to my email to the Council's employees about the tokens – a Beth Masters. She said that on her one and only visit to Beech Tree Orphanage she saw a token like ours on the Manager's desk.'

Richards smiled. 'I love this job, Sir. It's like spending all day finding the pieces of a jigsaw that you don't have the picture for, and then fitting them together at night like the Elves sewing the shoemaker's shoes.'

Parish screwed his eyes up and stared at her. 'Stop babbling, Richards.'

'Sorry, Sir.'

'What do those things tell us about the killer's motives then?'

'He's spent a long time watching each one of them. They're people that he knows. The tokens make the killings personal. Its about revenge isn't it, Sir?'

'Good, Richards. Revenge for what?'

Her eyes opened wide. 'Well, we don't know that yet. If we knew the why, we'd know the who?'

'Sometimes, Richards, I feel as though I'm talking to a presenter on the Crime Channel.'

Richards giggled. 'Sorry, Sir.'

'Do we know anything about why the killer has picked these people?'

She was quiet for some time.

Parish waited patiently whilst she went through the evidence in her mind. He loved this part of the job, teaching others to find a way through the forest.

'They're all old people, Sir. And something happened between 1982 and 1986.'

'Where?'

'Probably at Beech Tree Orphanage.'

'Excellent, Richards. What do we need to do now?'

'Tonight, Sir?'

'No, not now now, but the general now.'

'We need to find out about Beech Tree Orphanage, Sir. As you said to the Chief, that's probably the key.'

'And that's just what we'll do tomorrow morning. I've got the press briefing at nine o'clock, whilst I'm doing that you can pick up the pool car, and then we'll be ready to go by nine-thirty.'

'Go where, Sir?'

'To Martin Squires house in Abridge, and then to find Beech Tree Orphanage.'

'Okay.'

***

They went back to the station via 15 Buckingham Road, but the people who lived at the address – a Mr and Mrs Steven Petri – had never heard of Colin Jackson and didn't know where he lived.

It was six-twenty when they arrived back at the station. Parish told Richards to return the pool car and then go home. He went up to the squad room, which was deserted, to write his report for the Chief. He smiled as he remembered what the Chief had said earlier. The Chief Constable thought he was doing a good job. A bit of praise made everything bearable. He listed all the things that had happened today. If the Chief was keeping the Chief Constable in the loop then he'd better make sure the DCI shadowing him had all the information. He wrote about the suicide of Martin Squires, the destruction of financial data, Brian Ridpath's file, the email from Beth Masters, and the murder of Colin Jackson – if that was his name. Then he told the Chief that they were going to visit Martin Squires' house tomorrow morning (after the press briefing). He thought he'd add that so the Chief knew he hadn't forgotten. Then they would find out about Beech Tree Orphanage

He checked his emails again. There was another twenty-one from various departments. Didn't they have anything better to do than send him rubbish? If he tried to read everything they sent him, he'd never leave his desk, and he'd have to claim ten hours overtime a week as well. He deleted all of the emails except one about travel claims. There was no response from Beth Masters. Maybe he'd have to go and see her tomorrow morning. In fact, he decided to do that. If she had been to Beech Tree Orphanage then she had information he needed, quite apart from where it was. She had been in the Manager's office, so she could tell him the Manager's name. If anyone knew what had happened there, surely it would be the Manager.

Bloody hell! Where had the time gone? It was five past seven. He had to go home, get showered and changed, and then drive to Chigwell by eight o'clock. He did a dirty shut down of his computer, grabbed his coat and left.

***

Parish stood outside the *Gooseberry Restaurant* at five to eight pacing up and down like a sentry, and nibbling the nail on the little finger of his left hand. He'd stuck his head in the restaurant and spoken to the *Maître d'*, but Angie hadn't arrived before him. At first he was glad, but then he began thinking that maybe she'd had second thoughts. Maybe she'd changed her mind, spoken to her daughter and realised Jed Parish didn't measure up. Maybe Richards had found out about Carrie, about how he'd been unable to control his lust. If Angie did turn up, he swore silently that he'd be a better man in the future. What would he do if she didn't turn up? Richards would know what had happened. He'd be embarrassed knowing that she knew he'd been stood up. Why did he let these things happen? He should apply the same caution and logic to his private life as he did to his detective work. But no, where relationships were concerned, he was a complete amateur. They should run training courses. He'd go on all of them.

'I've not kept you waiting have I, Jed?'

She'd crept up behind him whilst he was pacing in the opposite direction. 'No, I got here early.' By the skin of his teeth, he thought. He kissed her on the cheek. 'Let's go in before we freeze to death.'

He let he go in first. They were shown to a table amongst the other diners, mingled in with the quiet conversation and the polite laughter. The waiter took their coats.

'You look beautiful,' he told her. She had on a dark green silk dress that plunged at the front and the back, with matching shoes and bag. He couldn't take his eyes off her. Strands of her hair had been braided at the temples and pulled backwards to keep the rest of it in place. Later, whenever he was asked, he would tell people that it was in the *Gooseberry Restaurant* that he had fallen in love with Angela Richards.

She smiled, but said nothing as he held the chair for her to sit down.

The waiter came back with the menus. Parish let Angie choose a bottle of red wine. Like relationships, he knew nothing about wine. In fact, when it came to dating and socialising, he knew very little about anything. He had spent all his time working, and apart from the few sorties into pubs and clubs as a student where he'd been mostly anonymous, he couldn't recall ever having had a social life.

He spent all day making decisions, yet when it came to choosing food from a list on a menu he was like a child faced with too many flavours in an ice cream parlour. They didn't make it easy for him because there was no fish and chips, no Chinese 55, or Indian 33. He didn't see a kebab on the whole menu, and the only pizzas were in the children's section. He should have checked the menu, carried out a reconnaissance. He'd left too much to chance. He should have come prepared as if it were an armed raid on a warehouse full of drugs.

'What are you having?' he asked her wondering whether he should order the same thing.

'Why, is there some way you can produce a criminal profile of me from what I eat?'

They both laughed. He knew this was going to be a good night. He should relax, open up, and be himself. 'If someone could do that,' he said. 'I'd be the worst criminal on the planet. My diet consists of...'

'Mary has told me what your diet consists of. You eat heart-attack food all the time.'

'It's like having my own dietician.'

'Mary thinks you're wonderful. She wants to protect you from yourself.'

He didn't want to talk about Mary. 'What about you, what do you think?'

'Fishing for compliments, Jed. I think my daughter has good taste.'

They both ordered prawn cocktail as a starter. For the main course Angie had a Chicken Milanese salad, he ordered an 8oz Grilled rump steak covered in peppercorn sauce. As the shadow of a frown crossed her face he asked for new potatoes instead of chips.

Angie wanted to know about him, but he kept moving the conversation back to her. 'Have you always been a nurse?'

'Yes, I never wanted to be anything else. What subject did you take at university?'

'Criminal psychology. Why haven't you married a doctor?'

'They have God-complexes. Why haven't you married?'

'Married who? The only women I meet are suspects, victims or criminals.'

'I'm none of those.'

'That's why we're out having dinner.'

For pudding he wanted a hot chocolate brownie with vanilla ice cream, but he ordered a tangerine cheesecake instead. He smiled. He wasn't being himself at all, he was trying to impress her by choosing what he thought were the healthier foods instead of what he would normally have selected.

She put her hand on his. 'Why are you smiling?'

'Because I really like you, and I'm ordering food that I wouldn't normally choose. I don't want you to think I'm an unhealthy person even though I am, and you know I am. I think it's the first time ever that I care what somebody thinks of me.'

'You're trying to talk me into bed, aren't you?'

'It's not a bad idea, but I want us to start off as we mean to go on. Yes we could go back to my flat and share a night of passion, but I think it's too soon. I think we'd both be doing it because we thought the other one expected it. I'm in no rush. I'd like our relationship to be about more than sex.'

'Keep talking Jed Parish, you're measuring up nicely.'

They were the last couple to leave the restaurant. He drove her the short distance home. They kissed as if they meant it and agreed to meet the next night at his flat. Although he had parked along the road from where she lived so that Mary wouldn't see his car, he stayed and watched her enter the house. He was just about to drive off when the bedroom light came on. She stood in the window and undressed. He knew that she knew he was still sat there watching her. He felt like a voyeur, but he

191

still wished he had his binoculars with him. After the light went out he stayed for another half-an-hour thinking about how beautiful she was.

When he arrived home, he decided to leave the Chief's report until the morning. He thought he might be in love, and he didn't want details of the case erasing that thought.

***

Tuesday, 21st January

Suddenly, he was suffering from tardiness. He couldn't remember the last time he had overslept. In fact, he didn't think he had ever stayed in bed beyond six o'clock. He'd never had an alarm clock because the nightmares had always woken him up. This morning though there were no nightmares, or he'd slept through them. When he woke at seven-thirty he had an erection like a flagpole, and a picture in his mind of Angie naked at her bedroom window. Even though he was late he didn't have the usual feelings of annoyance that accompanied getting up late. He sent his report to the Chief, and then took his time getting ready. As long as he was there for the press briefing at nine o'clock, what did a few stolen minutes matter. The Chief wouldn't mind, probably wouldn't even notice.

As he made himself presentable for his first press briefing in charge, what he was going to say ran through his mind. He knew he couldn't palm the press off with platitudes anymore. Two Directors at Redbridge Council had died. One had been murdered and the other had committed suicide. He'd directed police accountants to remove all their financial records. Discretion was hard to maintain when the removal men were traipsing in and out with boxes and leaving muddy boot prints on the carpets.

He turned on the television in the kitchen for the eight o'clock news whilst he ate his buttered toast. As he expected, the television crews were camped outside Redbridge Council offices speculating on the 'goings on' inside. The report was from yesterday afternoon and showed police officers transporting boxes full of files from the building and putting them into unmarked vans. The Town Clerk, Mr Traynor, appeared and said he had no idea what was going on. The police had informed him that there were irregularities in the accounts related to the murder of the Social Services Director, Diane Flint, and the suicide of the Finance Director, Martin Squires. He was sure the matter would be cleared up soon. In the meantime, the Council would be open for business as usual, which was not strictly true because their bank accounts had been frozen.

Representatives from the three main political parties, and some independent councillors appeared, but were even more in the dark than the Town Clerk.

Yes, he expected a grilling from the press this morning. They would want to know what was really going on. It was in the public interest to tell everyone the truth, especially if it was gory, scandalous, or juicy. The truth sold newspapers and increased television ratings. But there was only so much of the truth that he could tell them without it interfering with his investigation. He wouldn't tell them about the tokens, or the marlinspike. Those juicy details were for police eyes only. As far as the press was concerned, there had been one murder and a suicide. If he told them that the murders of Gregory Taylor, Brian Ridpath and Colin Jackson were connected to Diane Flint's murder, he'd have to discuss the way in which each was killed, what links them together, and about Beech Tree Orphanage. There would be a hue and cry about a serial killer, which would cause him serious problems. The press would start second-guessing him and he couldn't be doing with that. No, he would keep it focussed on Redbridge Council, on one murder and a suicide, probably related to the financial irregularities. Money was always a good smokescreen, he thought with a smile.

***

He arrived at the station at eight thirty-five. The squad room was unusually subdued. Richards hadn't appeared yet.

'What's going on?' he said to Kowalski, who seemed to have run out of stupid quips.

'You've not heard?'

'Would I be asking if I had?'

'The Chief was rushed into hospital last night.'

Parish swallowed with difficulty. 'Is he…?'

'No, not yet. Chief Inspector Naylor is acting Chief at the moment. He came in earlier and said he'd rung the hospital. The doctors weren't optimistic apparently. Naylor wants to see you by the way.'

In the back of his mind, he had known this day would come. After all the Chief had done for him, he wanted to spend some time thinking of the man, probably go to the hospital and give him some words of encouragement, but all he could do was think of himself. He hated CI Trevor Naylor, and the feeling was mutual. Everyone knew that Naylor was a slimeball who had got his promotions by trampling on the backs of the people who worked for him. He knocked on the Chief's door.

'Come in.'

Naylor was sat in the Chief's chair, getting his feet comfortable under the Chief's desk, drinking the Chief's coffee. Parish wanted to leap over the desk and thump Naylor in the face a few times until he bled profusely from the nose. He wasn't normally a violent man, but Naylor brought out the worst in him.

'What fucking time do you call this, Parish?'

Parish opened his mouth to reply.

'Don't fucking interrupt me. A week as a DI and you think you can come in anytime you fucking well please. Well, I'm here to tell you that the honeymoon period is well and truly fucking over. You've got five dead bodies now, Parish. How many more does he have to fucking kill before you fucking well catch him? I'm giving you ample warning, if he kills again you're fucking well off the case. Just give me an excuse. Do I make myself crystal fucking clear?'

'Yes...'

'I haven't fucking well finished yet. And that fucking stunt you pulled at the Council yesterday, Jesus fucking wept. I've had the Mayoress and the Leader of the Council on the phone complaining. Have you never heard of tact, diplomacy, or fucking stealth? No wonder the Chief's in fucking hospital fighting for his life. Where's your fucking press briefing?'

Parish took a folded piece of paper out of his pocket and slid it across the desk.

CI Naylor read it. 'If anybody mentions a fucking serial killer, or even hints at one, you'd better deny it until your tongue bleeds if you know what's good for you. You should never have been promoted as long as you had a fucking hole in your arse. I can't imagine what the Chief was fucking thinking of. If the Chief kicks the bucket and I get this job you'll be out on your fucking ear, Parish. I don't like you, never have. As far as I'm concerned you're too much of a fucking loner for my liking. Now, get the fuck out and catch the bastard before hell freezes over.'

The Chief's secretary, Debbie, pulled a sympathetic face and shrugged as he walked past her. He could see she'd been crying. The Chief was well liked throughout the station and Debbie had worked with him for fifteen years, she was his work-wife.

The meeting with CI Naylor had gone much as he had expected, although he was surprised to be still on the case. There was no room for manoeuvre now. If he made a mistake, or the killer struck again, Naylor would be adding his name to the transfer list, and Richards would be back on the beat.

EIGHTEEN

The press briefing room was stuffed to overflowing. Outside, the temperature had plummeted to –7°C, but in the briefing room it was like a sauna. With the spotlights and television cameras aimed directly at him he felt like a target. If he were destined to die of a heart attack, now would be a good time for it to happen, he thought. His cardiac pump was thrashing about in his chest like a Vietnamese pot-bellied pig in a sty without food.

Parish sat down at the table and unfolded the paper in front of him. He could hear his hair growing it was so quiet. Once he had read the briefing the shouting began. The Chief should have warned him about the damage to his hearing. He wondered whether he should wear ear defenders in future.

His hands went up in surrender. 'Please, one question at a time.' He pointed to a young woman with reddish hair and freckles standing up on the left by the wall.

'Catherine Cox from the Chigwell Herald. Are you investigating a connection between the two deaths at Redbridge Council and a number of other murders in the local area?'

Here we go, he thought. 'I'm sorry, Miss Cox, without knowing which murders you're referring to I'm unable to answer your question.' He was glad that no one seemed to grasp that the implication of non-denial was that they were investigating a link to other murders.

'Yes?' Parish pointed to a pretty young woman with glasses in the first row.

'Emma Potter from the Redbridge Times. 'Is it true that Mr Squires killed Mrs Flint, and then took his own life?'

It sounded like an accusation in Cluedo. He had to work hard not to smile as he finished the sentence: ...using the candlestick in the conservatory. 'We are still investigating what happened at Redbridge Council, Miss Potter. More than that, I'm not at liberty to say, but thank you for your question.'

He was enjoying answering questions without telling them anything, and he chose another pretty young woman from the third row with a blonde bob and sparkling grey eyes.

'Ruth Sandland from the Commuter. Do you know how much money was stolen?'

'At this point, Miss Sandland, we don't know that any money has been stolen.'

'It's Mizz Sandland, Inspector.'

'I'm sure it is,' he parried and immediately stood up. 'The next briefing will be at nine o'clock tomorrow morning. Thank you all for coming'

***

In the corridor he leaned against the wall and took a deep breath. Well, for a first briefing on his own he thought that it went okay. At least nobody mentioned a serial killer, so he didn't have to lie, and his tongue wasn't bleeding.

What was his plan for today? News of the Chief had really thrown him. He'd have to nudge everything backwards so that he could go and spend some time with him. Then he needed to visit Beth Masters to see what she knew about Beech Tree Orphanage, which meant running the gauntlet of reporters squatting outside Redbridge Council offices. Unless, of course, he rang her and met her for lunch, which would probably be safer.

Yes, he knew a bit about fucking stealth, especially where lunch was concerned!

He walked slowly up the stairs to the squad room. After speaking to Beth Masters, he should go and find out what this orphanage looked like, see what all the fuss was about. He still had no idea if the orphanage still existed. Beth Masters would surely know. It seemed to have mythical status, a place shrouded in mystery like El Dorado or Camelot. Then, of course, they still needed to go and search Martin Squires' house in Abridge.

'Morning, Sir.' Richards was sat at his desk going through his intray. She needed a desk of her own. If he survived until the end of the week and she was still his partner, he'd organise something for her. If not, neither of them would need a desk. 'Kowalski told me about the Chief.'

'Its worse than you think, Richards.'

'What do you mean, Sir?'

'I'll tell you later. First, find the number for Social Services at Redbridge Council.'

She rifled through the telephone book and then rang the number.

'Ask to speak to Beth Masters.'

After a while, Richards thrust the phone at him. 'On the line, Sir.'

'Miss Masters…'

'It's Mrs actually.' Didn't you just know it? Somebody with the right authority should fix that. How the hell could anybody tell whether it was Miss, Mrs or Ms. If he was stood in front of a woman the wedding ring was a bit of a clue. But when he was writing a letter or speaking on the telephone it was like throwing darts with a blindfold on.

'I'm Detective Inspector Parish from Hoddesdon police station. You sent me an email.'

'Oh yes, the one about the tokens?'

'That's right. Can we meet? I'd like to pick your brains about Beech Tree Orphanage.'

'I have appointments all morning, but you could buy me lunch. You won't get value for money though, because I don't know a lot about the orphanage'

'I'll be the judge of that. Where?'

'Do you know the *Marianna Restaurant* on Manford Way in Chigwell?'

'I'll find it. Twelve thirty okay for you?'

'Yes, that will be fine.'

'See you then, Mrs Masters.'

He passed the phone back to Richards. 'That's lunch organised.'

'Are we going to see the Chief now, Sir?'

'Yes, we are.'

'I knew we would be.'

In the car Richards said, 'Did you take my mum out last night, Sir?'

'I was in bed alone last night, Richards.'

'You're not answering my question, Sir.'

'That's because I don't have to.'

Her eyes creased up and her lips stretched into a thin line like a bulldog that had found the scent of fresh meat. 'Oh, I forgot to tell you, Sir, I did a database search for Brian Ridpath and Colin Jackson whilst you were briefing the press.'

He knew he should have done that, but what with one thing and another he had forgotten. 'And...?'

'There was nothing of interest on Brian Ridpath, but Colin Jackson died in 1981, Sir. He used to live at 15 Buckingham Road before he died, but that was a long time ago.'

'What do you think that means, Richards?'

'Colin Jackson isn't really the victim's name, Sir.'

'Yes, you're right. Give Doc Michelin a ring and ask him to run Jackson's fingerprints through the National Fingerprint Database, we'll see who comes back.'

Richards picked up the phone and rang the pathologist.

'There's no time is there, Sir?'

'That's what happens when a murder team consists of one man and a dog, Richards.'

'I'm the dog am I, Sir?'

'Yes, but a very cute pedigree dog with long silky hair.'

'Thanks, Sir, I think.'

'We'll try and get to Squires' house this afternoon, otherwise it will have to be tomorrow.'

***

Chief Superintendent Walter Day lay awake propped up with pillows. A thin clear tube disappeared up his nose, and another one carrying liquid ran into the back of his hand. His hair had been incinerated as waste long ago, and his skin was like translucent porcelain with blue cracks. In the office he usually wore a black woollen hat that hid his baldness, but didn't match his suit and tie. Nobody had the heart to tell him it looked ridiculous.

'Hello Parish, I saw you on the news earlier, good job.' His voice was soft like tissue paper.

Parish put the bottle of orange juice and the bag of grapes he'd bought on the bedside table. 'Thanks, Sir.'

'I see you're still smiling, Richards?'

'I was until I heard about you, Sir. Now I'm not smiling so much. I hope you're going to get better?'

'I feel like an ass, Richards. I mixed up my tablets last night, nearly killed myself. Of course, they think I did it on purpose, and who could blame me? But it was an

201

honest to goodness mistake. Anyway, as well as everything else, I'm on suicide watch now and I've got to have counselling twice a day. They're going to stabilise me again and make sure I'm not a danger to myself and others, and then they'll let me out. I should be back at work on Monday.'

'That's excellent news, Sir.' Parish said. He had decided in the car not to say anything to the Chief about his meeting with CI Naylor. The man had enough on his plate without Parish bleating like a weakling about being bullied.

Walter Day forced a smile. 'Come on, Parish, out with it?'

'Out with what, Sir?'

'Whatever it is that's rung the colour out of your face?'

'It was hearing about you, Sir.'

'It's Trevor Naylor, isn't it?'

Parish couldn't prevent his mouth from ratting him out. 'He dragged me into your office and told me my future.'

'If it's any consolation, Parish – and you never heard it from me – he won't get my job when I'm gone.'

'Unfortunately, Sir, he's got it now, and he's made himself very much at home in your office. By the time you come back on Monday your coffee will be gone, and Richards and I will be history.'

'He's coming in to see me this afternoon, I'll have a word.'

'I can sign a handgun out, Sir. It would be better to shoot him in the heart with a silver bullet.'

'I'm glad you've still got your sense of humour, Parish.'

'I'm just being cheerful for your sake, Chief.'

'So, are you any nearer catching the killer?'

'Well…'

'Let Richards tell me, Parish. We'll see how good your teaching is. Not only that, I prefer her voice to yours.'

Richards grinned. 'Thank you, Sir, I said to DI Parish you had good taste. We're meeting a Social Worker for lunch who knows about Beech Tree Orphanage. We still think it's the key to what's been happening. Then, if its still standing, we'll go and have a walk round.'

'Are you expecting the killer to be hiding out there?'

'No, Sir, but if the orphanage still exists then there might be some clues left for us to find.'

'What do you make of the latest victim being killed in the middle of the day?'

'We think the killer knows all the victims, Chief. He's been watching them and knows the best time to kill each one. The crime scenes are all isolated so there's little chance of him being seen or caught.'

'She sounds like a presenter on the Crime Channel, Parish.'

Parish smiled.

'We're also trying to find time to search Martin Squires' house, but we haven't got much of that, Sir.'

'I wish I could help you, Richards. In here I have lots of time.'

A rotund nurse with bright red hair and a dark blue uniform came in the room. 'You'll have to leave now, Inspector. Chief Superintendent Day needs his rest, and it's nearly lunchtime.'

Parish squeezed the Chief's arm. 'Don't worry about me, Chief, I can look after myself. You just concern yourself with beating this thing. Richards and I will pop back tomorrow to check up on you.'

'Thanks, Parish. By the way, the Chief Constable has taken a real liking to you. He's following your investigation with interest and is thinking of using it for training purposes, so keep sending your reports, but to his email address.'

'Ha!' Parish mumbled as he walked out. 'The perfect example of what not to do.'

Richards leaned over and kissed the Chief on the forehead. 'See you tomorrow, Sir.' She followed Parish along the corridor. 'What did this CI Naylor say to you, Sir?'

'He wanted to know how I'd lumbered myself with such a nosy partner, Richards.'

***

The *Marianna Restaurant* on Manford Way was a café pretending to be a restaurant. The food and the clientele were both cheap and cheerful, and there were no tablecloths on the Formica-topped tables. Parish ordered a full English breakfast to matching frowns from Richards and Beth Masters, who both ordered salads.

Beth Masters was in her late fifties, thin with spiked grey hair. She wore chunky colourful jewellery, and dressed like a hippie. Her clothes looked as though they were all offcuts from a patchwork quilt.

'It was a long time ago,' Masters said when Parish asked her about Beech Tree Orphanage. 'A couple of months before it was closed down, I think.'

'Why did it close?'

'I have no idea, Inspector. I went to the orphanage that one time to see a young girl who was being adopted. We sat in the Manager's office and had a chat, then I left. Whilst I was there, I recall seeing a token on the Manager's desk, like the one in the picture. It was unusual, that's why I remember it.'

'Do you recall the Manager's name?'

Parish could see Beth Masters dredging through memories that had not seen the light of day for many years. 'Pearson, I think. I only remember because his breath smelled terrible. He was fat and sweaty... Oh yes... and his office smelled of sweaty body as well, a really unpleasant man.'

Parish forked a mixture of bubble 'n' squeak, black pudding and baked beans into his mouth, and then washed it down with tea. 'Where was the orphanage?'

'You mean you don't know?'

He wondered why people did that. Why would anybody ask a question if they already knew the answer? 'No, I don't know.'

'After it closed, the orphanage was bought by Rushdon Property Management.'

'Never heard of it.' Parish said.

'Peter Rushdon was an orphan there apparently, but he's an old man now living in America. He made his fortune in the 1960s and 70s buying up land and building houses people could afford.'

'So he bought up the orphanage and built houses on the land?'

'No, I remember reading an article in the Chigwell Herald at the time. He just put a twelve-foot high metal fence around the whole damned place and went to live in America. As far as I know, nobody has seen him since.'

'So where is it?'

'Between the Cemetery and Chigwell Brook. You can get to it via Froghall Lane, but you won't get in.'

'What do you mean?'

'This morning, I thought I'd make a slight detour, between visiting clients, to have a quick look. The fence is still there, but it's hidden behind a forest of brambles, black thorn and hawthorn. You can't see the orphanage. Nobody knows it even exists anymore. Until I got that email asking about the tokens from you, I hadn't thought about Beech Tree Orphanage in twenty years, and I've never heard anybody talk about it either. I think Peter Rushdon made it disappear.'

'But why?'

Beth Masters shrugged. 'No idea. Listen, Inspector, thanks very much for lunch, but I have to go now, more appointments. They treat Social Workers like slaves these days.'

'You're welcome, Beth. Thanks very much for helping us.'

After Beth Masters had left, and Parish had finished slurping his tea, Richards said, 'Sounds a bit creepy, Sir?'

'Doesn't it,' he said.

***

Graham Pearson had seen the news concerning the murder of Diane Flint and wondered what was going on at Redbridge Council. When he read in the Redbridge Times a couple of days later that police had taken the Council's financial records away he became increasingly concerned about his pension. First, he tried to contact Brian Ridpath, but found out from the landlord at the *Two Brewers* that Brian had been murdered. He decided to go and ask Martin Squires what the hell was going on, and more importantly reassure himself that his pension was safe. It wasn't so urgent though that he shouldn't keep his booking at the Hainault Forest Golf Club of which he was a long-standing member. After he had hit fifty balls down the frozen driving range he celebrated with a couple of beers in the nineteenth hole, and then caught a taxi to the Council offices.

Having taken retirement in 1986, he had put on three stone in weight before taking up golf. Although he had only been forty-eight, he was able to negotiate a good deal with Martin Squires because of the videotapes he had secured in a safe-deposit box at the bank, which allowed him to live quite comfortably and take regular holidays to Thailand. He thought it was a great shame that the orphanage had been bought by that bastard Rushdon and then closed, but he had known that the long-running exclusive after-hours club would come to an end sooner or later.

He hadn't spoken to Martin Squires since negotiating his retirement package. In fact, he had avoided any contact with the other members of the club as a precautionary measure, but he was about to close a deal on a small place in Spain, overlooking a golf course, and he didn't want anything to go wrong.

The Council offices had been refurbished in 1999, and were a lot more welcoming than the Victorian heavy wooden doors and mosaics he remembered. He went straight to the lifts, stepped in and pressed for the sixth floor.

He found Martin Squires' pretty little secretary sat at her desk and said, 'Mr Squires please?'

'I'm sorry,' she said, 'but Mr Squires has died.'

'Thank you, Miss.' Died? He turned around and left. Died? Now what will happen?

***

Terry Reynolds was on duty. He hadn't planned to kill Graham Pearson until after work at the old man's house, but the fat smelly bastard had come into the Council for some reason. Terry got into the lift on the fifth floor, and Pearson was there on his own. He nearly didn't get on, but then changed his mind.

Even after all this time Pearson had recognised him. 'Well, well, little Terry Reynolds? Its you isn't it? You're the one killing them all. Right from the start I knew you were trouble.'

Terry punched Pearson in the throat, smashing his windpipe. He'd learnt how to do that in prison. The fat bastard slid down the side of the lift and sat on the floor like a blob of greasy blubber. He used his lift key to override the controls and take it down to the lower basement where he locked it. Thankfully, there was no one about. He went to his locker and retrieved the marlinspike and token number 43 from his bag. Back at the lift, he stabbed Pearson in the heart and slipped the token in his mouth.

'For Tommy Lonely,' he said. Then he unlocked the lift and sent it up to the top floor.

He was breathing heavy. Sweat snaked down his back, and he began to think of the CCTV cameras. There were none in the lifts, but there were a number in the lower basement, and one of them overlooked the lift doors. He'd have to go up to the security room and get rid of the computer disc. Trouble was, Ollie Townsend was up there. He didn't want to kill Ollie, but...

Terry was relieved when he went into the Security office and found Ollie dozing with the *Sun* open on his lap at Page 3. He took the disc out of the computer and put it in his pocket. Then he removed a clean disc from the pile and slipped it in the CD drive. Last, he took a lift key off the hook on the board. He knew that once the police had been called, and they worked everything out he would more than likely be searched. He went down to his locker, took out the marlinspike and remaining tokens, and put them in a plastic shopping bag with the CCTV surveillance disc and the lift key. Then he hid the bag in the toilet cistern.

When he returned to the Security office Ollie was still snoring. He helped himself to Ollie's newspaper, sat down and began reading about the strange 'goings on' at Redbridge Council.

***

Richards had driven to the end of Froghall Lane and parked up in front of a wire fence. It was five past three and the light was beginning to fade. The cemetery, like a snow-covered garden of bones, stood to their left. They were sat on the warm bonnet of the car looking across a field towards a twelve-foot wall of thorns.

'It looks like an enchanted forest, Sir.'

Parish grunted. 'You watch far too much television, Richards.'

'We're not going to go over there are we, Sir? We'll need wellies or something if we're going to go over there.'

'We'll be all right, Richards. I haven't finally found the orphanage and come all the way out here only to leave without taking a look.'

'You could give me a piggyback, Sir.'

'I'm the senior officer, Richards. You could give me a piggyback.'

She pulled a face.

'Your face will stay like that one of these days, Richards.'

She stuck the tip of her tongue out.

He pulled the top wire of the fence up so that Richards could duck underneath, and then they started across the field with Richards gripping Parish's upper arm. The frozen ground was uneven and it was hard trying to stay upright, but eventually they stood before the thorn enshrouded fence. They began to walk in an anti-clockwise direction around the wall of thorns until they came to the main entrance and an access road leading to Vicarage Lane. A sign instructed them to ring Rushdon Property Management on 0800 800 9785 for enquiries.

'I should have worn my snow boots this morning,' Richards said looking down at her shoes. 'It feels as though I've got blocks of ice at the end of my legs.'

'Stop whining and write the number down, Richards. It looks as though the only way we're going to get inside is if someone lets us in.'

Just then his mobile rang.

'Parish?'

'You just sit in your office waiting for me to call, don't you, Parish?'

'Hello, Doc. Yes, we're just playing Monopoly, and I've got hotels on Mayfair and Park Lane. Richards has just popped out for some pickled eggs to go with the beers, so don't make me come out in this horrible weather when we're having such a good time.'

'Yes, very funny, Parish. Put your riot gear on and meet me in the Reception at Redbridge Council.'

'Bloody hell, Doc, not again?'

NINETEEN

At quarter past four Richards slowed down in front of Redbridge Council as a herd of reporters ran into the road like Wildebeest and surrounded the car. Cameras flashed. Microphones scratched the car's paintwork and smashed into the side window in the crush trying to record any utterance Parish might make.

'They're like a pack of wild dogs, Sir.' Richards said. 'I'll have to explain any damage when I take it back to the garage.'

'The mechanics are used to it.' He smiled and pointed at the television camera aimed directly at them. 'At least you'll have television evidence to support your story.'

Richards smiled, pouted her lips and waved at the camera. 'You didn't tell me I'd be on the television, Sir. I'll have to get my hair done, and be more careful with my make-up in the mornings.'

'Stop boring me, Richards.'

'Sorry, Sir.'

Richards parked on the double yellow lines directly in front of the Council offices. Two constables held the mad dogs at bay as they ran up the steps to the entrance.

A thin familiar-looking security guard with dark hair and lazy eyes held the glass door open for them.

A great believer in politeness costing nothing Parish said, 'Thank you.'

Richards, breathing heavy, said, 'That was a bit scary, Sir.'

'I know, sometimes the press are worse than the criminals we're paid to arrest, torture, and lock up.'

Richards smiled. 'If you say so, Sir.'

Parish looked about and saw a group of Council staff milling around the Reception desk. Sergeant Ken Rice came towards him.

'Hello, Ken.' Parish said. He'd known Ken Rice since they'd attended the Sergeant's course together eight years ago. Married with three school-aged children, Rice was the same age as Parish, but had woken up eighteen months ago with white hair instead of black.

'Hi, Jed, or should I say, Sir? Congratulations on the promotion.'

'I'm sure they've promoted the wrong Parish by mistake, but thanks anyway, Ken. Were you first on the scene?'

'Yes, I got here shortly after it was called in.'

'What's been happening?'

'The victim's in the lift,' Rice said. 'Doc Michelin and that oddball Toadstone are over there in white suits. I called for some reinforcements and we've got the place locked down until you say otherwise, but it was a good hour before we were able to do that so I expect the killer is long gone.'

'I suppose you're right, Ken. Good job anyway. Are there any eyewitnesses?'

'None have come forward. A woman pressed for the lift, the doors opened, she screamed and fainted, but she doesn't know anything. What do you want me to do now?'

'Give me a minute to find out about the victim. I'll come back to you.'

Doc Michelin was waving at them. They walked over to where one of the lifts stood locked open and peered inside. A fat old man with straggly grey hair was slumped in the corner. Toadstone was on his hands and knees examining the floor with a magnifying glass.

'We've got something a bit different this time, Parish,' Doc Michelin said. 'Token number 43 in his mouth. Stabbed through the heart with a marlinspike, but… after he was already dead.'

'Go on, Doc don't leave us on the edge of our seats.'

'He had his trachea crushed first…'

'I wish you wouldn't use jargon, Doc.'

'Sorry habit, the windpipe… Then he was stabbed in the heart.' He knelt down and pointed at the entry wound. 'Notice the lack of blood.'

Parish turned to Richards. 'What do you think happened, Richards?'

She looked at the two men with shock etched on her face. 'Oh… Well, it could be that the killer was surprised. A bit like me now, Sir.'

Parish smiled. 'Keep going,' he encouraged her.

Richards swallowed. 'He wasn't ready to kill his victim with the marlinspike, so he hit him in the windpipe.'

'That would require someone with a lot of strength wouldn't it, Doc?' Parish asked.

'Not necessarily. If you knew what you were doing, you could kill someone fairly easily with a punch to the throat.'

'No help there then?' Parish said. 'Carry on, Richards. What do you mean, he was surprised? If the killer wasn't ready, why didn't he wait?'

'Because…. He had to kill the victim?'

'Why?'

'We already think that the killer and the victims knew each other, so this victim could have recognised him.'

'Okay good,' Parish said. 'I think we're getting somewhere. So the victim said, "Hey, I know you," and the killer thumped him in the windpipe. What did the killer do then?'

213

'Well, he stabbed the man in the heart, and then put the token in his mouth.'

'You're missing something, Richards. Where was the marlinspike when all this was happening?'

'In... Ah, I see what you mean, Sir. If he had it on him, why didn't he use it instead of hitting the man in the throat?'

'Exactly. We also have another problem.' He stared at Toadstone on the floor. 'Was he killed in the lift, or somewhere else, Toadstone?'

Toadstone sat back on his heels. 'There's no scrape marks on the floor and none on the victim's shoes either. He could have been lifted in, but considering the size of him that seems unlikely. I'd say he was hit whilst he was standing up in here, and then collapsed to the floor.'

'Thanks Toadstone, but if that's the case why did no one see anything? It's Tuesday afternoon, there are staff and visitors all over the place. Why haven't we got any witnesses?' He looked up at the CCTV cameras. 'What about the security disc? If the killer was recognised, then he might not have had his hood up. This murder could be the breakthrough we've been waiting for. Have we got the security disc, Toadstone?'

'The first thing we did was confiscate the disc, but it'll need analysing. I should have something for you tomorrow.'

'Tomorrow!' 'Parish was incredulous. 'Get somebody on it now, Toadstone. We've got this place locked down. The killer could still be here.'

Toadstone stood up, wandered out into the Reception and spoke to another white-suited figure. Then he came back and carried on with his examination of the lift floor.

'We haven't asked why the killer and the victim were here, Sir,' Richards said.

'Good point, Richards. Who is the victim, Toadstone?'

'According to his driving licence, his name is Graham Pearson, he's 72 years old, and he lives at 267 Forest Lane in Chigwell, which if I'm not mistaken overlooks the golf course..'

'Crap!' Parish said. 'I guess we won't be talking to the last Manager of Beech Tree Orphanage after all, Richards.'

'What was he doing here, Sir?' Richards said. 'And why now? Was he visiting someone at the Council?'

'You're asking some damn good questions this afternoon, Richards.' He walked over to speak to Sergeant Rice. 'Ken, the victim's name is Graham Pearson. We need to get everyone's contact details in the building, and whilst you're doing that I want to know who he was here to see. He didn't wander in off the street and get in the lift just for the hell of it; he came here to see someone. Once people have been interviewed and you've got their details, send them home.'

'Leave it with me, Jed.'

Sergeant Rice began organising tables and chairs in front of the entrance, and put one of his officers at each of the tables with clear instructions for obtaining the identity of every person, their contact details, why they were in the building, and if they knew the victim.

'I don't understand why the killer stabbed Pearson in the heart,' Richards said. 'If he was already dead, what was the point?'

The Doc scratched his stubble. 'Stabbing the victims in the heart with a marlinspike could have some symbolic meaning,' he suggested. 'He's used the same weapon for all the murders.'

'Interesting hypothesis, Doc. Suggestions?'

'Love, Sir?' Richards blurted out. 'Stabbing them in the heart could be about love.'

'What, you mean like: "I'm stabbing you in the heart because I love you?"'

'No, Sir. More like: "I'm stabbing you in the heart because you broke my heart."'

'Not four men and a woman, Richards. I don't think its revenge for a broken heart. We've agreed that it's about revenge, and that the tokens mean something in the context of Beech Tree Orphanage. Stabbing the victims in the heart with a marlinspike could very well mean something to the killer, but I don't think we'll find out what that is until we catch him.'

Just then a forensic officer came up and spoke to Toadstone, who then interrupted their speculation.

'The security disc is useless.'

'I'll pretend I didn't hear that, Toadstone,' Parish said.

'Whoever killed Graham Pearson also took the disc out of the computer and replaced it with a new one. In other words, there's no CCTV surveillance on the disc until after the murder.'

'How is that possible?' Parish said. 'The door into the Security office has a digital keypad. Only the security staff can get in there, can't they?'

Toadstone shrugged. 'I'll get back to work and leave you to find out what happened, Sir.'

Parish walked over to the thin security guard. 'What's your name?'

'Terry Reynolds, Sir.'

'How many security staff are on duty, Mr Reynolds?'

'Three, Sir.'

'Who's in charge?'

'Mr Townsend.'

'According to my forensics officer, the CCTV disc has been taken from the computer in the Security office and replaced with another one. If the door has a digital keypad and only the security staff knows the code, how is that possible unless one of you took it?'

The man looked away and shuffled his feet. 'I think you'd better speak to Mr Townsend, Sir.'

'Where is Mr Townsend?'

'Have you tried the Security office?'

'Okay, lets go there. Where's the other member of your team?'

'He should be in the office as well.'

Parish turned to Richards. 'Whilst I'm sorting this mess out, ring the number for Rushdon Property Management and ask them to meet us at the orphanage at eleven o'clock tomorrow morning with the keys.'

Richards nodded.

Parish headed towards the Security office behind the Reception with the thin security guard following him. A tall man with a paunch and cropped brown hair opened the door.

'Who are you?' Parish asked showing his warrant card.

'Ollie Townsend.'

'You're Head of Security?'

'Yes.'

'I've got Terry Reynolds here. Is the other member of your team in there with you?'

'Sol Campbell? Yeah, he's here. You'd better come in, Inspector.'

A thickset black man that Parish assumed was Sol Campbell stopped reading his newspaper and stared at him.

Once they were all in the Security office, Parish introduced himself and told them about the CCTV surveillance disc. 'Now, as I see it one of you three took the disc, or someone else had access to it.' Leaning against a filing cabinet he glared at them. 'Well?'

Nobody would look him in the eyes.

'This is a murder investigation, gentlemen. If you won't tell me the truth here, I'll take you all down to the station.'

Terry Reynolds looked at Ollie Townsend and said, 'You'd better tell him, Ollie.'

'I'll lose my job.'

'You'll lose your job if you don't tell me,' Parish said.

'I had a bit of a snooze.'

'And…?' Parish pushed.

'And the door to the office was propped open with the fire extinguisher.'

'Christ almighty! So what you're telling me is that anyone could have walked in, helped themselves to the disc, and trundled out again?'

Looking at the floor Ollie Townsend mumbled, 'Yes.'

'You're right, Mr Townsend,' Parish said. 'You will lose your job. The first chance we have of identifying the killer and you fall asleep in a secure area using a fire extinguisher to prop open the door. I suggest you tell your boss what happened before he finds out from me.'

Parish turned, opened the door and left. Out in Reception, Sergeant Rice caught his attention. 'What have you got, Ken?'

'The PA to the Personnel Director, a Mrs Carrie Holden, said she was standing in for the Finance Director's secretary who's off sick, and she saw the victim up there. He came in and asked for Mr Squires. He obviously hadn't heard about the suicide.'

Parish saw Carrie sitting at a table and walked over to talk to her. 'Hi, Carrie.'

'Hello, Inspector.'

He sat down on the table. 'What did you say when Graham Pearson asked for Mr Squires?'

'I simply said that Mr Squires had died.'

'Did he say anything?'

'He thanked me and left. That's all I know.'

'Are you okay, Carrie?'

'I'm all right, Jed.' She touched his hand. 'I've thrown him out and started divorce proceedings. He realises now that he made a mistake. The thing is, so do I. I should never have married the bastard. I'll make him pay through the nose now though.'

Parish stood up. 'Look after yourself, Carrie.'

'And you, Jed Parish. Thanks.'

He saw Richards watching them and walked over to her. He told her what had happened to the surveillance disc then said, 'What did Rushdon Property Management say?'

'They said we'd need a warrant, Sir. So I used my initiative and phoned DI Kowalski who told me how to go about getting a warrant. I've got to pick it up from the CPS offices at nine-thirty tomorrow morning. I then rang the management company back and told them I had a warrant and they were send someone to be there at eleven o'clock with the keys, or else.'

'Well done, Richards, I'll make a detective out of you yet. You didn't have to promise DI Kowalski anything before he'd help you, did you?'

Richards' lip curled up. 'I see you know him very well, Sir. Unfortunately, a spotty kid at a beach party in Cornwall stole my virginity five years ago. When I threatened to report DI Kowalski for sexual harassment, he couldn't do enough for me.'

'I'm seeing a different side to you, Richards.'

'I told you I could look after myself, Sir.'

'Well done. I think we've finished here now. What do you think?'

'We're not really any closer to finding the killer are we, Sir?'

'Not after those idiots in the Security office lost the CCTV surveillance disc.'

'I've been thinking about something, Sir.'

'Go on, Richards, let your imagination run free?'

'If the killer didn't have the marlinspike and the token on him when he killed Graham Pearson, where were they?'

'In a bag?' Parish suggested.

'What if the killer is a member of staff, Sir? What if he went to get the marlinspike and the token from somewhere in the building, then came back and finished what he'd started.'

Parish thought about Richards' 'what-if' scenario. 'The first murder was Gregory Taylor on Ralston Drive in Chigwell. At that time there was no connection to Redbridge Council. Right, Richards?'

'Right, Sir.'

'The second murder was Diane Flint in the car park here. There was no reason to suspect that the killer might be someone who worked here. In fact, we had no leads to suggest it was anyone. All we knew was that Diane Flint's murder was connected to Gregory Taylor's death, and it therefore diverted attention away from here. Okay so far?'

'Okay, Sir.'

'Then, Brian Ridpath was killed in an alley, and still there was nothing to suggest the killer might work here. What we did get with Ridpath's murder was a link back to the Finance Department, and then Martin Squires committed suicide after destroying the Council's financial data. It was then that we found out about Beech Tree Orphanage. Agreed?'

'Agreed, Sir.'

'The fourth murder was Colin Jackson in an alley at the back of the *Pepper Pot* café, but again there was nothing to suggest the killer worked here. All we knew was that each of the victims once worked for Redbridge Council. Do you go along with that?'

'Yes, Sir. Except…'

'Except what?'

'We don't know yet whether Colin Jackson, or whoever he is, worked for the Council.'

'Okay, a minor point, but can we move beyond that?'

'Yes, Sir.'

'Finally, we've got Graham Pearson who was killed in a lift here. Although everything is connected to Redbridge Council, there's no reason to believe the killer works here. We've had two murders committed here, but in public places. The other three murders were committed elsewhere.'

'If we think that Graham Pearson recognised the killer, what were both of them doing here at the same time? I find it hard to believe it was a coincidence.'

'Maybe the killer followed Pearson in off the street?'

'If that were the case, Sir, he'd have had the marlinspike and the token with him. Also, and this really spooks me, if he killed Pearson in the lift with a punch to the throat, and then had to go and get the marlinspike and the token, how come no one saw Pearson's body? As soon as the killer stepped off the lift, someone would have pressed the button and whoosh, the dead Graham Pearson was travelling from floor to floor. He'd have been found by someone long before the killer could come back and stab him in the heart and put the token in his mouth.'

'Unless…?'

'Unless they had a key to take the lift out of service.'

221

Parish grasped Richard's upper arms and kissed her on the cheek. 'You're a genius, Richards.'

She blushed like a solar corona. 'I've been trying to tell you that for a week, Sir.'

'And the only people who have keys to the lift are employed here?' Parish said.

'Yes, Sir.'

'You could have said something before, Richards. We've sent most of the staff home now.'

'We only need to talk to the ones who have a key to the lift.'

'Yes, you're right.' He strode back to the Security office and knocked.

Ollie Townsend opened the door. 'Yes?'

'Mr Townsend, do you keep a record of the staff who have a key to the lifts?'

'Er yes, Inspector.'

Ollie Townsend stood there not moving.

'Could you give me a copy?'

'Oh sorry. Yes, of course.' He went back into the office and took a file from the top of a filing cabinet and pulled out a page. 'Seven security staff, the Town Clerk, the three maintenance engineers, and six Directors, a total of seventeen people altogether.' He passed the sheet of paper to Parish and said, 'You can have that one. It obviously needs updating, I'll print off another copy.'

Parish looked at the list, which had five columns. The first column was the date of issue, then a key number, the name of the person it was allocated to, their job title, and lastly a signature. He noticed Martin Squires had a key, but Diane Flint's had been returned.

He was just about to take the list outside and give it to Sergeant Rice when something occurred to him.

'It says here that there should be twenty keys. Seventeen were issued, one has been returned, so you should have four left, is that right?'

Townsend went to a board with numbered hooks on and said, 'Number 83 if memory serves.'

'Are there any missing?'

Townsend looked at hook number 83 and his face dropped. 'There's only three, Inspector.'

Parish took a pace forward until he was only an inch from the Head of Security's face. 'I should arrest you and throw away the key, Townsend.'

Townsend looked away.

Even though he wasn't hopeful of a result, Parish took the list out to Ken Rice and said, 'I'd like you to gather as many of these people in Reception as you can find, Ken.'

'Okay Jed, leave it with me.'

It took Ken Rice and three of his officers fifteen minutes to round up eight of the seventeen people. The Town Clerk had remained in the building like the Captain of a sinking ship. The three Security staff were also still on duty. Only one of the maintenance engineers was available – a Mr Bogdan Krawiec. One had already gone home, and the other one was on holiday. Of the six Directors, those of Social Services and Finance were dead. The Director of Personnel was sunning himself in California. Of the other three, only the Director of Environmental Services had remained. The Director of Education was out visiting primary schools; and the Director of Crime and Public Safety was in Finland to see how they were able to maintain such a low crime level.

Parish addressed them all. 'It's possible that the killer might work here and have a key to the lift,' he said. They all looked at each other as if the culprit could easily be identified. 'What I'm going to do is ask that you volunteer to have yourself and your possessions searched.' He waited, but no one objected. 'Thank you. One of my officers will be with you shortly.'

Whilst the search was being carried out he spotted Susan Tollhurst, the Finance Manager, at one of the tables.

'Susan…'

'Oh hello, Inspector.'

'Did Pocahontas recover your financial data?'

'That girl is a bloody genius. She was worth all the food I had to go out and buy for her, and more. If we'd called in a company to do what she did, it would have cost us tens of thousands of pounds. She knew exactly what had happened, and was familiar with the software that bastard Squires had used to delete the accounts. She had us back up and running within three hours, and had re-established our off-site back-up account as well.'

'So everything's as it should be?'

'Nearly. The forensic accountants have a copy of our computer accounts now, and they still have our paper-based records. We're also no nearer finding out why Brian Ridpath was being paid £2,000 a month, but its certainly not the disaster we thought it would be.'

'I'm glad. Have you any idea when you'll be getting your records back?'

Her eyebrows knitted. 'Don't you know?'

'They'll only contact me if they find something relevant to my investigation.'

'And you've heard nothing?'

'Not a word.'

'It seems as though that bastard Martin Squires knew how to hide something.'

It was forty-five minutes later by the time everyone had been searched. No marlinspike or tokens were found.

Parish realised that whether the killer worked at the Council or not, he had evaded them.

'Let's knock it on the head, Ken,' Parish said to Sergeant Rice. 'Send those remaining home, and let the security staff lock up. We've done all we can here. Thanks for your help, and thank your men for me.'

'No luck then, Jed?'

'He's like an eel. I thought we might have struck lucky this afternoon, but he's slithered through the cracks again.'

'Bad news about the Chief.'

Parish's heart began racing. 'What news?'

'That he was rushed into hospital last night.'

'Oh yeah. Richards and I went to see him this morning, he said he'd mixed up his medication.'

'Well, you couldn't blame him if it wasn't an accident. You get to the end of your working life and pack your Union Jack shorts and a cooler bag full of beers for the beach, and then some jobsworth tells you you've got cancer. A crappy retirement package, if you ask me.'

'He said he'll be back to work on Monday.'

'The man's a saint in my book, Jed. Anyway, I see you've got yourself a hot-looking partner at last.'

'I hadn't noticed, Ken.'

'Yeah right. You're the only one that hasn't then.'

'See you tomorrow Ken, and thanks again.'

Parish checked his watch. It was quarter past seven. 'Come on, Richards, let's get out of here.'

TWENTY

They ran the gauntlet of reporters.

In the car, Richard's mobile activated. Looking at his watch, Parish waited impatiently whilst she listened to whoever was on the other end of the connection. He had to go back to Hoddesdon station, collect his car, and then drive back to his flat. He needed to shower and change before Angie came at eight o'clock. At this rate, he'd get home just before she knocked on the door. Being a homicide detective was definitely not dating friendly. He was used to the long hours and hadn't minded in the past because he'd had no social life to speak of, but now he wanted one. Unfortunately, he'd really picked the wrong time to start wanting a social life. Now that he'd been promoted to DI he needed to focus all his energies on proving that the Chief had been right in recommending him for promotion. The trouble was, he wanted Angie as well. Was it possible to have both?

Richards disconnected the call and said, 'That was my mum, Sir. She said she'll be a bit late tonight.'

'Okay, lets…'

'I knew you two were seeing each other, Sir,' she said laughing and starting the engine.

'You're a scheming cow, Richards. That wasn't your mother on the phone at all was it?'

'No, Sir. I sent myself a fake phone call.'

'Well, now that you know, Richards, I'll have to get myself another partner.'

She stopped laughing. 'No, Sir, don't say that.'

'You're too nosy for your own good, Richards. Our working relationship will change now.'

'No it won't, Sir. I promise I won't start calling you 'Dad'.' She grinned.

'See, it's started already. You think of me now as your mother's boyfriend instead of your boss. No, you should have left well alone, Richards. Don't say anything else. I need to think. Drive.'

'I promise…'

'Which part of 'don't say anything else' don't you understand, Richards?'

'Sorry…'

He glared at her.

At the station he said, 'Your job in the morning is to sign out the pool car, to go and collect the warrant from the CPS, and then to come here and pick me up. Do you think you can do that without getting into any more trouble, Richards?'

'Yes, but can't we pretend I never found out, Sir?'

'Its too late for that now, Richards. You've burned your bridges, smashed your boats beyond repair, there's no going back.' He climbed out of the car and slammed the door.

Once she'd driven off he smiled. That would give her something to think about over night. If he were still a DI in the morning, after he'd seen CI Naylor, he wouldn't really get rid of her. She'd proved today that she had an enquiring mind even if it did extend to his private life. He knew he couldn't blame her though, she was looking after her mother like any good daughter would.

He laughed all the way home. A bloody fake phone call. He would never have thought of that. She was becoming an asset. Getting the warrant for Beech Tree Orphanage without being asked proved that. He'd need to have a word in Kowalski's ear though. Propositioning Richards in return for information was an abuse of his position.

***

When he answered the door, he was still wet from the shower and had a towel wrapped around his waist. It wasn't what he'd planned, but what else could he do? In his mind he'd cooked spaghetti bolognese with Parmesan cheese and garlic bread. A bottle of Yarra Valley Pinot Noir red wine was breathing at room temperature on the table next to the candle. And after eight mints sat in a box waiting to be devoured. He'd already showered, wore a black suit and open-necked shirt, and had switched the electric blanket on ready.

'Is this your way of saying let's go straight to bed?' Angie said looking him up and down as she stepped inside.

He kissed her on the lips and shut the door. 'It's my way of saying I've only just got in.'

'Yes, I know. Mary rang me in tears. She says you're going to get another partner because she found out about us.'

Helping her off with her coat he said, 'She tricked me into giving our secret away. Anyway, let me go and get some clothes on before you think about taking advantage of me.'

She followed him into the bedroom. 'I've got a better idea,' she said taking off her dress. 'Let's take advantage of each other?'

Parish didn't need asking twice, and he was glad that the quilt cover was only a couple of days old. They fell on the bed kissing and groping like teenagers. The first time was always the same, he thought. Always rushed and nerve-wracking, wondering if you'll match up to previous lovers, whether you're too quick, too small, too noisy. Having sex was not for the faint-hearted that was for sure.

Afterwards, under the quilt, when they lay in each other's arms in the darkness, he said to her, 'If I thought you were trying to bribe me, you know I'd have to arrest you.'

'I don't have to bribe you, Jed Parish,' she whispered. 'I know you won't get another partner, but if you want to arrest and torture me some more I suppose it would be foolish of me to resist.'

He pulled her tight and kissed her. 'After two dates, you're suddenly an expert on Jed Parish.'

Her hands strayed to his erection. 'Yes, otherwise I wouldn't be here.' They made love again without the panic, and he knew then that he wanted to spend the rest of his life with this woman.

'You're right, I'm just teaching your nosy daughter a lesson. She's got to remember that I'm her boss, and playing tricks on your boss can have serious consequences.'

'You're being mean, she really likes you, Jed.'

'I know, but she'll get over it.'

Angie switched the bedside light on and threw back the quilt.

Parish watched her walk naked to the wardrobe and put on one of his shirts.

'All this lovemaking has made me hungry,' she said. 'I hope you've got some food in?'

'Ah, well…' He hadn't really had chance to do any shopping. As far as he could remember there wasn't much of anything in.

Angie went into his kitchenette. He heard her rummaging around in his cupboards and drawers, but stayed in bed embarrassed that those cupboards and drawers belonged to him.

She came back and stood in the doorway smiling. 'I can see that a woman's touch is needed in this flat.'

229

'I just park myself here when I'm not working,' he said defensively. 'I really did mean to get some supplies in, but Mary will tell you that we didn't have much time today.'

'I'm not criticising you, but I'm still hungry. What about a Chinese takeaway?'

He smiled, climbed out of bed and began getting dressed. 'Now you're talking.'

'Don't think we're going to eat fast food on a regular basis because we're not, but it's okay in an emergency and looking at the green furry things in your fridge this is a dire emergency.'

He found the menu for the local takeaway and gave it to her. 'Choose what you want, I'll ring in the order, and then pop out and get it.'

It wasn't the evening he'd planned, and he thought he'd ruined any chance of a long-term relationship with his lack of planning and preparation. Women like Angie should be the centre of the universe not an afterthought, but as he drove her home she said, 'I'd like us to do that more if that's all right with you, Jed Parish?'

He realised he'd been holding his breath forever and breathed out. 'I'd like to do it more as well, Angela Richards.'

They agreed that making love with Mary in the house would just be too weird for both of them, and so they decided that their lovemaking should be restricted to his flat. She would come round again tomorrow night and bring some food with her.

They were kissing goodnight in the car when Parish heard tapping on the roof. He opened the window and peered out.

'I'm sorry, Sir, please don't get rid of me.'

'Richards! I'm in here with your mother. You standing out there watching us through the window like a voyeur is bordering on the obscene. I'm not going to get another partner, but my relationship with your mum is off limits, do you understand?'

'Oh yes, Sir. Thank you, Sir.' She pushed her arms through the opening and pulled his head towards her, but as she kissed him on the eye his head clanked on the glass. Then she ran off back into the house squealing.

'Thanks, Jed,' Angie said.

'Tell her when you get inside the house that I'd better not end up regretting my decision.'

Angie leaned across and kissed him on the lips. 'You won't regret any decisions you've made tonight, Jed Parish.'

***

Wednesday, 22nd January

He thought he'd beaten the nightmares, but they returned with a vengeance during the night. He sat up in bed with a scream on his lips at ten past four. Sweat dripped off him as if he'd been lying in a sauna, and his heart was on its way to bursting. He tossed and turned until six o'clock and then he got up. What the hell was going on? He was thirty-six for God's sake, long past the age when nightmares should be troubling him. He stood in the shower with his eyes closed and forcibly shifted his thinking away from the dark tunnel that he never seemed to reach the end of to Angie. He thought of her warmth, her softness, her whispering as he made love to her and began to get an erection.

Out of the shower and dried by ten past six, he threw on some clothes. Breakfast, that's what he needed, but to make himself breakfast he had to go to the Mart and get some food.

It had been snowing during the night. He thought the bad weather was over, but clearly he was wrong. An inch of snow had settled over the existing frozen slush, and the pavements were like glass. With great care, he managed to walk the half-mile to the Mart where he bought the essentials: bread, milk, sugar, coffee, butter, bacon and eggs. He was sure he had some baked beans in the cupboard, but he bought a tin anyway. He also bought a newspaper so that he could read about the case. On the way back, he slipped and banged his elbow and hip, but he managed to make it home.

In the flat, he cooked himself a breakfast with four pieces of toast and read the paper. At seven he switched on the television. He thought the local news crew would have edited out Richards waving at the camera, but they hadn't. It seemed to trivialise the investigation, and he wondered what CI Naylor and the Chief would make of it. She had an excuse because she was new, but he'd have to speak to her about it. Although they were in their little part of England trying to solve these murders, people across the UK, and for that matter across the world, were peering in at them through the window of television. They were specimens under a microscope, and she had to bear that in mind at all times.

***

CI Trevor Naylor sat behind the Chief's desk and stared at Parish as if he were a turd someone had thrown into the Chief's office as a bad joke. Parish felt extremely uncomfortable as Naylor continued to stare at him, and his mind began to wander. He thought the Chief Inspector had the look of Humphrey Bogart, thin and angular with dark hair slicked straight back. All he needed was a cigarette in the corner of his mouth, a double-breasted suit, and a trilby hat, and he could get a part in Casablanca.

The Chief had said he'd speak to Naylor, but maybe he hadn't. Maybe the Chief had forgot, or worst case scenario the Chief was dead. Maybe Naylor had been given the Chief's job – God help us all. Maybe slimeball was enjoying torturing him – but what was he thinking? There was no maybe involved in that. There were too many maybes for his liking. Maybe he should resign and become a taxi driver.

'I've got the press briefing at nine, Sir,' he said trying to hurry CI Naylor along. His feet were going numb.

'You've got the fucking press briefing at nine if I say you've got the fucking press briefing at nine, Parish.'

'Have I got the press briefing at nine, Sir?'

'I haven't made up my fucking mind yet. You went and bleated to the Chief like a fucking crybaby. The Chief asked me to leave you alone, note I said 'asked'. I'm in fucking charge until the Chief comes back, if he comes back. I can't make up my fucking mind whether to leave you alone, or kick your fucking arse so far out of the door you'll end up on the beat in Yorkshire. I said you'd be fucking history if there was another murder, and as sure as fucking eggs is eggs there was another fucking murder. Now, you know me Parish, am I a liar?'

'No…'

'Don't fucking interrupt me. You're a fucking slow learner, Parish.'

'Sorry…'

'Jesus fucking wept, Parish. How you even got promoted to Sergeant is beyond me. And don't think I didn't see that stupid fucking cow you call a fucking partner waving at the cameras like a fucking celebrity. You two are a good fucking match for each other. Together you probably make half a brain. Out of respect for the Chief I'm going to fucking pretend you don't exist until he comes back, Parish. I'm going to ignore your fucking stupidity, I'm going to play along with the Chief's madcap fucking idea that you're a good detective, and I'm going to pray that you stumble over some evidence that will help you solve the case and makes me look good. Five murders and a fucking suicide, Parish! A blind man with a fucking wooden leg and a donkey could have solved it by now, but the Chief wants you and that stupid fucking bitch on it. I must be out of my mind. I can hear the Chief Constable asking me why I didn't put you at the head of the fucking euthanasia queue. And you know what Parish? I have no fucking idea. I'll blame the Chief, of course, but that's not the real reason. The real reason is, I'm fucking curious to see how long the Chief will let you bumble along before he does something about you.' He thrust his hand out. 'Press briefing?'

Parish put his folded press briefing on the table.

Naylor read it and pushed it back. 'I shouldn't have to repeat myself, but you're not a normal fucking person, Parish. Don't mention a serial killer.'

'What serial killer, Sir?'

'Get the fuck out. Same time tomorrow, Parish.'

'Have a good day, Sir.'

Outside the Chief's office he smiled and said into the microphone on his lapel, 'I hope you got all that, Toadstone?'

He strolled up to forensics. 'Well?'

Toadstone passed him a memory stick, which he slipped into his jacket pocket. 'Its in WAV format, Sir.'

'You've sent it to the Chief Constable?'

'Sat in his inbox like a grenade waiting for the pin to be pulled.'

'They won't be able to track it back to us?'

'I'm not stupid, Sir. If anyone puts a trace on it, they'll discover it came from a region of China that has only one computer, which doesn't work.'

'Good job, Toadstone, I owe you one.'

'On that, Sir... Do you think you could put a good word in for me with your partner?'

'I can do that, Toadstone, but I think she's way out of your league. She's Premiership, you're Southern Conference.'

'Do you think so?'

'Definitely, but that's only my opinion. I'll say some nice things about you and we'll see what happens.'

'Thanks, Sir.'

He patted his pocket. 'Least I can do.'

Parish didn't really need to go to the toilet, but he knew that as soon as the press briefing began he'd be bursting at the seams and then it would be too late, so he went and squeezed a few drops out. As he washed his hands, the man in the mirror stared back at him like a hedgehog caught in the main beam of a car's headlights.

Amazingly, he was still a DI. The Chief had come through for him again. He wished he had a cure for the Chief's prostate cancer, but he didn't. All he could do was solve this case, prove that the Chief had been right in recommending him for promotion, right in continuing to have faith in him.

How CI Naylor had risen to the position he had, and remained there was beyond Parish's comprehension. The man was an anachronism who belonged to a time when people didn't matter. What surprised him was that nobody had done anything about the man. Everyone seemed to be scared of him, scared of how he could ruin their career with a word, the swish of a pen, or a non-recommendation. Parish wasn't scared of Naylor, the man was a bully. As he straightened the red and white striped tie in the mirror, and ran steady fingers through his gelled hair he hoped the Chief Constable would act on the tape Toadstone had sent him.

He walked along the corridor, down the stairs, and into the press briefing room. It seemed that everyone was interested in the 'goings on' at Redbridge Council. His report was brief:

'Yesterday afternoon, a man called Graham Pearson aged seventy-two years old, was stabbed in a lift at Redbridge Council and was declared dead at the scene. As far as we know, there is no connection to the deaths of Diane Flint and Martin Squires, but our investigations are continuing.'

'Inspector Parish?' This came from a man with a goatee beard and beady eyes. The man pushed a microphone towards him. 'Andrew Peterson from the Beeb,' he drawled like a Texan. 'Can you tell us please, whether you have any suspects for either of the two murders? Or, whether Mr Pearson's murder is connected to the missing money? Or, if there will be any further murders?'

'That's a handful of questions, Mr Peterson. No, we have no suspects, but then it is still early days. We haven't yet established that there is any money missing from Redbridge Council. Lastly, my crystal ball is in for repair.'

A weak ripple of laughter told Parish he wouldn't make a living as a stand-up comic.

The young woman with the freckles and the nervous smile from the Chigwell Herald stood up, pen poised over a fat notebook. 'Catherine Cox, Inspector. A number of sources have provided me with details of three similar murders in the local area. Isn't it true that you're really looking for a serial killer, and are keeping the truth from us?'

Mayhem ensued. After it had quietened down Parish said, 'I don't know who your sources are Miss Cox, but you have to remember that this is Essex not America.'

There was a smattering of laughter again, and his tongue wasn't even bleeding.

'Answer the question,' someone shouted from the back.

'No,' he responded.

'No what? No, you're not looking for a serial killer? Or no, you're not keeping the truth from us? Or, no you're not answering the question?'

'Yes.' Even as he said it, Parish was admiring how slippery he had become.

The reporter from the Redbridge Times squinted at him through her designer glasses as she stood up. 'Emma Potter, Inspector.'

Looking her up and down like a client in a lap dancing club he smiled and said, 'Yes, Miss Potter, I remember you?'

She blushed. 'Can you tell us why you have obtained a warrant to search Beech Tree Orphanage?'

People swivelled left and right to find someone who might know something about the orphanage, but apart from Emma Potter nobody appeared to.

How the hell did they find out these things? He was just glad they didn't know about the marlinspike and the tokens. He knew he didn't have long before they found out he'd been keeping the truth from them. Then he'd be front-page news with a stake through his heart.

'Because the people who own it wouldn't let us in. Now unfortunately, that's all the questions I have time for, but thank you all for coming.' He stood up to a hail of shouted questions and walked into the corridor where Richards was waiting for him with a mug of steaming coffee.

'I thought you might need this, Sir.'

'Four…?'

'Yes, four sugars, Sir.'

'Thanks, Richards, you're a lifesaver. Did you…?'

'Yes, Sir, the warrant is in my bag.'

'Good. We'll go…'

'…and see the Chief now, Sir?'

'Yes, Richards, and stop finishing my sentences. It's getting like…'

'…we're married, Sir?'

'God forbid. And talking of marriage, did you know that Toadstone is madly in love with you?'

'You're kidding?'

'He asked me to whisper sweet nothings in your ear about him.'

'He's ugly, Sir.'

'Well, I did mutter something about Beauty and the Beast.'

'I hope I was Beauty?'

'I was hardly going to say Toadstone was beautiful was I, Richards? So, I'll leave you to tell him yes or no.'

'Thanks, Sir.'

'You're welcome. Did Mrs Taylor turn up?'

'Yes, Sir.'

'What did she say?'

'She knew that her husband had worked at the Council as a Rent Advisor, but it was before they met. He never spoke to her about his time there.'

'Had she heard of Beech Tree Orphanage?'

'No, Sir.'

'Not much help then?'

'No help at all, Sir. What did CI Naylor say?'

'He thinks we're doing a fantastic job, but he asked that you refrain from waving at the cameras again. He thinks you're far too beautiful to be grabbing all the media attention.'

'Did he really say that, Sir?'

'What do you think, Richards?'

***

Tim ELLIS

Chief Day looked a lot better. He was wrapped in a hospital blanket and sat in a high-backed chair positioned by the side of his bed. The tube disappearing up his nose had been removed, but the one in the back of his hand continued to dribble liquid into his emaciated body.

It was ten to ten. Parish didn't have long before he and Richards had to make their way to Beech Tree Orphanage for the grand opening at eleven o'clock.

'How are you feeling, Chief?' Richards asked.

'Much better for seeing your smile, Richards.'

'I'm glad, Sir.'

'You're still on the case than, Parish?'

'Just, Sir, thanks to you. Chief Naylor is Lucifer in disguise.'

'He isn't that bad.'

'He's worse, Chief. I wouldn't speak to a dog the way he speaks to me.'

'Yes, he does have a way with words, doesn't he?'

'That's putting it mildly. Anyway, enough about the replacement from hell, what have the doctors said? And don't fob us off with any lies, Chief.' Over the course of the week, he and Richards appeared to have become Walter Day's surrogate family.

'I had a CT scan yesterday. The cancer hasn't spread to the bones or lymph nodes.'

'That's good, isn't it?' Parish asked.

'Very good. It means I have a chance of getting through this in one piece.'

Richards sat on the arms of his chair, put an arm around his shoulders, and began to cry. 'I'm very happy for you, Chief.'

'Thanks, Richards, but you don't need to cry. We're past the crying stage, we're at the praying stage now.'

240

'I say a prayer for you every night, Chief,' Richards said wiping her eyes with a paper tissue the Chief had given her.

'Do they know if the treatment is working yet, Chief?' Parish said.

'They won't know for another month whether they've caught it early enough. In the meantime, whilst I'm having the treatment, I feel as though I'm descending through Dante's nine levels of hell. I'm in limbo at the moment.'

Richards hugged his face to her breasts.

'I'm beginning to feel better already, Richards,' he said, 'but I think I just plummeted into the second circle.'

'Which one's that, Sir?'

'You don't want to know, Richards.'

'Do you need anything, Sir?'

'I've heard marijuana is good for prostate cancer, Parish.'

'I'll see what I can do, Sir, Vice owe me one.'

'How's the case going? Any nearer a solution?'

'I hope we're going to get some answers when someone from Rushdon Property Management lets us into the orphanage this morning,'

'You've said for a while that the orphanage is the key to solving the case, Parish. I hope you're right.'

'So do I, Sir.'

The Chief sucked orange juice through a straw. 'I saw you on the news last night, Richards,' he said. 'Nice wave.'

'Thank you, Sir. You didn't think it was too pretentious did you?'

'No. The news is always so miserable. I'm sure it made people smile, and that's a good thing.'

'Don't encourage her, Sir. Right, Richards, say goodbye to the Chief and lets get going.'

241

She leaned over and kissed the Chief on the cheek. 'Goodbye, Chief.'

'Goodbye, Richards.'

***

Parish directed Richards to drive up Vicarage Lane and turn into the disused main entrance to reach Beech Tree Orphanage at five to eleven. A tall spotty office boy, wearing a grey suit like a coathanger, waited for them outside the overgrown entrance.

Suddenly, Parish didn't feel very optimistic. 'I hope you've got the keys to open this place up?' he said to the boy as he stepped out of the Mondeo.

'No, Sir,' the young man shouted as if he were an American Marine, and thrust a folded piece of paper towards Parish.

'What's this?' Parish said taking the paper.

'An injunction, Sir.'

'Issued on what basis?'

'Evidentiary burden of proof.'

The office boy walked to an Audi TT, did a handbrake spin on the icy road, and zoomed away.

'What does it all mean, Sir?' Richards asked.

'Rushdon Property Management have persuaded the old fogies in the High Court that we have no evidence to make them open up the orphanage, and what's so annoying is that they're right.'

'But why would they prevent us from seeing inside?'

'That's a very good question, Richards.'

'A better one, is what are we going to do now, Sir?'

'Well, what we're not going to do is take this lying down, Richards. There are answers waiting for us in there, and we need to get in. Let's go back to the station. Along the way we'll drop into the CPS offices and find out what went wrong with the warrant, and what we need to do to fix it. Then, out of interest we'll go and see who or what runs Rushdon Property Management…'

'What do you mean, "What?" Sir.'

'I have an idea that Satan runs Rushdon Property Management, Richards, and the orphanage is the gateway to hell that he's guarding.'

'And you think I watch too much television, Sir?'

'…and then we'll go and get some lunch.'

'Is it my fault, Sir? I made a mistake with the warrant, didn't I?'

'No, Richards, its not your fault.'

'Are you sure? I won't mind if you tell me what I did wrong?'

'When you requested the warrant, we expected to gain access. What we didn't expect was that they would go to the High Court for an injunction to stop us. We might need to provide more compelling evidence to support our request for the orphanage to be opened.'

'Have we got more compelling evidence, Sir?'

'That's why we're going to the CPS, Richards.'

'We've got Mr Pearson now, Sir. If he was the Manager, he might have some compelling evidence at his house.'

'Yes, he might, we need to go there as well.' Parish opened the door of the Mondeo, looked up at the twelve-foot high fence wreathed in thorns and snow and said, 'One way or another we'll get into that orphanage even if it is the gateway to Hades and Cerberus is waiting for us on the other side.'

'Do you think there really was a three-headed dog, Sir?'

'Why not, Richards, why not?'

***

Tim ELLIS

The Crown Prosecution Service offices were situated on Orange Tree Hill in Havering-atte-Bower overlooking Kiln Wood. They arrived at eleven-forty just as Ms Juliette Langley LLB returned from the courts in Redbridge.

In her early thirties, Juliette Langley had long unruly brown hair that looked as though she had tied it up with parcel string in exasperation. Parish wondered how she made the obligatory wig look presentable in court.

They were shown into Ms Langley's office. Parish accepted a coffee whilst Richards sipped iced water.

'You want to know how we're going to overturn the High Court injunction,' Ms Langley asked. 'Am I right?'

'You're right,' Parish said.

'They have argued successfully that you have insufficient evidence as justification to search Beech Tree Orphanage, so you need to find the evidence to overturn the High Court decision. Have you got more evidence?'

Parish emptied his cup and poured himself another coffee from the pot on the table in front of them. 'What did we put on the warrant as justification for the search in the first place?' he asked.

Ms Langley went to her desk and found the warrant. 'Yes, here it is. All you had was that someone – a Mrs Beth Masters – saw something similar to the tokens, that are being left on the victims, in the Manager's office of the orphanage twenty-four years ago – a bit tenuous to say the least.'

'What more do we need, your honour?' Richards said.

Juliette Langley laughed like a hyena. 'I'm not an old fossil like those Judges in the High Court, Constable. Ms Langley will do just fine.'

'Sorry, your… Ms Langley.'

'You need more evidence linking Beech Tree Orphanage to the murders.'

Parish began to think that he was never going to get into the orphanage, or solve the murders. 'The last Manager of the orphanage was murdered yesterday, will that do?' he said.

'The fact that he was the Manager of the orphanage twenty-four years ago is hardly evidence linking the murders with the orphanage. Talk me through the murders. Let's see what we can come up with.'

'Go on, Richards,' Parish said. 'You like talking.'

Richards blushed. 'Are you sure, Sir? I might forget something.'

'That's why I'll be listening.'

'Okay. The first murder was Gregory Taylor. He was a teacher at Chigwell Secondary School, but we found out that he also worked at Redbridge Council between 1982 and 1986.'

'Is there a link to Beech Tree Orphanage?' Ms Langley asked.

'Only the token put in his mouth.'

'Lets forget about the tokens for the moment, shall we?'

'Next, there was Diane Flint. She was the Director of Social Services at Redbridge Council, and she also worked there as a Social Worker at the same time as Mr Taylor.'

'You'd have more chance of getting a warrant to search the Council offices than the orphanage,' Langley said. 'Did the Council control Beech Tree Orphanage before it was closed?'

Parish interrupted. 'Yes, but they didn't just close it, they sold it to Rushdon Property Management, and they closed and sealed it up in 1986.'

245

'A strange sequence of events,' Langley said. 'And apart from the Manager being murdered, none of the other victims are linked to the orphanage?'

'I haven't finished yet, Ms Langley,' Richards said.

'Oh sorry, please carry on, Constable.'

'Brian Ridpath was murdered next, and we thought he was a school caretaker, but we found a letter in his flat from someone at the Council asking him to remove his effects from a locker in the Caretaker's Lodge at Beech Tree Orphanage.'

'Hardly evidence that would stand up to judicial scrutiny,' Langley said.

'Then Mr Colin Jackson was murdered, and we don't know anything about him because Colin Jackson is not his real name. We're waiting to see who his fingerprints belong to.'

'Nothing there then,' Langley said.

'Oh, let's not forget Martin Squires who killed himself and destroyed all the Council's financial records held on computer, including the backups.'

'Why did he do that?'

'Because Mr Ridpath was being paid £2,000 on the first of every month by the Council, and we wanted to know why. Ridpath was only a Caretaker, after all.'

'And as a result of that, you seized the Council's paper-based financial records and forensic accountants are examining them now?'

'Yes.'

'You have no suspects?'

Richards looked at Parish who merely shrugged. 'No.'

'So all you really have that points you in the direction of Beech Tree Orphanage are possibly the tokens, and possibly two victims that used to work there twenty-four years ago? Getting an injunction was a no-brainer. Anything else I can do for you, Inspector?'

'But...' Richards looked at Parish again. 'Can't you do something, Sir?'

'Like what, Richards? Ms Langley is quite correct. We need considerably more evidence than we've got. We were trying to take a short cut, but let that be a lesson to you, there are no short cuts in police work.' Parish stood up and proffered his hand. 'Thanks for seeing us, Ms Langley,' he said. He thought she might have asked him to call her Juliette, but she didn't. 'Come on, Richards, time to get our hands dirty.'

Outside the CPS offices Parish rang Toadstone. The time was twelve twenty and it had just started snowing again.

'Is that you Toadstone?'

'Yes. Hello, Inspector, what…'

'Listen, Toadstone, do you work in forensics?'

'Well… yes, but…'

'And what's your job in forensics, Toadstone?'

'I…'

'Isn't it to collect and analyse things, and then provide the detectives with evidence that will stand up in court?'

'Some…'

'What I'd like to know, Toadstone, is why I have no evidence linking the murders to Beech Tree Orphanage, and what you're going to do about it?'

'Me…?'

'Yes you, Toadstone. Have you been to Graham Pearson's house yet?'

'No, but…'

'Richards and I will meet you there at two o'clock. Is that all right with you, Toadstone?'

'Yes…'

'Good. I'm also going to interrogate you about this lack of evidence, Toadstone, so make sure you're able to tell me why you've been firing blanks since we began this case.'

Parish disconnected the call.

'You weren't very nice, Sir,' Richards said.

'There you go with that *nice* word again, Richards. When CI Naylor hauls me in and asks in similar words, "Why haven't you solved the case yet, Parish?" Do you think he'll consider how *nice* I was? Do you think he'll grade me along a number of continua such as, ability to solve cases – zero, ability to find evidence – zero, ability to ferret out suspects – zero, ability to be *nice* – ten. And then he'll say in similar words, "Oh you're such a *nice* person, Parish. Everybody says so, especially those who work for you. Toadstone, the man in forensics who has found no evidence at all, particularly thinks you're a really *nice* person. As a detective you're completely useless so I'm only going to give you easy cases from now on, but well done for being such a *nice* person."'

'Now you're not being nice to me, Sir.'

'Get in the car, Richards, and drive to Chigwell. For the rest of the day you're banned from using the word *nice*.'

'I'm not going to speak to you at all, Sir.'

'Don't make rash promises you can't keep, Richards.'

'I…'

'See.'

'Huh.'

Parish opened up the injunction and said, 'Rushdon Property Management are located on Station Road, opposite Chigwell tube station.'

Richard's lips were screwed up tight. She didn't look at Parish, but focused on her driving.

He sat back and closed his eyes. Who was this Peter Rushdon? Why did he buy the orphanage and then shut it down? Why did he surround it with a twelve-foot high fence, and plant thorns all around it? Why didn't he demolish the orphanage and build houses on the land? Why was the orphanage so different from all of his other building projects? Why force them to get a warrant, and then block it with an injunction? What was behind that fence that Peter Rushdon didn't want him to see?

Questions, so many damned questions! He knew he shouldn't really go and harass the people at Rushdon

Property Management. They were only following the instructions of Peter Rushdon, but he was curious about who they were. In the ten years he had been at Hoddesdon he had never heard of Rushdon Property Management, had never seen any signs, or building projects, or reports. What did they do? Why did they need premises in Chigwell?

He'd get Richards to drive past slowly, peer in through the window. Maybe stop, get out, and look at the houses for sale or the advert for their services. Under no circumstances would they go in. The office boy with the Audi TT would recognise him, call the police, and he'd get taken to court for harassment. No, they wouldn't go in.

Richards nudged him.

He opened his eyes as she pulled in opposite Chigwell tube station.

'Drive past slowly, Richards, lets see what the premises are like.'

To the annoyance of other drivers Richards crawled past the building, but Parish saw no sign up for Rushdon Property Management.

After completing a triangle involving Hainult Road, High Road and Station Road, Richards returned to where she'd started.

'Park the car,' Parish said. 'We'll amble past nonchalantly, and find somewhere to eat lunch.'

Richards did as she was told, but Parish could see she was struggling with her vow of silence.

They walked along Station Road until they reached a doorway, which had an obviously new brass sign with Rushdon Property Management engraved on it screwed on the wall.

Parish peered through the grubby glass, but saw only stairs covered in a worn-out carpet leading upwards. He knew he had to go in. 'We'll have to go in, Richards.'

Richards shook her head violently.

'Stop being childish, Richards. We're grown-up detectives trying to solve a multiple murder case, and you're refusing not to talk to your partner. How ridiculous does that sound?'

'All right, Sir.'

Parish laughed. 'I knew you wouldn't be able to keep it up, Richards.'

'I'm going to tell my mum what you're really like, Sir,' Richards said jutting out her bottom lip like a petulant child.

Parish mimicked her then pushed her through the door. 'Get your backside up those stairs and stop being a spoilt brat.'

'You… You…'

'Some kinda wonderful?' Parish suggested.

'…horrible person.'

They reached a small landing with a door.

'Open it then,' Parish said.

'Are you sure you want to do this, Sir?'

'I'm sure, Richards. We need to look the enemy in the eyes.' He wasn't sure at all. In fact, he knew it was going to end in disaster, but he was here now and he had to take a look inside.

Richards opened the door slightly and peered through the crack. Then she opened it fully and stepped inside.

Parish followed her.

They were stood in an empty room. The floorboards creaked beneath their feet. There were no people, no furniture, and no Rushdon Property Management.

'Why is there no one here, Sir?'

'I expect they needed an address for the injunction, this is it.'

'But who was that skinny man that gave us the injunction?'

'I assumed he worked for Rushdon, but now I think of it he probably worked for Rushdon's solicitors.'

'So Rushdon Property Management is just a telephone number?'

'So it would seem, Richards. We'll…'

'…find out who the number belongs to?'

'Ring your boyfriend, ask him to do the honours.'

'Stop being mean, Sir. You know he's not my boyfriend. Can't you do it?'

'Haven't you spoken to him yet?'

'I haven't had chance, Sir.'

'Now would be a good time then.'

Richards clucked and pressed Toadstone's number in her contact list.

Parish could only hear Richards' side of the conversation, and she kept it short and to the point.

'You didn't tell him he's too ugly for you then?'

'I thought I'd better not, Sir. Maybe I'll tell him when the case is over. If he thinks I don't like him, he might not be as quick analysing things as he would if he thought I did like him.'

'And you talk about me being mean, Richards? Let's go to lunch, you're paying.'

'Me, Sir?'

'Your reward for re-establishing communications.'

'Reward?'

'You're getting the hang of it, Richards. All this tutoring makes me hungry.'

'Tutoring?'

'Stop pretending to be a parrot, Richards.'

In the *Subway* café, Parish ordered two bacon toasties with brown sauce and a large coffee with four sugars. Richards had a bottle of water and turned away saying, 'I can't watch, Sir.'

'You don't know what you're missing, Richards,' Parish said wiping the grease running down his chin with a paper napkin. A bacon toastie is akin to nectar from the Gods.'

'Sulphur from Satan, more like.'

'Right, enough about my eating habits. Where are we, and don't say the *Subway* café in Chigwell?'

The café was busy. They'd had to fight for a table with two chairs. People were queuing at the counter for takeaways, and the door kept opening letting in the cold. They both kept their coats on, and tried to ignore the noise from the other customers.

'We're no further forwards than we were this morning are we, Sir? In fact, we've wasted a whole morning chasing shadows.'

'Not necessarily. 'We know that we need a lot more evidence to link the murders to Beech Tree Orphanage if we want to get in there. We also know that Rushdon Property Management doesn't really exist, its probably a telephone number going back to Peter Rushdon himself. I'd like to talk to him face-to-face, I know that.'

'You'd have to go to America, Sir.'

'That wouldn't be a bad thing, Richards. If the local politicians can swan off on all these conferences and fact-finding missions, I'm sure that I could go to America to question a vital witness.'

'I could come with you, Sir?'

'There's someone else I'd much rather take, Richards.'

'I thought we weren't going to talk about my mum, Sir. And anyway, if you took her it wouldn't be a working trip would it?'

'Who said I was talking about your mum?'

'Sirrr…?'

'We wouldn't be allowed to go to America anyway, Richards so stop going on about it. What loose ends have we still got to tie up?'

She took out her notebook and flipped through the pages until she reached the one she had the information on. 'I made a list last night whilst I was watching Ed Gein on the Crime Channel, Sir.'

'Is he one of the presenters?'

'You're teasing me, Sir. Do you know he made trophies out of skin, such as a belt studded with women's nipples?'

'Do you mind, Richards I'm still eating,' Parish said pushing the last of the bacon toasties in his mouth. 'And what have I said about watching the Crime Channel?'

'I like to watch it, Sir.'

'We all have our vices I suppose, Richards. I have bacon toasties and you have the Crime Channel.'

'At the top of my list is Colin Jackson's fingerprints.'

Parish pulled out his phone and found the Mortuary in his contact list.

'Michelin?'

'Hello, Doc.'

'Parish! You don't love me anymore. You don't ring me. You never visit. Is it something I said?'

'You're not my type, Doc.'

'I'm heartbroken. What can I do for you?'

'Fingerprints?'

'I want a large chocolate donut next time you're visiting, Parish.'

'You've got news?'

'Big news, came back half-an-hour ago. Colin Jackson was really Evan Hughes.'

'Not someone I know personally, Doc.'

'He got ten years in the Scrubs for kidnapping and sexually abusing a boy of eight.'

'The pieces are beginning to fall into place, Doc.'

'I thought you might be pleased, Parish. He was released in 2000 and promptly disappeared.'

'Now we know how. I'll drop by later with a box full of chocolate donuts, Doc, thanks.'

'It's my mission in life to make your life easier, Parish.'

'What did he say, Sir?' Richards asked when Parish had disconnected the call.

'Colin Jackson was a man called Evan Hughes who got ten years in the Scrubs for kidnapping and sexually abusing an eight year-old boy.'

Richards' mouth dropped open like a drawbridge. Parish was sure he could hear the cogs whirring, chains crunching, and blocks shunting into place.

'Beech Tree Orphanage! Crap… oops sorry, Sir. It's all beginning to make sense isn't it?'

'So it would seem, Richards. I think we have our breakthrough.'

'Its still not enough to get us into Beech Tree Orphanage though, is it, Sir?'

Parish shook his head. 'No, Richards. Even if we find out that Evan Hughes worked at the orphanage before it shut down, there's still no evidence that what's happening now is related to then. What's next on your list?'

'Graham Pearson's house, which we're going to see soon so I can tick that one off.' She made a tick in her notebook.

'Very efficient.'

'Its important to be organised, Sir.'

'Keep going?'

'Did you know that only Mr Taylor was married?'

'Meaning?'

'I was just saying. It seems odd that most of the victims lived alone. They had no partners, no relations, and no next of kin.'

'There are lots of us that have no next of kin...'

'Ah, don't you have anyone, Sir?'

'We're not talking about me, Richards.'

'I'm sure my mum would be happy to be your next of kin if you asked her, Sir.'

'Carry on with the list, Richards, and stop rummaging around in my private life.'

Richards' mobile vibrated on the table. She picked it up. 'Hello, Paul.'

Parish mouthed, 'Paul' and smiled.

She listened then disconnected the call.

'Paul says that Rushdon Property Management's telephone number is untraceable. He said to tell you it's routed through China.'

'Another dead end then.'

'What did he mean, it's routed through China, Sir?'

'He was speaking in code, Richards so that you wouldn't know what he was referring to. In view of that, I'm not likely to tell you am I?'

'I'll find out, Sir.'

'Good luck with that, Richards. What else have you got on your list?'

'Martin Squires' cottage.'

'Okay, here's what we'll do. After we've ransacked Graham Pearson's house we'll go straight to Martin Squires cottage in Abridge, and your boyfriend can follow us.'

'I'm not speaking to you again, Sir.'

'I'll look forward to that, Richards.'

***

Richards parked the Mondeo outside 267 Forest Lane in Chigwell. The unmarked forensics van had arrived before them. It hadn't snowed all day, but now the heavens opened up.

'It could have waited until we'd got into the house, Sir.'

'I thought you weren't talking to me, Richards?'

'I'm not, Sir.'

Snow swirled about them as they slithered down the drive and through the open front door. They found Toadstone in the kitchen.

'How's it going, Toadstone?' Parish said.

'Nothing of interest up to now, Inspector but…'

'I like buts…'

'Mr Pearson has a key on his key ring that opens a safe-deposit box.'

'Oh?'

Toadstone pulled the keys out of his pocket and juggled the safe deposit key off the key ring. 'You'll need a warrant to gain access to it,' he said as he passed it to Parish.

'Richards, ring the CPS.'

'Which bank, Sir?'

Parish raised his eyebrows at Toadstone.

'The Bank of Croatia on the High Street in Redbridge.'

'Have they got a bank, Toadstone?'

'Just a small one, Sir.'

'I hope they're not covered by diplomatic immunity, or anything ridiculous like that?'

Toadstone shrugged.

Tim ELLIS

Whilst Richards rang the CPS and Toadstone continued his search, Parish had a walk around the house. The kitchen was quite spacious, and through the window he could see the golf course beyond the long snow-covered back garden. He walked into the hall where a set of golf clubs sat in a trolley. Upstairs, there were four bedrooms, but it appeared that only the master bedroom had been in use. The three other bedrooms were used as storage rooms. Parish remembered what Beth Masters had said about Pearson being smelly. A pungent odour invaded his nostrils in the main bedroom. The quilt had been thrown back on the double bed, and the bottom sheet was filthy. On the bedside cabinet was what appeared to be a stack of pornographic photographs. He pulled out his latex gloves, put them on and picked up the photographs. After looking at the first three he put them down disgusted and horrified. They were photographs of young boys in various states of undress.

Is that what this case is about – young boys? A lot of the clues seem to point towards that conclusion. Gregory Taylor worked at a school, Diane Flint worked with children, Evan Hughes kidnapped and sexually abused an eight-year-old boy, and now Graham Pearson who was the Manager of Beech Tree Orphanage with pornographic photographs of young boys. Where does the killer fit into all of this? Is he a victim? A victim's relative? Did something happen at Beech Tree Orphanage? Were all the victims involved in something between 1982 and 1986? How does Diane Flint fit into that scenario?

He knew they were close to the pot of gold, but a lot of it was guesswork without any substance. He needed evidence to get into that damned orphanage.

'Tomorrow afternoon, Sir,' Richards said standing in the bedroom doorway.

'Is that the best they can do?'

'Ms Langley is in court all morning. She wants to see you at one-thirty to make sure you've got sufficient justification to open someone's safe-deposit box.'

'Didn't you…?'

'I told her everything, Sir, but she insisted.'

'Okay, good job, Richards.' He pointed at the photographs on the bedside cabinet and said, 'Put your gloves on and tell me what you think of those?'

She did as she was told, then turned and stared at him. 'They're all paedophiles aren't they, Sir?'

'At the moment, we only have evidence that Hughes and Pearson were paedophiles. Taylor was married, although that doesn't preclude him from being one, and where does Diane Flint fit into your theory?'

They both stared out of the bedroom window at the swirling snow. Everywhere was draped in a mantle of white.

'Couldn't she have been a paedophile as well?'

'It's possible, Twenty percent of paedophiles are women, but I think it's unlikely in this case.'

'Then I don't know, Sir.'

'What about Ridpath and Squires?'

'I bet they both were.'

'That's hardly objective evidence is it, Richards?'

'Shouldn't you tell Vice, Sir?'

'What, and have them come in at the eleventh hour and solve the case when we've done all the hard work? They'll take all the credit and we'll be left out in the cold. No, I don't think so, Richards, this is our case and we'll solve it. We're nearly there, we just need a break.'

'Won't you get into trouble, Sir?'

'I…'

His mobile activated.

'That could be our break, Sir,' Richards suggested optimistically.

The screen displayed 'Unknown Caller'.

'Parish?'

'This is Peter Rushdon, Inspector.' The voice sounded as though it was oozing through a crack in an ancient tomb. 'I'm somewhere over the Atlantic at the moment, but I hope to arrive at Heathrow sometime tonight. I've returned to give you the guided tour of Hell, or what we both know as Beech Tree Orphanage. Meet me there at four o'clock tomorrow afternoon, I'll be the one in the wheelchair wearing an oxygen mask. I also suggest you have a light lunch.'

He was about to say something like, 'Why now?' or 'How did you get my mobile number?' but the line went dead.

'Who was it, Sir? You look as though you've been listening to a ghost.'

'Maybe I have, Richards. That was Peter Rushdon. He wants to meet us at the orphanage at four o'clock tomorrow afternoon.'

'But…?'

'I don't know, Richards.'

'It'll be dark and scary at that time, Sir. Why couldn't he meet us in the morning?'

'We're detectives, Richards, not frightened little children. We'll take torches with us.'

'If you say so, Sir. Did he tell…?'

'He didn't say anything other than what I've told you, Richards.'

'Okay, Sir. I was only asking. Have we finished here?'

Parish walked out of the bedroom and down the stairs. In the living room he found a computer, scanner and photographic printer. He went back into the hall, and then into the dining room where Toadstone was rifling through an expensive antique sideboard.

'Make sure you take the computer equipment, Toadstone,' he said. 'Upstairs, on the bedside table in the main bedroom, there are a heap of pornographic pictures of children.'

'Have you called in Vice yet, Sir?'

'No, Toadstone, and I'd be grateful if you didn't say anything to them either. I'll have this case nailed down by the weekend.'

'Fine by me, Sir.'

'Thanks. Have you found anything?'

He turned and opened a lever arch file sitting on the Queen Anne dining table. 'Bank statements. Mr Pearson also received a substantial monthly payment from Redbridge Council - £5,000.'

'Bloody hell, £60,000 a year!' Parish said. 'No wonder there are so many potholes in the roads, Toadstone. Still nothing relating to Beech Tree Orphanage?'

'Nothing yet.'

'Good work anyway, Toadstone. We're going to Martin Squires' house in Abridge, can you bring your team there when you've finished here?'

'It'll be a while, but we'll be there.'

'If you've not arrived by the time we're ready to leave, I'll put the key under the mat.'

'Okay, Sir.'

Parish and Richards headed towards the door, but Toadstone cleared his throat and said, 'Mary, can I have a word?'

'I'll be outside, Richards,' Parish said.

TWENTY-THREE

Lance Hobart had just woken up from his afternoon nap when the doorbell rang. Coco, his black and white Shitzu, began wagging her tail. Although Coco was a dog she had an uncanny knack of telling the time, and three-thirty was usually the time Lance took her for a walk.

He pushed himself out of the armchair and headed towards the door. Yapping with excitement, Coco followed him. Lance Hobart had been retired ever since he'd collapsed outside the newsagents three years go. A kind Samaritan had called 999 and the paramedics arrived within minutes. They gave him a clot-busting drug before rushing him to the Accident & Emergency at King George Hospital with the siren clanging in his ears. The doctors had told him he was lucky to be alive because they'd had to shock him back to life with the defibrillator three times. That night, a team of cardiologists had carried out an angioplasty and inserted bare-metal stents into his narrowed coronary arteries. Now, he liked to think of himself as bionic, but he had to take five lots of drugs so that he didn't have another heart attack. Trouble was, the drugs sent him to sleep in the middle of the day, and if he didn't go to bed before ten o'clock at night he turned into a pumpkin.

Nursing had been his life until 1981. He had applied to run the medical centre at Beech Tree Orphanage where he would be his own boss. Yes, the doctors would pop in every now and again, but the medical centre belonged to him. He was responsible for all aspects of its operation. It was the job of a lifetime. The pay was good, and he had his own flat next to the medical centre.

If he was asked he couldn't say exactly when things had changed, but it was certainly during the first three months that he realised he was enjoying his job more than he should be. Then the Manager, smelly Graham Pearson, had asked him if he wanted to join the exclusive club. At first he wasn't sure, but that night he had been given a taster, and he knew there was no going back. He was disgusted with himself, but knew he could never stop.

A thin man dressed in black stood at the door. It took him slightly longer than it would have done had he not been taking the drugs, but eventually he recognised the visitor and knew that his life was over. He didn't try to avoid the strange-looking weapon as it came towards him. If the truth were known, he had been expecting this visit. He didn't normally watch the news, but he had caught the tail end of a report on Redbridge Council and heard the names: Diane Flint, Martin Squires, and Graham Pearson. He had no idea why Diane Flint was murdered, but the other two had been in the club. Then he had looked at the back-issues of the free newspapers he kept in the house for Coco's little accidents and found the names of Greg Taylor, Brian Ridpath, and someone called Colin Jackson, which he suspected was that arsehole Evan Hughes.

His heart exploded, and as he crumpled to the floor he thought that the pain was a lot worse than when he'd had his heart attack. He wondered why the bare-metal stents hadn't saved him, wasn't he meant to be bionic?

Coco barked at Terry Reynolds as he leaned over Lance Hobart and slipped token number 55 into his mouth. 'For Jed Parish' he said, and closed the door of 12 Ingleby Mansions in Chigwell Row.

***

Terry Reynolds expected to be arrested as soon as he saw Jed Parish at the Council offices. He was surprised when

Jed didn't even recognise him. Admittedly, Jed was the youngest of them all, but they had been friends. Terry had tried to protect him, but he was only nine and couldn't protect himself. He guessed that Jed had somehow been able to blot it all out, forget about everything that had happened to them. Terry wished he had been able to do that. Instead, his life had been destroyed by the demons at Beech Tree Orphanage.

He knocked on Mr Hobart's front door. Heard the dog barking. As soon as the door opened he saw recognition and resignation in Hobart's face.

'Time to die, Mr Hobart,' he said as he pushed the marlinspike through the old man's shirt and into his heart.

Once he had slipped the token into Hobart's mouth, he closed the door and made his way down the stairs and out into the street.

He could nearly reach up and touch the heavy black clouds, but he knew that if he did a ton of snow would fall out of the tear. He liked this weather, there was a hopelessness about it. For a man without a future, this weather was just perfect.

Terry Reynolds caught the bus back to Redbridge, back to his flat where he put a heavy black cross through Lance Hobart's picture.

There was only one token left, only one more on his 'To Kill List'. How ironic that it was Jed Parish's job to catch him. Maybe Jed had recognised him at the Council offices, but chose not to arrest him. Maybe they were partners again, still fighting the demons of Beech Tree Orphanage.

***

Richards drove into the *cul de sac* and parked outside 5 Willow Close in Abridge. Mrs Wilson had been right, Martin Squires' thatched cottage was beautiful.

Parish crunched through the untouched snow, which lay on the path leading up to the front door. He found the key in his pocket, opened the door and went in. He expected the house to be cold, but it was warm. He saw the thermostat on the wall outside the kitchen, which was set at twenty-five degrees and could hear the boiler working. He looked at his watch. It was five-twenty. He expected that the boiler was on a timer and had activated between four and five.

They switched all the main lights on. Parish went upstairs, whilst Richards stayed downstairs.

There were three bedrooms and a bathroom. The master bedroom was *en suite*. He assumed that the rooms would have beams and slanted walls, but there were no beams and the ceiling and walls were all right-angled and squared up.

He also expected to find paedophile memorabilia littering the master bedroom, but again he was disappointed. Upstairs, at least, gave him the impression of a house owned by a conservative middle-aged man. The only evident perversion was a liking for John Grisham novels and blue ties.

Richards started to ascend the stairs as he was descending.

'Oh, you've finished up there, Sir?'

'No, I'm coming down because I'm feeling lonely. Of course I've finished. What about you?'

'I was feeling lonely as well, Sir.'

'So you found nothing?'

'No, Sir?'

They sat down together on the fourth stair.

'Isn't there a computer down here?'

'Not that I could find.'

'For an accountant, that's odd.'

'He might have been someone who left his work at work.'

'Mmmm,' Parish murmured. 'Okay, let's go back to the station. I've still got a report to write for the Chief Constable.'

'And my mum's coming…'

'What have I said about your mum, Richards?'

'I was only reminding you.'

'It's off limits.' He headed outside. At the bottom of the steps he turned and said, 'Put the key under…'

'…the mat, Sir?'

'Did you find a cellar door during your search of downstairs, Richards?'

'No.'

Parish signalled her to come down the steps, then he pointed to a thin slit of a window just above ground level with wire mesh welded over the glass. He squatted and tried to see inside, but it was too dark. 'Let's go back inside and find the entrance to the cellar.'

They started in the hall, then moved to the kitchen, the pantry, the dining room and the living room, but found no door.

'Are you sure there's a cellar, Sir? The window could be a vent or something like that.'

'I know the difference between a vent and a window, Richards. Let's start in the hall again.'

Parish was on his hands and knees examining the floor, whilst Richards strained her neck to inspect the ceiling. When they were in the kitchen, Parish found something in the pantry.

'This pantry is too small, Richards.'

'Are you thinking of buying the house, Sir?'

'Look inside at the depth, and then outside.'

She did as she was instructed. 'I see what you mean. It's got a false back, hasn't it?'

'It certainly has.' Parish began touching, pulling, pushing… until he twisted what looked like a large pepper mill and heard a click. The back of the pantry opened. Shelves, tins of beans and all, swung towards him. He opened the door fully to reveal a set of stairs disappearing into the darkness. His heart began to race uncontrollably. Without a light he knew he could never go down there, and looked around for a switch. He found one on the wall to the left of the stairs and flicked it.

He stepped out of the pantry. 'You go first, Richards.'

'Me, Sir?'

'There's nobody down there. It's just that I'm not very good with tunnels and cellars. I'll be right behind you.'

'Okay, if you say so, Sir.'

She began walking down the stairs. Parish followed her.

The cellar consisted of one large room with a cornucopia of the latest computer equipment. One wall had shelves from floor to ceiling stuffed with books, magazines and stacks of DVDs. There was an alcove that looked like a photographic studio with lights on stands, a muted abstract backdrop on the wall, and a Leica digital camera on a tripod. Against the other wall was a single bed. A Sanyo video camera sat on another tripod positioned so that it overlooked the bed.

'The bastard brought children down here, Richards.'

'They're all dirty scumbags, Sir.' She picked up a magazine off one of the shelves. 'It's full of children, Sir. By the writing, I'd say it comes from Eastern Europe. We're not going to look through all of this are we, Sir?'

His face was set hard. 'This place is a paedophile's haven. Let's leave it to Toadstone, he's used to sifting through filth.'

'Its definite now isn't it, Sir? We're dealing with a bunch of paedophiles aren't we?'

'Yes, I would say so, Richards, but we've known that for awhile haven't we?'

'Yes, Sir. Do you think that all the victims were involved in abusing the children in the orphanage, and the killer was one of those children, Sir?'

'That's a good working theory, Richards. We're still nowhere near identifying a suspect though, are we? We have no records of the children who were put in there; no information about the staff who worked there; and no details of what went on in there. We don't even know what the orphanage looks like.'

'We should get some answers tomorrow when we meet Peter Rushdon, shouldn't we, Sir.'

'I doubt he will be able to tell us who the killer is, Richards. I'm beginning to think we'll never find him.'

'It's not like you to give up, Sir.'

'I'm not giving up, Richards, I'm simply voicing my thoughts out loud. That's why you're here, to give me feedback. Let's go,' he said pushing her towards the stairs. 'I don't like cellars, they give me the heebie-jeebies.'

Richards squealed as she stepped out of the pantry. Toadstone was stood in the shadows of the kitchen like the Grim Reaper waiting for her.

'Sorry, Mary, I didn't mean to scare you.'

'Well you did, you idiot,' she said walking towards the front door.

'That's no way to win the fair lady's heart, Toadstone.'

'I didn't do it on purpose. You'll tell her that won't you, Sir?'

'I'll tell her, but every time she sees you now she'll be reminded of how you made her heart flutter, and not in a good way either.'

Toadstone's shoulders slumped. 'Oh well, as you said, Sir, she's probably out of my league.'

'Don't give up so easily, Toadstone.'

'Do you think there's still a chance, Sir?'

'There's always a chance.'

'Okay, thanks, Sir. What's in the pantry besides food?'

'A secret door, stairs, and a cellar. In that cellar is filth of the highest order, which you will have to wade through to provide me with a report. I don't envy you, Toadstone.'

'More shit on children?'

'I'm afraid so.'

'Some of my officers are rooting for the killer, Sir. They think he's doing a good job getting rid of these perverts.'

'Well tell them to stop rooting, Toadstone, and just do the job. As much as we dislike this type of thing, the law is the law. Imagine what type of world we'd be living in if there was no law.'

'I know, Sir. Don't worry, they'll do their job.'

'Good. Richards and I are going back to the station now.'

'I doubt you'll get a report on this before Monday of next week, Sir.'

'There's no rush, Toadstone. Goodnight.'

'Goodnight, Sir, and say goodnight to Mary for me.'

***

Richards was sat in the car with the heater on.

'Toadstone says goodnight, Richards,' Parish said as he climbed in. 'He was ready to give up on you, but I persuaded him that he might still be in with a chance.'

'So let me get this right, Sir. Your relationship with my mum is off limits, but you can meddle in my relationships?'

'That sounds about right, Richards. I didn't realise you were already having a relationship with Toadstone though. Maybe you ought to tell him.'

She put the car in gear, and set off towards the station with a face like a pinched peach.

The digital clock on the dashboard displayed ten past six. He was running out of time again, and was glad that Angie planned to bring some food because he hadn't had time to buy any.

Is that what this case boils down to, he wondered, revenge for being abused? He still had no idea what relevance the marlinspike and the tokens had in the scheme of things. The tokens had obviously been used for something in Beech Tree, but what? Was abuse rife in the orphanage, or was it just the killer who was abused? With so many victims it seems likely there were a number of abusers and a number of children being abused. How were the abusers able to get away with it for so long? There were still so many questions that remained unanswered. Maybe tomorrow he would get some answers. Surely the Chief Constable wouldn't allow him much more time?

Richards pulled into Hoddesdon station car park.

'Pick the car up in the morning, park up and then come into the station. Whilst I'm seeing CI Naylor and doing the press briefing, you can consolidate what we've got and summarise where we are. Construct a list of the things we still haven't got answers for, and so on.'

'Okay, Sir.'

'Is your nose out of joint, Richards?'

'What could possibly have caused that disfigurement, Sir?'

'I'm sure I don't know. Goodnight, Richards.'

'Goodnight, Sir.'

He stamped up the back stairs to get the snow off his shoes. Some of the lights had been switched off to save electricity. He felt like a sightless person and had to adjust his eyes to accommodate for the dimness.

'Parish, as I live and breathe.' Kowalski said popping his head above a partition.

'Hello, Ray, how's it hanging?'

'You didn't bring Richards back then?'

'Gone home, but I heard about you propositioning her when she asked for help on how to do a warrant.'

'It was a joke, Jed.'

'You're gonna get yourself locked up if you're not careful, Ray. In future, I'd appreciate it if you kept your sexist jokes for your wife.'

'Everything's changed, Jed. There was a time when you could have a laugh with stuff like that, but now you have to be whiter than white. I keep wondering where it all went wrong. Maybe I need to get out of this job and find something more suited to my sense of humour.'

'What you need to do, Ray, is treat people as equals. The only legitimate targets we've got now are the criminals.'

'Don't get me started on those bastards, Jed. I used to be able to do some persuasion to get at the truth, but now you can't touch them. They have more rights than the bloody victims. It makes me sick to my stomach when I see them walk out of court because they hired a slick barrister. Sometimes... sometimes, I think I'll buy a sniper's rifle and pop them as they come out of the courthouse. Splatter a 7.62 round into their smirking faces.'

'I think you should go home, Ray, get some rest, take some time off. I've never heard you talk like this, what's happened?'

'The little shit that killed that seven-year-old girl with the car he stole walked free this afternoon. Weeks of work down the drain, and my reputation in the shredder.'

'I'm sorry to hear that, Ray. Still, you need to gain some perspective. Go home and get drunk.'

'Interested in joining me at *Dirty Nelly's*?'

'Sorry, Ray, I'm seeing someone tonight, and I'm already late.'

'I suppose I'll have to go home and talk to the wife then.'

'See you in the morning, Ray.'

'Yeah.'

Parish walked to his desk, but found the computer had been switched off. He didn't have the time to wait for the damned thing to come back to life, so he decided to do his report in the morning.

TWENTY-FOUR

Angie was stood outside his door leaning against the wall when he walked up the stairs to his flat. It had only been four days since Carrie had stood in the same place waiting for him. This woman was different though. She had on an Arctic coat with the hood up that swallowed her whole, a pair of snow boots and jeans. On the floor were two reusable bags full of food. He hugged and kissed her.

After unlocking the door, he picked up the bags. 'We could sleep in your coat tonight.'

'Who said sleeping was on the agenda, Jed Parish?'

'You've come with an agenda? I'd be interested in taking a look at that.'

'I'm sure you would,' she said taking off her coat. 'Go and get showered, I'll make us something to eat.'

'What're we having?'

'I thought chilli con carne with rice.'

'Sounds good. You could sleep here tonight instead of rushing home?'

'Not yet. We need to talk first.'

'Talk? Is that on the agenda tonight?'

'Not tonight, at the weekend.'

He stripped off his clothes in front of her. 'You seem to have everything organised.'

Half way through his shower she joined him. Her hands were instruments of magic, able to turn flaccid flesh into iron.

'I hope you're not ruining the chilli con carne and rice?' he said.

'Do you care?'

'No.'

They washed each other, and he took her from behind.

As he dried her she said, 'I'm turning into an immoral woman, Jed Parish.'

'Do you care?'

'No.'

She'd bought a cheap bottle of Californian white wine to go with the chilli con carne and rice. He wasn't really a wine-drinking type of person, but he drank it anyway.

'When are you back at work?' he asked her.

'Tomorrow night.'

'Oh!'

'I'm on permanent night duty on the Intensive Care Unit. I do a week on, and a week off. It suited me before I met you, Jed Parish, but now my life is a mess.'

'Think of me as your psychotherapist.'

She laughed.

After swirling the food around on her plate she said, 'Are we together now, Jed Parish?'

'Is this the weekend talk that's been rescheduled on the agenda for now?'

'Yes.'

'Cards on the table?'

'All of them, none up the sleeve.'

'Well, Angela Richards, I knew you were the woman for me from that first night in the restaurant, and I hope you feel the same way?'

'I feel the same way.'

'Then we're officially together.'

She walked the short distance that separated them and sat in his lap. She wore one of his shirts. The towel he had wrapped around his waist came undone. They made love there, on the chair, with the smell of chilli con carne in their nostrils and love in their eyes and their hearts.

She stayed the night. He held her in his arms and listened to her soft breathing in the darkness. She had said she wasn't staying, but he began reasoning as people do at one in the morning. He convinced himself that she didn't want to stay before, but now that they'd had their talk she would thank him for not waking her up.

***

Thursday 23rd January

'Jed?'

He sat upright sweat dripping off him.

Angie stared at him, concern on her face. 'What's wrong?'

'Now you know my darkest secret. I have nightmares.'

'What about?'

'Sometimes I'm being dragged down a dark corridor to somewhere terrible, but I always wake up before I get there. That's all I ever remember.'

'Nothing else?'

'No.'

'I know a good therapist.'

He looked at his watch. It was quarter past five. Swinging his legs over the side of the bed he said, 'I don't think so, but thanks anyway.'

'What are you afraid of?'

'The truth, probably.' he said heading for the toilet.

When he came back she said, 'Tell me about your childhood?'

'Oh, so you're the good therapist?'

'I've done a course, but no it's not me. It's a friend, a woman.'

'You're not worried she'll take me away from you?'

Angie laughed. 'When did you start having these delusions that women are attracted to you?'

He put his head in her lap and his feet up the wall. 'What do you think my chances of a full recovery are, Doctor?'

She pulled a face. 'Do you have any other symptoms?'

'At the moment, I've got this erection I can't seem to get rid of.'

'Haven't I treated you for that before, Mr Parish?'

'Yes, Doctor, but it keeps coming back.'

She took hold of him. 'I'd better examine this recurring symptom more closely, Mr Parish.'

'Thank you, Doctor.'

Afterwards, in the shower, they made love again. Parish would have spent the day with her if he could, but he knew it was impossible.

She made him scrambled egg on toast whilst he sent his report to the Chief Constable.

'We still haven't got to the bottom of your nightmares?' she said after they'd eaten. 'What happened in your childhood?'

'I have no memories before being adopted at the age of eight. All I was told was that my parents died in a car crash when I was two. They left me nothing, and I had no near relatives. I went into the care system. From there, a family who wouldn't let me have a puppy adopted me.'

'That sounds terrible.'

'It was. I saw the very puppy I wanted, but they wouldn't let me have it no matter how much I cried and stamped my feet.'

On her way to wash up, she stroked his cheek. 'Poor Jed Parish.'

'It left me damaged.'

'I can see.'

276

He drove her home. As no subterfuge was necessary, he parked directly outside her house. Richards opened the door and waved at him. He ignored her.

***

CI Naylor looked as though he'd been searching through the rubbish in a landfill site. He was unshaven, and his usually slicked-back hair was all over the place. The suit had gone, in its place were a pair of filthy crumpled jeans and a worn out old T-shirt with *Fuck the Police* on the front. He had his dirty trainers on the Chief's desk, and his hands wrapped around a coffee mug.

'You're a fucking bastard, Parish.'

'I'm sorry, Sir, I have no…'

'I don't know what you fucking did, but I know it was you. The Chief Constable says I'm a fucking dinosaur. He's put me on gardening leave before they force me to take early retirement.'

'I…'

'Still haven't fucking learned not to interrupt a senior fucking officer when he's talking down to you. The only one here that's worth anything is Ray Kowalski, the rest of you should have joined a fucking knitting circle. Well, don't fucking worry, Parish, you'll get yours. I phoned a few mates last night and put the fucking word out on you. One day, when you're not fucking expecting it, someone will get shot and your fingerprints will be all over the fucking murder weapon. I'll be dragging you down to hell with me if it's the last thing I do. Now, get the fuck out and let me enjoy my coffee in peace.'

Parish left. Debbie, the Chief's secretary smiled at him. It was the first time he'd seen her smile in days.

***

277

Parish sat down. He made himself comfortable and then read his briefing: 'Ladies and gentlemen of the press thank you for coming this morning.' There was a strategic advantage in stroking their egos. 'I'm afraid all I can say is that our investigations are continuing.'

'Surely you can do better than that, Inspector?' the shy retiring freckled redhead from the Chigwell Herald said.

'I'm sorry, Miss...?'

'Catherine Cox, Inspector, as you well know.' She puffed herself up to her full height. 'I'm wise to your strategies of obfuscation. I'd like you to tell us all why you have not mentioned the murder weapon, and the item the killer puts in the victim's mouths.'

Miss Cox sat down, her task complete. Uproar ensued. Who had leaked the information?

Parish held up his hand for quiet.

'I am sure you are well aware, Miss Cox, that were certain information available in the public domain, it would hamper our investigation?'

Catherine Cox stood up again. 'Don't think I've finished with you yet, Inspector. I understand that you're afraid of copycat killings, but throughout this investigation you've blatantly withheld information, which the reading public had a right to know. For instance, I recall asking you whether you were searching for a serial killer, and you made fun of me.'

'I...'

'Yesterday, you said that the death of Graham Pearson was not related to the deaths of Diane Flint or Martin Squires. Yet, to date, there have been six people who have been murdered by the same man in the same way. Would you like me to name them, Inspector?'

'That won't...'

'I think that if you want the co-operation of the press you need to stop treating us like fools.'

'I apologise for…'

'My sources also tell me that Peter Rushdon has returned from America to meet you. Have you anything to say about that, Inspector?'

People looked around with, 'Who is Peter Rushdon?' on their lips.

'Who are your sources, Miss Cox?'

'You know I can't divulge that.'

The only people who knew about his meeting with Peter Rushdon were Richards and Rushdon. It must be Rushdon who had leaked his return to Chigwell.

'If I may speak, Miss Cox?' He paused and she sat down.

'You are quite correct, we are looking for a serial killer, but this killer targets specific individuals and there is no danger to the general public. And yes, I am concerned about copycat killings, so it is accepted practice to… keep certain information out of the public domain to ensure that we can identify a fake when we see it.'

'And Peter Rushdon?'

'I have been convinced that the murders are related to Beech Tree Orphanage, which, as you know, Rushdon Property Management own, and Peter Rushdon owns Rushdon Property Management. At first, we had to get a warrant to gain access to the orphanage, but we were prevented from entering by a High Court injunction. Now, Peter Rushdon, for whatever reason, has agreed to act as our tour guide.'

Emma Potter from the Redbridge Times stood up. 'When you say that the murders are related to Beech Tree Orphanage, what exactly do you mean by that, Inspector?'

'We think that the whole case revolves around child abuse at the orphanage during the 1980s. Certain evidence has been found, which suggests we are dealing with a group of paedophiles.'

'Are you any closer to identifying a suspect, Inspector?' Catherine Cox asked.

He decided he had nothing to lose. 'I am hoping to arrest the killer within the next forty-eight hours.' If he didn't, he wouldn't have a job anyway. 'Now, I have to conclude the briefing for today, it has taken considerably longer than I expected thanks to Miss Cox's revelations.'

Catherine Cox smiled. 'You're welcome, Inspector.'

He smiled back. 'Same time tomorrow for round two.'

Outside in the corridor he leaned against the wall and closed his eyes. His heart pounded in his ears.

'Are you all right, Sir?'

'No I'm not, Richards.'

She passed him a steaming coffee.

'Thanks. It was harrowing. I feel like I've been experimented on by aliens.'

'Have you got a chip in your neck, Sir?'

'You didn't get that off the Crime Channel, did you?'

'Scully in the X-Files has a chip…'

'Stop talking, Richards.'

'Sorry, Sir.'

They set off back to the squad room, but before they got there Richards touched his arm. 'I didn't like sleeping in the house on my own last night, Sir.'

'How is that any of my concern?'

'You could come and live with us.'

'Are you out of your mind, Richards?'

'My mum would like it.'

'I'm not having this conversation with you.'

'Yes you are, Sir.'

'Since when have you been giving the orders?'

'Since you took my mum away from me, Sir.'

'You were the one that threw us together.'

Tears sprouted from her eyes. 'Yes, but I wanted us to be a family. Instead you've taken my mum away.'

He put his arm around her shoulders. 'I haven't taken your mum anywhere, Richards.'

'I never see her, because she's always with you. If you lived at our house I could see you both.'

As usual he tried to be flippant, but it didn't work. 'You should get yourself a man, Richards. Go out with Toadstone, he'll look after you.'

'I don't want a man, I want my mum.' She ran down the corridor and into the ladies toilet.

Oh shit! Now what was he going to do? This was what he'd been afraid of. What choices did he have? He could finish with Angie. That was hardly an option when he'd told her last night how much he loved her. And, he doubted it would save his partnership with Richards if he did that. He could send Richards back to Cheshunt. She'd be back on the beat instead of a trainee detective. That would destroy Richards. It would also destroy his relationship with Angie, and he'd no doubt have to keep seeing Richards if he were still seeing Angie. Or, he could move in with both of them. He'd end up seeing Richards twenty-four hours a day. She'd move out sometime though, she'd find a man, settle down. Would moving in with them work? He had manoeuvred himself into such a position that the choice had already been made for him, and if he was being honest it was what he wanted.

He stuck his head in the ladies. 'All right, Richards.'

PC Heather Walsh came out of the inner door and gave him a look of disgust.

'All right what, Sir?' Richards asked.

'All right let's go and see the Chief, and I'll move in with you and your mother.'

Richards bolted out of the door and hugged him. People passing by gave them strange looks.

'Will you put me down, Richards. This is not the way partners behave.'

'Sorry, Sir.'

'And you're not to say anything to your mum.'

'Why not, Sir. I think she'll notice you snoring next to her sooner or later.'

'Oh yes, very droll, Richards. Do you realise how strange all this is, the daughter asking her mother's boyfriend to move in? Your mum and I have to discuss it before you start blabbing all over Chigwell.'

'Okay, Sir. You'll speak to her soon though, won't you?'

'Tonight.'

***

'What have you done, Parish?' Walter Day said as Parish and Richards strolled into his room at ten to ten. The Chief was looking much better. He had colour in his cheeks, and there wasn't the look of defeat in his eyes.

'Me, Sir? Are you referring to the case?'

'You know damn well I'm referring to CI Naylor, Parish.'

Richards stared at him. 'What have you done, Sir?'

'It was either him or me, Chief.'

'You should have spoken to me, first.'

'I think you've got enough to worry about without me coming to you about CI Naylor.'

'You don't understand, Parish. He's a dangerous man. There's a fine line between a policeman and a criminal. Naylor has crossed that line so many times he could have spent his career in prison, but instead he blackmailed people into protecting him.'

'What are you saying, Chief?'

'I'm saying, you've made yourself an enemy who doesn't play by the rules. He'll either kill you, or end your career.'

Parish shrugged. 'Well, its too late to do anything about it now. I'll just have to keep looking over my shoulder.'

'And under your bed, in the cellar, behind the sofa...'

'I get the idea, Chief. Anyway, you're looking a million percent better.'

'I didn't have a choice. The Chief Constable came to see me late last night to tell me what you'd sent him, what he'd done about it, and that I had to stop taking things easy and get back to work.'

Richards put her hands on her hips as if she would have taken the Chief Constable to task if he'd been standing in the room. 'But...'

'It's all right, Richards, the Chief Constable and I are old friends. We talked about CI Naylor, and I was coming back to work tomorrow anyway. If you'd only have waited, Parish.'

'It wasn't necessarily about me, Chief. The man was a bully and I decided to do something about him. I don't like bullies, never have.'

'Well, you'll end up paying sooner or later. Naylor never forgets people who cross him. Anyway, enough about Naylor. I saw you on the news earlier. Now, forgive me if I'm not fully in the picture, Parish, but didn't you say you'll be arresting someone tomorrow?'

'Yes, Sir.'

'Anyone particular in mind?'

'Hopefully the killer, Chief.'

'Hopefully?'

'Well, as I see it, I either find the killer tomorrow, or I'm out of a job anyway.'

'You remind me of the Japanese kamikaze pilots in the Second World War, Parish. It's not even been two weeks yet. You're doing what all good detectives do, which is collect evidence until a breakthrough occurs.'

'But there's been five murders and a suicide, Chief?'

'And each death has added to the evidence you've been collecting. If a killer doesn't want to be found then there's only so much you can do. As I said to you, the Chief Constable is really impressed by the way you've gone about this investigation, but God only knows what he's going to think about your statement to the press. I should imagine that if you don't find the killer by tomorrow night, you *will* be out of a job. No luck with the marijuana then?'

'What with one thing and another...'

'So, tell me why Parish feels so optimistic, Richards?'

'I'm glad you're feeling better, Chief.'

'They call it a remission. I'm keeping my fingers crossed its going to be long term.'

'We had a phone call from Peter Rushdon. We're meeting him at four o'clock today, and he's going to let us into Beech Tree Orphanage and give us a guided tour.'

'At last. See, Parish, patience is its own reward. Go on, Richards.'

'We found explicit photographs of young boys in Graham Pearson's house, and a hidden cellar with terrible things relating to children in Martin Squires' house. Then we found out that Colin Jackson was really Evan Hughes who had been convicted of kidnapping and abusing an eight-year-old boy. They were all paedophiles, Sir.'

'Just because they are paedophiles now, doesn't mean they were then.'

'We think it does, Sir. Pearson also had a key to a safe-deposit box, which we're going to open this afternoon before we see Rushdon, and he was being paid £5,000 a month by Martin Squires at Redbridge Council.'

'I can see why you're feeling optimistic, Parish, but just because you know the why, doesn't necessarily give you the who. Throughout this investigation you haven't had a single suspect. What now?'

Parish answered. 'I'm hoping there are still records in Beech Tree Orphanage, Sir.'

The Chief gave a strangled laugh then took a sip of orange juice. 'After twenty-four years? If there were something going on there, the records would have been destroyed when the place closed.'

'Let's wait and see, shall we?'

'What do you think Pearson kept in a safe-deposit box, Richards?'

'Evidence, Sir. He was the Manager, whatever was going on in Beech Tree Orphanage, he must have known about it, and was probably involved in it. I think he kept his insurance policy in the box and used it to blackmail Squires into paying him money each month.'

'She's getting good, Parish.'

'Don't say that, Chief, I'll never hear the last of it.'

'You know you should be getting Vice involved in this investigation now.'

Parish cupped his ear like a profoundly deaf person. 'I'm sorry, Chief, I didn't quite catch that.'

'Oh well, you'll either be a hero tomorrow, or the Chief Constable will tell me to put you in charge of the recycling initiative and the case will be given to Vice.'

'Say goodbye to the Chief, Richards and wait outside for me.'

Richards kissed the Chief on the cheek. 'I'll see you tomorrow, Sir.'

'Good to see you're doing so well, Richards.'

After Richards had gone out Parish said, 'I'm concerned about Kowalski, Sir.' He told the Chief what had happened in the squad room last night.

'Thanks for that, Parish. I'll talk to him tomorrow, see about sending him for counselling or something.'

'I'm glad, Sir. Kowalski's an ass, but he's a damned good copper.'

'I agree. Now, are you going to procrastinate the day away in here, or go out and arrest somebody?'

'See you tomorrow, Chief.' Parish squeezed his arm. 'I'm glad you're back in the saddle.'

'Get out, Parish, before I burst into tears.'

TWENTY-FIVE

It was ten forty-five when they left the Chief's room. Parish told Richards to wait in the car whilst he did something else, and was surprised when she didn't ask what he was going to do. He then went up to the hospital restaurant on the third floor and bought a bag of chocolate donuts, which he delivered to Doc Michelin in the Mortuary. Unfortunately, the pathologist wasn't in so Parish left the donuts in the middle of his stainless steel post-mortem table like body parts in a bag.

It was quarter past eleven when he returned to the car. Richards had the heater blowing on the penultimate setting with her coat on. Parish could have toasted hot-cross buns in the car if he'd had any with him.

'I'm all for keeping warm, Richards,' he said when he'd climbed in the Mondeo, turned down the heater to the first setting, and opened the window to let some cold air in, 'but this is taking it too far.'

She didn't say anything, but pulled out of the car park and headed west on the A12.

'Why have you started moving, Richards, I haven't told you where we're going yet?'

'My house, Sir, to see my mum. You won't be able to talk to her tonight because she's back on night duty, and we've got two hours before we have to be at the CPS offices.'

'You think you have it all worked out, don't you, Richards?'

'Yes, Sir.'

'Well, let me tell you, young lady that I know when I'm being manipulated.'

'Oh?'

287

'You're used to sleeping alone in the house because your mum is on night duty every other week.'

She grinned. 'I'd forgot about that, Sir.'

'As if.'

He knew damn well he was dancing to Richards' tune, but if it made her happy, then he was happy to go along with it. Wasn't it what he'd wanted all along – a family? Going home to the warmth and laughter of a home was definitely preferable to parking himself in the cold garage of his flat. Yes, it would take some getting used to. He had been his own man for so long with no responsibilities. Had looked after himself without thinking about the consequences for other people. Now, he'd have to think before he did everything. He certainly wouldn't be able to fart when he felt like it, would have to clean up as soon as he'd made a mess, would have to ask whether anyone wanted the last chocolate eclair before he stuffed it in his mouth. Yes, things would be very different.

'Are you sure this is what your mum wants, and its not just about what you want, Richards?'

'My mum and me are best friends, Sir, we tell each other everything.'

'Everything?'

'Everything, Sir.'

'I don't know whether I like that, Richards.'

'It's all good, Sir.'

'Oh, that's all right then.'

'I knew when my mum met you she'd fall in love with you, and she has. You're the man my father would have been if he hadn't been murdered.'

'So I'm a replacement for your father?'

'It's been a long time since I needed a father, Sir, but every now and again, I'd like someone to hug me and say everything will be all right.'

'I'm beginning to fill up, Richards.'

'And my mum has been without a man for so long I thought we'd never find anyone that would be good enough.'

'You've known me for less than two weeks, Richards. I could be the Illford axe murderer, or a vampire for all you know.'

'They caught the Illford axe murderer, Sir, I saw it on the Crime Channel, and vampires don't come out during the day.'

Richards pulled up in the slush outside her house. Suddenly he felt nervous.

'Your mum might say no, Richards.'

'I've already phoned her, she knows we're coming.'

'Don't I get a say in this?'

'No, Sir, you shouldn't have made my mum fall in love with you. Now, you have to face up to the consequences.'

He followed Richards into her house. Angie stood in the hall waiting for him.

They held each other tight and kissed. Richards disappeared into the kitchen.

'Are you sure you want a man in your house, Angie?'

'I'm sure,' she said. 'If only to shut Mary up.'

'Oh, so it's her idea?'

'It's what we both want, Jed.'

'When?'

'Sunday.'

'I'll begin packing.'

'Coffee in here, Sir,' Richards called from the kitchen.

He walked through with his arm around Angie's waist. 'I hope…'

'…no, Sir. There are only three sugars in this coffee. You'll have to start eating and drinking properly now that you have two good women looking after you.'

'And so it begins,' he said wrapping his hands around the proffered mug, but he felt something that he had never felt before.

***

After a lunch of pasta salad, which he thought was probably the worst meal he'd ever eaten, they set off towards the CPS offices at Orange Tree Hill in Havering-atte-Bower and arrived at exactly one-thirty.

Juliette Langley was waiting for them.

'You do realise that opening up somebody's safe-deposit box goes against everything democracy stands for,' she said even before they'd sat down and helped themselves to the coffee and biscuits.

Richards was quick to jump in. 'The man was a paedophile, and anyway he's dead, Ms Langley.'

'Being a paedophile does not nullify a person's rights, Constable Richards.'

'Well, it should.'

'What about you Inspector, are you standing next to the Constable on the extreme right with a noose in your hand?'

'I'm not far away.'

'So, before I sign this infringement of rights, tell me why I should?'

Richards described what they'd found in Pearson's house and in the hidden cellar beneath Martin Squires' idyllic cottage in Abridge. She told the barrister about how Peter Rushdon had phoned Parish and agreed to let them into Beech Tree Orphanage and show them round. And she put forward her theory of blackmail as if it were fact concerning the amounts of money both Ridpath and Pearson were paid by Martin Squires.

'All right, I'm willing to sign the warrant, but it better not come back to bite me on the backside. If it does, I'll never trust either of you again.'

Richards smiled at her small success. 'Don't worry, Ms Langley, no one is going to come in here and bite your bum.'

***

They were on their way to the Croatian Bank on the High Street in Redbridge to open Graham Pearson's safe-deposit box when Parish's phone grunted in his pocket.

'You need to change that ring tone, Sir, it sounds disgusting.'

He scrabbled in his pocket to reach his phone. 'If you change anything else about me, Richards, I won't be able to find myself when I get lost.'

She had no opportunity to reply before he was speaking to the caller.

'Parish?'

'Thanks for the donuts, Inspector, very tasty.'

'Glad you liked them, Doc.'

'That's not why I rang though.'

'Oh?'

'I'm at 12 Ingleby Mansions in Chigwell Row.'

'A bit early in the day for a party, Doc, and not really the weather for a barbecue.'

'Neither of those pleasant pastimes are what brought me here, Parish, as you well know. Lance Hobart has been stabbed in the heart, and a token with the number 55 stamped on it is sitting on his tongue like a parasite.'

'This is getting beyond a joke now, Doc.'

'Tell me about it, Parish. Due to the recession I only have so many shelves in my freezer, and you've been using them all up on your own. There's no room for the people who die from accidents and natural causes anymore. I'm having to double-up, and that's not what they pay National Insurance for.'

'You could start means testing them, Doc. I know the current government would applaud your initiative. You might even get a gong, or peerage out of it. Lord Michelin of Chigwell has a nice ring to it, don't you think.'

'You should have been a stand-up comic, Parish.'

'I've often thought I might travel down that road one day, Doc.'

'This should be the last victim shouldn't it?'

'What do you mean?'

'Well, according to that look-a-like on the news, you're going to arrest someone tomorrow, aren't you?'

'That's the plan.'

'There's a plan? Excellent, then there shouldn't be any more bodies.'

'Let's hope not. We'll be with you in about an hour.'

'An hour, Parish?'

'Got to open a box first, Doc.' He disconnected the call as Richards stopped outside the Bank of Croatia and parked on the double yellow lines.

A parking attendant darted over as they climbed out of the Mondeo. 'It's more than my job's worth to let you park there.'

Parish flashed his warrant card, but said nothing.

'I'm sorry, but you know the law better than me. Not even the police are allowed to park on double yellow lines.'

'Listen jobsworth, if you don't go and harass someone else, I'll arrest you for impeding a police investigation. I'm trying to catch a murderer, and all you can do is bleat on about parking restrictions, get the hell out of my way.'

The overweight attendant shifted to one side to let Parish pass.

'Wise decision, jobsworth,' Parish said.

'He was only doing his job, Sir,' Richards said as they entered the bank through the automatic doors.

'Don't defend parking attendants, Richards, they're worse than local politicians and should have excrement thrown on them.'

'They uphold the law like we do.'

'You're not saying that us superior beings feed from the same trough as parking attendants and local politicians are you, Richards? Next, you'll be arguing that we should throw excrement over ourselves?'

They had to cease the banter because they'd arrived at a desk where a dark-haired young woman wearing a blue skirt and jacket stood in front of the red and white Croatian chequered coat of arms hanging on the wall.

'How can I help?' she said.

Parish was glad she spoke English, because his knowledge of Croatian was limited to Ožujsko, which was a beer made at the Zagreb Brewery and sponsored the Croatian national football team. With nothing better to do, he'd once got drunk on it at a party towards the end of his degree at university.

He showed her his warrant card and handed over the search warrant. 'Detective Inspector Parish,' he said. 'That is a warrant to look in one of your safe-deposit boxes.' He pulled the key from his pocket and examined it. 'Number ninety-seven, which belonged to a Mr Graham Pearson.'

Just before she disappeared through a security door, she smiled and said, 'Just one moment, Sir.'

She came back accompanied by a tall man with thinning hair. He extended his hand towards Parish and said, 'Victor Valdez. I am the Manager, please follow me.'

He led them through the security door he had appeared from. After walking along a corridor they descended down a set of marble stairs. A uniformed security guard stood up as they approached and opened a metal gate at a nod from the Manager. They passed through the gate into a medium-sized room. In front of, and attached to, each of the four walls was a cabinet containing 8 x 8 inch doors with a keyhole in the centre of each. Victor Valdez opened the door to number ninety-seven, pulled out the box inside, and placed it on the table in the middle of the room. He nodded and said, 'I will wait outside should you need anything else, Inspector.'

'Thank you, Mr Valdez.'

'Come on, Sir,' Richards said. 'I can't stand the suspense.'

'Your middle name isn't Pandora is it?'

'Did my mum tell you, Sir?'

'A wild guess, Richards.'

He put the key in the lock and turned. The mechanism clicked and he stepped to one side. 'Do you want to do the honours?'

Her eyes opened wide. 'Do I, Sir?' she said pulling the oblong box towards her. She lifted the lid, and all of the excitement drained from her face.

'Surprise me, Richards,' Parish said.

'It's empty, Sir.' She put her hand inside and felt the smooth interior as if she couldn't believe what her eyes were telling her brain.

'So much for your theory about blackmail, Richards.'

She banged the lid closed. 'No, Sir.'

'No? Don't say, "No," to me, Richards.'

'Pearson must have paid the safe-deposit box monthly charge for a reason.' She called out for Mr Valdez to come in. 'Do you have records of when Mr Pearson last accessed his box?'

'It will be on computer, Miss, please follow me.'

They followed him upstairs to a small office. He sat at the desk and logged on to the bank's network. Eventually he said, 'Yes, here it is. Mr Pearson came into the bank and accessed his box on the 17th of December last year.'

Richards screwed up her eyes. 'When was the last time he accessed the box before then?'

'Never. He purchased it in 1991 shortly after we opened a bank here, and apart from his monthly payments we have had no further contact with him.'

'Pearson kept something in the box, Sir,' Richards said to Parish, 'which he must have removed last month.'

'What is this something? And where is it?'

'I don't know what, but if he was blackmailing Squires then maybe we're looking for photographs or videotapes. If he took them out of the box last month, then maybe they're at his house. Maybe we missed them, but maybe Paul found something.'

'There are a lot of maybes in there, Richards. Maybe you should give your fiancée a ring, and ask him if he found photographs or videotapes at the house.'

'You're being really mean, Sir. I'll phone Paul in the car.'

They thanked Mr Valdez for his help and left the Bank of Croatia. When they reached the car there was a parking ticket under the windscreen wiper.

Parish looked around and saw the fat parking attendant waving at him from across the road.

Tim ELLIS

'I'll drive, Richards. Killing someone with a car is still classed as a Road Traffic offence. I'll probably get three points on my licence for squashing a parking attendant.'

'You will not drive, Sir, and don't think I'm going to pay the parking fine either. You're the Inspector so you keep telling me, so you can pay it. You should never have talked to him like that, and you know you'll only have to pay £30 if you pay it within the next fourteen days.'

He screwed the ticket up and thrust it in his pocket as he climbed in the car. 'Haven't you rang Toadstone yet, Richards?'

'I'm going to.' She pulled out her phone. 'Hello, Paul.'

Parish glared at the parking attendant as he walked along a line of parked cars liberally writing up tickets. In fact, he thought, excrement was too good for parking attendants.

'No, that's all right, Paul. You just frightened me that was all. The Inspector and me have just opened the safe-deposit box, and there was nothing in it. Pearson took whatever was in there out last month. Did you find any photographs or videotapes in his house, Paul?'

'He says no, Sir.'

'Well, tell him to go back and have another look, they could be hidden somewhere.'

'He says he'll do that, Sir.'

'This afternoon, tell him.'

'Thanks, Paul. Maybe, let's wait until I've solved this case.'

She disconnected the call. 'He heard you, Sir.'

'And?'

'He's at the Hobart crime scene, but he says he's finished what he was doing and he's on his way back to Pearson's house now.'

'Good. So, you're going to solve this case are you, Richards? I may as well take some leave, go somewhere hot with your mum so that she can wear her skimpy bikinis, and I can drink beer all day by the pool.'

'Sirrr.'

'Drive, Richards. We don't want to keep Doc Michelin waiting, do we?'

***

It was two forty-five when they scrambled out of the Mondeo at Ingleby Mansions in Chigwell Row, entered the block of flats, and climbed the stairs to number 12.

'Go and knock on some doors, Richards. Find out if anyone heard or saw anything. I'll be in the flat picking Doc Michelin's brains.'

'Okay, Sir.'

Parish found Doc Michelin in the kitchen drinking Hobart's tea and eating his chocolate biscuits.

'Bored, Doc?'

'You've noticed, Inspector. I could have been back at the Mortuary an hour ago catching up with my post mortems if it wasn't for the fact that I had to wait for you and... Where's that beautiful partner of yours?'

'Knocking on doors.'

The Doc put his head in his hands. 'And you deprive me of her smile as well. It was a cold day in hell when I met you, Parish.'

Parish sat down opposite the Doc at the small kitchen table. A dog barked.

'Oh yes, Lance Hobart had a dog. We've called the RSPCA, and they're on their way.'

Coco stood on its back legs up against Parish's legs and stared at him. He picked the dog up and sat it on his lap.

'I always wanted a dog, Doc,' he said stroking Coco's head.

'Take that one.'

'Unfortunately, my current situation prevents me from making life-changing decisions without consulting her indoors.'

The Doc nearly choked on a mouthful of his chocolate biscuit. 'You're not married, Parish.'

'I know. Yet, I find myself under the yoke of feminine wiles.'

'Sounds painful.'

'I'm sure I'll get used to it. So, anything for me?'

'Same old, Parish. This killer is meticulous to the point of boring. Apart from that mistake he made in the lift at Redbridge, he never does anything different.'

Parish saw a white-suited forensics officer and waved him in. 'A word?'

'Yes, Sir?'

'Who did Mr Toadstone leave in charge?'

'Me, Sir.'

'And you are?'

'Sally Vickers.'

Parish was taken aback. He hadn't noticed he was talking to a female. She was shapeless in the white suit, and her voice behind the mask sounded male. Maybe it was him. Maybe when you agree to live with someone, you lose the ability to distinguish between the sexes. 'Have you found anything?'

'We've found lots of things, Sir. What specifically did you have in mind?'

'Specifically, items that a paedophile might keep such as, photographs, tapes, a computer full of downloaded images of children, that type of thing.'

'We've found photographs, Sir. He had a computer and we'll be taking that back with us to analyse.'

'Okay, thanks.'

'You're welcome.'

Richards strolled into the kitchen. 'Hello, Doc.'

'Hello, Constable. You're smile makes my day worthwhile.'

'That's very nice of you to say so, Doc'

Parish put the dog down. 'Come on, Richards, we'll take a quick look at the body, and then get over to Beech Tree Orphanage.'

Richards squatted when she saw the dog. 'Ah, it's a dog, Sir.'

'I do know what a dog looks like, Richards.'

She picked it up and cuddled it. 'I love dogs.'

'Then why haven't you got one?' he asked her.

'It wouldn't be fair when my mum and me are both out at work all day.'

'Put it down, Richards. Let's do what we have to do and go on our way.'

She put the dog down. 'You have no heart, Sir.'

'That useless organ was removed a long time ago.'

They walked through into the living room. Parish crouched down and pulled back the sheet covering the corpse. Lance Hobart was a man of about sixty, with a crew-cut, a cardigan, and an expanded waist.

Coco waddled up beside Parish and barked at her master's dead face. Richards picked the dog up and covered its eyes. 'Poor thing must be traumatised,' she said.

'It'll probably need counselling,' Parish suggested and smiled.

'Stop being mean, Sir.'

'What have I told you about that *mean* word, Richards?'

'That was yesterday, Sir.'

'Stop splitting hairs.' He stood up. 'Right, put the dog down and let's go. Our work here is done.'

'You didn't do any work, Parish,' Doc Michelin said.

'Work comes in different shapes and sizes, Doc.'

'Oh, by the way, when I was doing Martin Squires' post mortem this morning, guess what I found?'

'A token?'

'You're no fun at all, Parish. Number 37. The killer had pushed it right back into Squires' throat. I only found it by accident.'

'You know what that means, Sir?' Richards said.

'The killer works at Redbridge Council.'

'Yes, Sir.'

It was only when they were sat in the car and Coco barked from the back seat that they realised they had a stowaway.

'I thought I told you to put that dog down, Richards. I certainly didn't say bring it with you.'

'It followed us, Sir.' She picked it up and took it back inside.

During the journey to the orphanage Richards said, 'What did you send to the Chief Constable about CI Naylor, Sir?'

'I have no idea what you're talking about.'

'I think you do, Sir. Whatever you sent him I think Paul helped you, and it went via China like he said.'

'Haven't you got anything better to think about, Richards?'

'No, Sir.'

TWENTY-SIX

Peter Rushdon arrived shortly after Parish and Richards reached Beech Tree Orphanage. Rushdon had two helpers in white jackets that climbed out of the Volkswagen Caravelle first to remove the wheelchair from the back of the vehicle and prepare it for use. There was also a young man carrying an attaché case who got out of the front passenger seat and stood to one side. Parish assumed he was an assistant.

The driver remained in the van. He kept the engine running and the lights on because as well as day making way for night snow began to fall again. At first, the weather wasn't sure what it was doing, but then the snow became heavier and heavier until it was nearly a whiteout. It was below freezing, and Parish was glad there was no wind.

With the help of a walking stick and one of his helpers, a wrinkled bag of skin in a hooded quilted coat tottered down from the vehicle and sat in the wheelchair. From an array of bottles and wires strapped to the back of the chair Peter Rushdon was passed an oxygen mask, which he pressed to his face and began taking deep breaths. The helpers wrapped blankets about his shoulders and legs.

'Inspector Parish?' the young assistant asked with an American accent.

Parish stepped forward. 'I'm Detective Inspector Parish, and you are?'

'Roger Anderson,' he said extending his hand. 'Mr Rushdon's personal assistant.'

Parish shook it and introduced Richards. He then stepped up to the old man in the wheelchair. 'You must be Peter Rushdon?'

The old man nodded and coughed, but ignored Parish's proffered hand.

'Please excuse Mr Rushdon, Inspector,' Anderson said. 'His excuse for being rude is that he's dying.'

Anderson walked up to the ivy-covered metal gates and put a large key into the bulky lock holding a thick chain together. It took him some time, but eventually the lock came apart and the chain clanked on the ground.

Parish went up to help him drag the gates open. It was, after all, his idea that they go into the orphanage.

Feelings of despair and hopelessness washed over him as he lifted his head and stared at the brick and concrete single-storey buildings that made up Beech Tree Orphanage. It was hard to see, but everything appeared to be covered with ivy and snow.

'Welcome to Hell, Inspector,' Peter Rushdon said. 'The building straight ahead of us is the administrative block. All the other buildings are either male or female dormitories, except the one on its own to the left, which housed the medical centre, the laundry, and the kitchen and dining room.'

The paths were all overgrown. Parish realised that he and Richards had come unprepared. They'd forgotten torches, and they probably should have worn boiler suits, wellies, hard hats, and probably breathing masks.

'Come on you two useless bastards, push.' Peter Rushdon was talking to the two helpers who had now donned winter coats. One of them had a hefty rucksack slung over one shoulder. They began to push the wheelchair through the deep frozen snow with considerable difficulty towards the administrative block.

'Why do you call the orphanage Hell, Mr Rushdon?' Richards asked.

'You'll understand why soon.'

'What we don't understand is why you didn't knock it all down and build houses on the land?' Parish said.

Peter Rushdon ignored him, and Parish didn't bother to ask anymore questions. He presumed Rushdon would tell the story in his own time.

They reached the administrative block. Roger Anderson used a key from a bunch he took out of his coat pocket to unlock the door.

Peter Rushdon's two helpers lifted the wheelchair up the set of four steps, onto the porch, and wheeled it in through the front door.

'You'll find all the records of the children and the staff in the cabinets in the office.' He waved to his left. 'But what you really want to see is in the Manager's office.' He pointed a withered finger towards a door on the right. 'Over there,' he rasped. 'Come on hurry up you useless bastards, I'll be dead before you pull your fingers out.'

Parish guessed that it wasn't much fun working for Peter Rushdon. He imagined that the old man must have been paying the helpers a fortune to work for him. Rushdon reminded Parish of CI Naylor, and decided that he didn't like the old man.

Again, Anderson unlocked the Manager's office with a key from the bunch he held in his hand.

'Get the torches out,' Rushdon said.

The helper with the rucksack slid it on the floor, unzipped it, and handed torches with handles to everyone. Parish and Richards both switched theirs on.

'You two useless bastards can stay here,' Rushdon said to the helpers. 'Anderson can help me now. Strap the mobile oxygen on my back.' The old man pushed himself up out of the wheelchair, shrugged off the blankets, and wriggled into the oxygen backpack that the helpers held for him.

303

'Where are we going, Sir?' Richards whispered.

'I have no idea,' Parish whispered back. He shone his torch around the lobby. Besides the doors left and right, there was another door directly ahead of them, which lead to the male and female toilets.

'Follow me,' Rushdon said, and he hobbled into the darkness of the Manager's office with the help of Roger Anderson.

Parish and Richards looked at each other nervously and followed Rushdon, who was hanging heavily on Anderson's arm, inside. It was a large room with twenty-four years worth of cobwebs dangling from the ceiling.

Richards squealed and flapped at her face with her hands. 'Oh, I hate spiders, Sir.'

'I'm not that keen on them myself, Richards,' Parish said, glad that he'd be going home after this to shower and change.

There was a glass-fronted cabinet against the wall on the left. Ornaments sat behind the glass on shelves. Next to it stood a bookcase stacked with books. In the middle of the room was a large table with a desk lamp, a heap of files, a coffee mug, and a pot stuffed with pens and pencils. To the right were three easy chairs and a coffee table. The way the room had been left as it was twenty-four years ago reminded Parish of the ruins at Pompeii. He shone his torch over the desk and saw a small pile of tokens, which he picked up. There were seven tokens with numbers 21, 23, 35, 38, 49, 50, and 59 on them. He began adding them up. Carlgren had forty-five, six had been used in the murders, one had been found in Martin Squires, and he held seven in his hand. There was one missing.

'This office is the gateway to Hell, Parish,' Rushdon said pulling something under the desk. 'Don't you remember?'

Parish heard a sound like a coffin opening from inside, and when he turned he saw that the bookcase had come away from the wall. 'I'm sorry, I…'

Richards' phone activated, she found it in her coat and moved back towards the lobby to talk in private. 'Hello, Paul…'

Rushdon, his feet scraping on the floor, went over to the bookcase and opened it fully. Anderson's torch lit the way down a set of steps into the darkness.

They began to descend the steps. Rushdon and Andrews went first, and Parish followed them. He looked behind, but Richards was still talking to Toadstone on the phone. She'll follow on, he thought.

At the bottom of the steps there was a corridor that led towards the north-east. The cold air smelled of mould and wrapped itself around them like a stinking old blanket. Rushdon began shuffling along the corridor. 'Nearly there,' he said through his oxygen mask.

With each step Parish began to feel a panic he had only ever felt in his nightmares. A dark hand gripped his insides and squeezed. This was his nightmare come to life.

'Do you remember now, Parish?' Rushdon said over his shoulder.

Tears came to Parish's eyes. He slid down the wall and sat on the cold concrete.

'Sir?' Richards shouted from the top of the steps. 'You have to come back, Sir.'

But it was too late. The wall in his brain, that he had built many years ago to protect himself from the truth, came crashing down. The memories flooded back and paralysed him, washed away everything else. All he was, all he would ever be, was that little boy of five being dragged screaming along this dark corridor to a room with a bed to satisfy the perverted desires of men. He remembered his friends: Johnny Tomkins, Joseph Dobbs, Liam Preston, Ronnie Sanders, Frank Landon, Tommy Lonely, and… Terry Reynolds. Their faces swam before him as if it were only yesterday. They were the special children with tokens. He was number 55 on the menu. He remembered the bastards that dragged him up this corridor and did terrible things to him as well: Gregory Taylor, Brian Ridpath, Evan Hughes, Martin Squires, Graham Pearson, and… Oh God…

***

From out of the darkness, a man dressed all in black knocked Anderson to the ground. With one hand he grasped Rushdon around the neck, with the other he held a marlinspike to the old man's sagging flesh.

'Hello, Mr Rushdon, remember me?' Terry had entered the underground complex through a secret entrance in his old dormitory.

'You're the driver,' Anderson blurted out. 'What…?'

'I knew you'd be here somewhere, Terry Reynolds,' Rushdon hissed. 'You always were trouble.'

'Time to die, Mr Rushdon.'

'Before you do, let me tell you why.'

'What does it matter now?' Terry said. 'All that matters is that you pay for what you did to me, to Jed Parish, and to all the others you used and then buried in the graveyard in unmarked graves.'

'I was one of you,' Rushdon said softly. 'It didn't start with you, you know, Terry. It had been going on for years. I wasn't the first, but afterwards I came back and joined Pearson's club. I didn't mean to, I hated myself for doing it. In the end, that's why I sealed this place up, why I never pulled it down and built on it. I knew that one day, we would all have to pay for our sins, and that the boys we killed deserved to rest in peace.'

Richards had reached them. She crouched down and put her arm around Parish's shoulders. 'Are you all right, Sir?'

Parish was crying silently. He was a little boy of five in the dark again with no one to help him.

'You don't have to kill Rushdon, Terry,' Richards said. 'He'll pay for what he did.'

'You can arrest me afterwards. My life ended in this place and Rushdon's will as well. You'll have to look after Jed though, if he's not going to end up like me. We were friends you know.' He began crying. 'I tried to protect him, but I couldn't protect myself.' He spun Rushdon round and stabbed him in the heart. 'For me, you bastard,' he said slipping token number 7 in Rushdon's mouth. 'A life for a life.' The marlinspike clattered on the floor and Terry Reynolds sat down against the wall.

After handcuffing Reynolds, Richards had to go back along the corridor and up the steps to get a signal. She phoned for Doc Michelin, Paul Toadstone, and two ambulances. She then rang DI Kowalski to come and take charge so that she could go to the hospital with Parish.

***

Aftermath

Kowalski arrived first. He formally arrested Terry Reynolds and took him back to Hoddesdon police station for processing. A confused Roger Anderson accompanied them and provided a witness statement before he was permitted to return to America.

Richards went with Parish in one of the ambulances and held his hand. For once she had nothing to say.

Toadstone had told her that they'd found sixty-nine videotapes hidden in a wall recess at Graham Pearson's house. The tapes had boy's names on them, and one of those names was Jed Parish. Toadstone was the only one that knew about the tape. Richards convinced him to destroy it. He wasn't keen on the idea of destroying evidence, but she persuaded him in the end that it was the right thing to do. With all those other tapes, she argued, they didn't need that one.

Doc Michelin arrived and took charge of Peter Rushdon's body. He noticed Toadstone hadn't arrived yet, so he also put the marlinspike in an evidence bag and slipped it in his pocket. Although the marlinspike would be used as evidence when the case went to trial, he hoped that someone would let him keep it when it was all over.

On Friday 24th January, the day after Parish was admitted to the medical ward of King George Hospital, Angie Richards and her daughter, Mary, signed him out against the advice of doctors and took him home to 38 Puck Road.

The forensics' team took everything away from Beech Tree Orphanage and analysed all the records. Most of the children had lived their lives and died, but there were a few who were able to corroborate what had happened. They found some of the old staff, but none of them had known what was going on, or so they said.

In Chigwell Cemetery, on the boundary next to the orphanage, they found twenty-seven children's bodies in unmarked shallow graves. Nobody knew who they were, but names from the files were put on their headstones when they were buried much later.

Peter Rushdon had amassed a twenty-three million-pound fortune. When his will was read, they found that he had no family and had donated the entire amount to children's charities in England. The unemployed Roger

Anderson went back to America wondering what had happened.

Two weeks after Terry Reynolds had been arrested, the forensic accountants rang up and told Richards that Martin Squires had hidden a number of 'pensions' in the accounts. The total amount he had fraudulently paid out over the course of twenty-four years was £1.2 million. Everyone at Redbridge Council, past and present, was stunned. No one, so they said, knew anything about the payments. The current Chairman of the Finance and General Purposes Committee resigned.

After it was all over, only a handful of people knew the truth about Parish. Richards made them all, even the Chief Constable, swear never to reveal what they knew. The Chief Constable was so impressed with Richards that he ignored his own procedures, and arranged for her to attend the next three-phase competency-based National Investigator's course.

***

Wednesday, 24th February

It was six-thirty in the evening. He was sat in the living room watching the Champion League Highlights that he'd taped last night. Angie came in and sat beside him on the sofa. 'There are two people to see you,' she said holding his hand. 'I've kept them away up to now, but I think you're well enough.'

He pressed the pause button and kissed her. 'Send them in.'

'If you're sure?'

'I'm sure.' He stroked the two-month old black and white Schnauzer puppy Richards had bought him. You're right, it's time.'

Tim ELLIS

Angie let the first visitor in.

'Parish, as I live and breathe.'

Parish smiled, and with each kind word, he moved further and further from the darkness. 'Hello, Kowalski, I've missed your big mouth.'

'That's a hell of a welcome. Back to work on Monday, I hear?'

'Somebody has to come in and do something productive,' he said.

'You've been reading the newspapers?'

'I've glanced at them.'

'So modest. They've made you into a bloody hero, Parish, especially that Catherine Cox from the Chigwell Herald. The rest of us are trailing in your wake. I hear the Chief Constable is ruing the day he ever promoted you. He knows damned well he'll have to move over to make room for you soon.'

'Have I ever told you that you talk a load of crap, Kowalski?'

'On numerous occasions, Jed. The wife and kids send their regards.'

'Thank them for me.'

'Right, Kowalski get the hell out. Go and wait in the car and tell yourself how wonderful you are.' It was the Chief with a ruddy complexion, and small tufts of hair on his head.

'See you Monday, Parish,' Kowalski said. 'Remind me to tell you what Richards and I have been getting up to in the broom cupboard.' They could hear his laughter all the way to the car.

'How are you feeling, Parish?'

'Never mind me, Chief, what's with the hair?'

'They've given me the all-clear. I beat the damned thing.'

'That's the best news I've ever heard, Sir.'

310

'Listen, Parish, I was hoping to ease you back in gently, but...'

'Hello, Chief,' Richards said coming into the room. 'My mum said you were here with that octopus Kowalski.' She leaned over. 'What's that on your head, Sir?'

'Hair, Richards. The cancer's gone.'

Richards burst into tears and hugged Walter Day. 'I'm the happiest girl alive, Sir.'

'Have you got nothing else better to do, Richards? The Chief and I are trying to have a serious conversation here.'

'Stop being mean, Sir. You know I've had requests from other people to be their partner, don't you?'

Parish laughed. 'As if, Richards.'

'I'll leave you two squabbling.' The Chief passed Parish a manila folder. 'Take a look at that, Parish, it's your next case.'

Parish opened the file. Inside there was a colour photograph of what looked like a middle-aged woman hanging upside down with a meat hook through her ankle. Maggots crawled in her empty eye sockets, mouth and nose. There was evidence of a multitude of stab wounds on her torso. Her abdomen had been slashed open, and her intestines were protruding through the wound. She was naked from the waist down, and her blouse had been pulled up to expose her breasts.

'A human being shouldn't have to look at things like that,' Parish said closing the file.

'Chief, you know DI Parish is recuperating.' She snatched the file off Parish and slipped it under her arm. 'I'll read it and brief him on it when he's ready.'

'See you, Monday, Parish,' the Chief said.

'I can't wait, Chief,' Parish said.

Tuesday 2nd March

Parish sat across the table from Terry Reynolds in the visitor's centre of HMP Wormwood Scrubs on Du Cane Road, London.

'Hello, Jed.'

'Hello, Terry. How are they treating you?'

'Good. Yeah, I'm a bit of a hero in here. Nobody likes paedophiles.'

'I can't condone what you did, but thanks for trying to protect me.'

'You remember?'

'Yes.'

'Don't let it destroy your life like it has mine.'

'I've got some good people round me.'

'That's important. I had no one.'

There was nothing more to say. Parish stood up.

'Thanks for coming, Jed, enjoy the rest of your life.'

'I will, Terry. By the way, why did you use a marlinspike? I've tried to think, but I don't remember anything.'

'It was a paperweight on Pearson's desk. I stole it and kept it. That's all.'

'What about Diane Flint, why did you kill her?'

'She was the Social Worker who put me in there.'

'Did she know what was going on?'

'If she didn't, she damned well should have done.'

'Goodbye, Terry.'

'Goodbye, Jed.'

***

DI Jed Parish and PC Mary Richards tackle their next case in *The Wages of Sin*, the first chapter follows:

THE WAGES OF SIN

Tim ELLIS

For the wages of sin is death.

Romans 6:23

ONE

Monday 1st March

'Right, Richards,' Detective Inspector Jed Parish said as he pulled away from the curb outside 38 Puck Road in Chigwell. 'I've recovered from my traumatic ordeal in Beech Tree Orphanage, and I'm now driving toward the station. You're the constable pretending to be a detective, and I'm your brilliant and exceptionally good-looking boss, so I'm ordering you to brief me on the case the Chief gave us last week. I promise I won't have a relapse.'

PC Mary Richards looked at him, scepticism etched on her fresh young face. 'Only if you're sure, Sir.'

'I'm sure, Richards. Stop mollycoddling me.'

From memory she said, 'It was an unsolved case dating back to 2003, Sir, but another corpse has turned up.'

Parish wondered where the killer had been, and what he'd been doing for seven years. 'When you say, "another corpse," do you mean a fresh one?'

'Yes, Sir, last Tuesday, the day before the Chief gave you the case. A woman was found hanging upside down in an abandoned warehouse on the outskirts of Redbridge. She'd been sexually assaulted like the last one, stabbed over forty times, and slashed across the abdomen.'

'With a meat hook through her ankle?' He grimaced as he recalled the details from the photograph that he had briefly seen in the file last Wednesday before Richards had snatched it off him. A middle-aged woman suspended upside-down. Maggots crawling in her empty eye sockets, mouth and nose. There was evidence of a multitude of stab wounds on her torso. Her abdomen had been slashed open, and her intestines were protruding through the wound. She was naked from the waist down, and her blouse had been pulled up to expose her breasts.

'Yes, Sir. Her eyes were missing, and there was another message.'

'A message?'

'The first victim had a message as well.'

'You didn't tell me about a message, Richards.'

'I'm telling you now, Sir.'

'This is like trying to squeeze orange juice out of a grapefruit, Richards. If you're not going to brief me properly, I'll stop the car and read the file myself.'

'Okay, Sir. I just don't want you to have a mental breakdown or something. My mum made me swear that I'd take extra special care of you. If anything happened to you, I'd never hear the last of it.'

Her mum, Angie Richards, had made love to him this morning as if he was never coming back. She'd clung to him, cried, and wouldn't let him leave until he promised to return in one piece.

'Well, you can stop worrying, Richards. I feel great. Nothing's going to happen to either of us today, because all we're doing is paperwork and catching up with everything. Now, do you think you can stop pretending to be a nurse and go back to being a trainee detective, or should I begin interviewing for another partner?'

'That doesn't work with me anymore, Sir. You wouldn't get rid of me, I've made myself irreplaceable.'

Inside he smiled. He knew she was right, they were like father and daughter now. 'I'd replace you with a crash-test dummy at the drop of a hat, Richards.'

She laughed. 'As if, Sir.'

'Well?'

'The first victim was a woman of forty-three. That was the photograph you saw in the file.'

'How long had she been dead?'

'Three months, Sir.'

'Go on.'

'Two ten-year-old boys found her hanging in a derelict school in Woodford Green. Her name was Tanya Mathews, she was a Social Worker...'

The car swerved as Parish turned his head to see if she was joking. 'Not another bloody Social Worker, Richards? People don't seem to like Social Workers very much.' He was referring to their previous case and the murder of Diane Flint, the Director of Social Services at Redbridge Council.

'People don't like the police very much either, Sir. You want to see the men run when I tell them I'm a copper.'

'If they're stupid enough to run in the wrong direction, Richards, they're obviously not intelligent men.'

'I know, Sir, but I still haven't found anyone decent like you.'

'You will, Richards. Anyway, how did we get onto your love life?'

'That's just the point, Sir, I haven't got a love life.'

'So, this Tanya Mathews was a Social Worker...?'

'Yes, Sir.'

He was becoming exasperated. 'And...?'

'Oh yes. A DI John Lewin investigated the case.'

Parish had heard that John Lewin was an uninspiring DI, but then he had never worked with him. He did recall though that the man had died in suspicious circumstances, and wondered if it had anything to do with the case.

'Hang on, Richards. You said there was a message before?'

'Pinned to her left breast, Sir, through the nipple.'

'And the message said?'

3

'Nobody knows, Sir. It was in a strange language and the investigating team couldn't decipher it.'

'How do you know it was a message then?'

'What else could it be?'

'What's the point in sending a message that nobody can read?'

'The Zodiac Killer did it, Sir.'

'You've been watching that damned Crime Channel again, haven't you, Richards?'

Her face reddened, and she looked at the gloved hands in her lap. 'No, Sir.'

'You must think I live up a tree. What have I told you about using the Crime Channel as a replacement for training? Pretty soon you'll be able to apply to join the FBI, but you'll know nothing about police work here, Agent Richards. So, now we've got two messages that need deciphering?'

'Yes, Sir.'

'Well, that's why they've put us on the case, Richards. We'll find out what the messages say, or die in the attempt.'

'I don't think I want to die Sir, and my mum wouldn't want you to die either. You've only just started shacking up with her.'

'You're the one who fixed us up together, and then forced me to move in with you and your mum, Richards. And for future reference we're not "shacking up" as you call it, we're living together.'

'Kowalski says you're "shacking up" with my mum. He makes it sound so sordid. It would be much better if you two got married, Sir. Then we'd all know where we stood.'

'What do you mean? You know where you stand now.'

Richards stuck her bottom lip out. 'I feel like an orphan, Sir.'

God, she was a scheming cow, he thought. 'Stop trying to manipulate me, Richards. What do you mean the messages are in a strange language?'

'I don't know, Sir, I didn't do languages at school.'

'You've got the messages at the top of your list, haven't you Richards?'

'Yes, Sir.'

'I knew you already had a list. I bet you've been lying in bed watching the Crime Channel, and trying to solve the messages like a bloody celebrity crossword puzzle out of one of your women's magazines.'

She blushed and turned away. 'I haven't, Sir.'

'You couldn't lie to me if your life depended on it, Richards. I'm a detective. I know exactly what you've been doing. So when you do get yourself a man, remember that.'

'Sirrr.'

'Get on with it then. It'll be the weekend before you've finished briefing me on this case. What did DI Lewin find out?'

'Not a lot, Sir. All of the information on Tanya Mathews is in the file. She worked in the Mental Health team. DI Lewin investigated the cases on her caseload, but didn't find anything that would merit someone killing her.'

'What about the recent body?'

'Susan Reeves. Two men were thinking of organising a rave at the warehouse. They went to see if it was suitable, but found the body of Susan Reeves instead.'

'I hope you haven't been investigating this case on your own, Richards?'

'I did go…'

Tim ELLIS

'I bloody well knew it. Have I taught you nothing? This case is about women being murdered. Unless you haven't noticed, you're a woman, Richards. That's why we have partners, so that we can protect each other's back. If you ever…'

'DI Kowalski went with me, Sir.'

'Yes well… So you'd rather be working with Kowalski? And what have I said about Kowalski, Richards? He's only after one thing and…'

'He was a perfect gentleman, Sir.'

'Now I know you're lying, Richards. Kowalski hasn't got that word in his dictionary.'

'You know Kowalski wouldn't do anything to me, Sir, he likes you too much.'

'Kowalski likes women too much,' Parish mumbled as he pulled into the car park at Hoddesdon police station. The clock on the dashboard showed five to nine. It was an hour fast because he hadn't synchronised it with the atomic clock at Greenwich. At the end of March he knew it would right itself for British Summer Time.

'Before we go up to the squad room, Richards, lets finish the briefing. Tell me about Susan Reeves?'

'She was a twenty-nine year old estate agent. A Mr Simpson called her office to arrange a viewing of a house in Chigwell. She kept the appointment, and that was the last time anyone saw her alive.'

'And Mr Simpson doesn't exist?'

'No, Sir.'

'Okay, Richards start another list.'

Richards took off her gloves, and pulled out her notebook and pencil.

'We've got two female bodies that have been hung upside down with meat hooks pushed through their ankles. Write down victim profiles, locations, fingerprints and meat hooks. Both women were sexually assaulted,

6

write DNA, hair, and fibres. The victims were also stabbed and slashed, write weapon and pattern. The eyeballs were removed, write method and eye colour. There was seven years between the murders, write identify prison and asylum releases, and investigate DI Lewin's death. Both victims had messages pinned to their breasts, write messages and GCHQ.'

'That's a brilliant idea, Sir.'

'Thanks, Richards. We also need to see Doc Michelin about the post mortem of the last victim, and find out if he discovered anything that isn't obvious from the photographs. We'll get a copy of the PM report for Tanya Mathews and ask the Doc to compare the two reports. We might need to exhume Tanya Mathews' body, but we'll check with the Doc. Have I missed anything, Richards?'

'It seems that the sick leave hasn't dulled your mental capacities, Sir.'

'Don't try and flatter me, Richards. I'm still angry with you for starting to investigate the case without my expert supervision and guidance. As good as Kowalski is as a detective, Richards, he isn't me.'

'I'm sorry, Sir. I won't do it again.'

'Just see that you don't. I'd hate to have to send you back to Cheshunt police station as a reject with the words, "Loose cannon" or "Disloyal," typed on your report in bold capital letters. Well, what did you and Kowalski find at the warehouse?'

'Nothing, Sir. It's just a dirty abandoned warehouse. There's nothing special about it.'

'Am I to take your word for that, or do I need to visit the warehouse myself?'

'You should take my word for it, Sir.'

'What type of detective would I be if I did that, Richards?'

Parish was glad that the snow had melted. The weather still resembled a Siberian winter, but at least he could walk properly and the roads were clear of slush and ice.

***

Parish had no idea what to say to anyone when he was cheered and clapped as he walked into the squad room. A wave of emotion swept over him and tears ran down his cheeks. He shook hands with people and thanked them for their kindness.

DI Kowalski slapped him on the back, and nearly sent him flying into the toilets. 'Parish, as I live and breathe. Welcome back.'

'Still got bugger all to do, Kowalski?'

'You really know how to hurt a guy, Jed. I've been waiting to say hello to you. Now that you're here, Richards and I have an appointment in the broom cupboard.' His laughter reverberated around the squad room.

'Don't listen to him, Sir. I would never go in a broom cupboard with DI Kowalski. Broom cupboards always have horrible things in them.'

Bunting had been put up welcoming him back, and his desk looked like a repository for cards, letters, and faxes wishing him a speedy recovery. He didn't realise he knew so many people. Someone had moved his desk back slightly, and a similar desk had been pushed right up against the back of it. On top were a computer, phone, and in/out trays. It looks like Richards has made herself at home, he thought.

'You knew about this didn't you, Richards?'

'Who me, Sir?'

'Richards organised the whole damned shebang,' Kowalski said still laughing.

'You're a rat, Kowalski,' Richards said. 'If there was ever a chance of you getting me in the broom cupboard, you've just blown it.'

Kowalski clutched his chest. 'Rip my heart out and stamp on it why don't you, Richards.'

Chief Superintendent Walter Day walked into the squad room, and people began returning to their desks. Parish hardly recognised him. Now that he had been given the "all clear" for his prostate cancer he looked like a new man.

They shook hands.

'Welcome back, Parish.'

'Bloody hell, Sir, you've got a full head of hair, some colour in your face and the grip of a grizzly again.'

'Like you, Parish, I'm getting there.'

'I'm really pleased for you, Sir.'

'Thanks, Parish. What about you?'

'I'm glad to be back, Sir. Sitting at home was driving me crazy.'

'With two women in the house, and one of them being Richards, I can imagine.'

'Excuse me, Chief,' Richards chirped in. 'Without me and my mum, DI Parish would have been on his own.'

'There is that, Parish, being on your own is not much fun. I can vouch for that.'

'Next Sunday, Sir,' Richards said.

The Chief scratched his new head of hair. 'What's happening next Sunday, Richards?'

'Roast dinner, Sir. You're invited to our house.'

'Thank you, Richards, very kind of you.'

'I'm free on Sunday as well, Richards,' Kowalski said.

'Only if you bring your wife and children, Sir?'

'You're not serious?'

'I am, Sir. I can't be helping my mum, and watching where you've got your hands as well.'

'Okay, they'll like that, thanks.'

'You're welcome, Sir.'

'In the meantime, Richards,' Parish said. 'We've got work to do. You know how I like my coffee?'

'Two sugars, Sir, not four?'

'You'll only tell your mum if I have four, so I suppose I'd better have two.'

Richards wandered off to the kitchen.

'Has she briefed you on the case, Parish?' the Chief asked.

'I finally got it out of her. A bit gruesome.'

'I know, but it'll take your mind off everything else.'

'I'm okay, Sir, I'm coming to terms with what happened. I still get the nightmares, but they're becoming less frequent. Angie and Mary Richards found me just in time. I think I would have been lost if I'd still been on my own.'

'Yes, Richards is a lifesaver that's for sure. She likes to spread happiness wherever she goes. Whilst you were on the sick she was at a loose end, so she's been organising me. Making sure I'm taking my medication and putting all of my outpatient's appointments in her diary, so that she can remind me to attend. She's been coming to my house and checking up on what food I've got in, and what I've been eating. Its like living in a warden-controlled house.'

They both smiled.

'Yeah, she's great isn't she, Sir?' Parish said.

'You found a diamond when you found Richards, Parish.'

Richards came back with two mugs of coffee. 'Where are we going to sit, Sir?'

'I'll let you get on with it then, Parish. Come in at four-thirty and brief me. Oh, and you'd better arrange a press conference for tomorrow morning, they're already out for blood.'

'Okay, Sir, see you later.' He took the steaming mug of coffee Richards held out to him and said, 'I see you've made yourself comfortable?'

'I was beginning to feel like a squatter, Sir. The Chief told Kowalski to sort something out for me.'

'You're getting a bit too close to Kowalski, Richards. Next, you'll be telling me he loves you, and that he'll leave his wife and kids. You'll run away to Cornwall, spend the summer making love on the beach, and then it'll all turn to a bag of onions. His wife will take him back, then you'll find out you're pregnant. Sometimes Richards, the future can be a scary place.'

'You tell a good story, Sir.'

He turned serious. 'Make sure it is a story, Richards. If I get even a hint that your relationship with Kowalski is anything more than verbal sparring, you will be going back to Cheshunt. Do I make myself clear?'

'If you married my mum you could be my dad for real, Sir.'

'Do I make myself clear, Richards?' he repeated.

'Yes, Sir.'

'Good, lets sit here,' he said indicating the two desks. 'You can start a database search for prisoners released in the last three months. Whilst that's running, start making some phone calls. Phone the Press Officer and ask her to organise a briefing for nine o'clock tomorrow morning. Give Doc Michelin a call, and ask him if he can make himself available for a twelve o'clock working lunch in the hospital cafeteria – I'll pay tell him. Then, after lunch, we'll come back and visit Toadstone in forensics.'

'What are you going to do whilst I'm doing all the work, Sir?'

'You don't want me to do myself a mischief on my first day back, do you, Richards? I'm going to delete my emails and make inroads into my intray.'

CPSIA information can be obtained at www.ICGtesting.com
Printed in the USA
LVOW100354120112

263377LV00001B/5/P